### The Murderer's Tale

*Dame Frevisse's respite at Minster Lovell turns deadly when murder visits the quiet manor . . .*

"The period detail is lavish, and the characters are full-blooded in this sixth book in an exceptionally strong series." —*Minneapolis Star Tribune*

"Good tension and high drama . . . Fans of Ellis Peters' Brother Cadfael mysteries will relish a similar setting and atmosphere here." —*The Bookwatch*

### The Prioress' Tale

*When the prioress lets her family stay at St. Frideswide's, the consequences are deadly . . .*

"Frazer is generous with her details of abbey life." —*Publishers Weekly*

"Will delight history buffs and mystery fans alike." —*Murder Ink*

### The Maiden's Tale

*In London for a visit, Frevisse finds that her wealthy cousin may have a deadly secret . . .*

"Great fun for all lovers of history and their mystery." —*Minneapolis Star Tribune*

*Berkley Prime Crime Books by Margaret Frazer*

# The Reeve's Tale

## MARGARET FRAZER

BERKLEY PRIME CRIME, NEW YORK

This is a work of fiction. Names, characters, places, and incidents are either the product of the author's imagination or are used fictitiously, and any resemblance to actual persons, living or dead, business establishments, events, or locales is entirely coincidental.

THE REEVE'S TALE

A Berkley Prime Crime Book / published by arrangement with the author

PRINTING HISTORY
Berkley Prime Crime hardcover edition / 1999
Berkley Prime Crime mass-market edition / September 2000

All rights reserved.
Copyright © 1999 by Gail Frazer.
This book, may not be reproduced in whole or in part,
by mimeograph or any other means, without permission.
For information address: The Berkley Publishing Group,
a division of Penguin Putnam Inc.,
375 Hudson Street, New York, New York 10014.

The Penguin Putnam Inc. World Wide Web site address is
http://www.penguinputnam.com

ISBN: 0-425-17667-3

Berkley Prime Crime Books are published
by The Berkley Publishing Group,
a division of Penguin Putnam Inc.,
375 Hudson Street, New York, New York 10014.
The name BERKLEY PRIME CRIME and the
BERKLEY PRIME CRIME
design are trademarks belonging to Penguin Putnam Inc.

PRINTED IN THE UNITED STATES OF AMERICA

10  9  8  7  6  5  .4  3  2  1

*To my Mother who makes so much possible.*
*To my Father who never ever told me I couldn't.*
*To Mary who gave me the chance.*

*Soothly synnes been the weyes that leden folk to helle.*

G. Chaucer, *The Parson's Tale*

# Chapter 1

he last clouds of yesterday's rain were no more than high white wisps across the summer-vaulted sky, tattered out and carried away on a warm west wind that bid to hold fair for the next few days and the weather with it, perfect for the haying that needed to be done before St. Peter and Paul.

Seated on the bench under the squat-trunked oak at the church-end of the village green, Simon Perryn let the satisfaction of that almost-certainty sink deep into him along with the day's June warmth.

If all held as it was, there'd finally be a harvest worth the name this year, after three years of rain and cold and more of the crops rotting in the fields than ripened. It had been a famine winter this last year, with everything brought near to the bone; but not so near as it would have gone if the nuns had not done their part, somehow managing to buy rye from somewhere the harvests hadn't been as bad and sharing it out with the village, and even then word was that they had been living on the hunger side of things, too.

Not that the hunger was over yet nor would be until harvest was safely done and the granaries, please God and St. Peter-in-Harvest, full, but the year was well enough on now that the early peas were ready in the pod and the young onions well up and there were greens to be had for those who went gleaning the field and hedge and wood edges for them and now and again a plumped-out rabbit if someone cared to set a snare when no one else was looking; and the villagers were most marvelous-skilled at not looking.

Not at snares anyway. Everything else they seemed to see well enough and too well, Simon thought, eyeing the cluster of folk in front of him. He was Lord Lovell's reeve for Prior Byfield and mostly glad of it. On the whole, it was better to be reeve than not, set to overseeing village matters rather than being overseen except for when Master Spencer, Lord Lovell's bailiff for his properties in northern Oxfordshire into Warwickshire, came twice yearly to sort out troubles, collect fees, and check records, or when—very much more rarely, thank the Blessed Virgin for mercy—Master Holt, Lord Lovell's high steward, came on his circuit, making general survey of his lord's properties. Happily, Lord Lovell held lands through most of England, with Prior Byfield one of the least of his holdings and not often worth Master Holt's visiting, so long as its due services and fees were accomplished and no great troubles arose.

Dealing with troubles before they became great was one of Simon's tasks as the manor's reeve, for which he was excused his own fees and most of the services he owed Lord Lovell for holding of his house and lands, an exchange that he found to his good, even on days like this when it was time to hold Prior Byfield's three-month court and sort out whatever village matters had collected since the last one. At least the weather could not have been better, letting them be out here in the oak shade instead of cramped into the alehouse or being chill in the church.

Beside him on the bench, Master Naylor shifted, glanced up to judge the time by the sun's slant through the leaves, and asked, "That's the most of this lot, then?" of Father Edmund, the village priest who sat to one side with paper, pen and ink at a table carried out from his house, keeping record of what was decided in each matter.

Father Edmund finished scratching down that Bess Underbush had been fined two pence for breach of the assize of ale, having begun to sell a brewing before the village's ale taster—presently Philip Green, who was never one to let a chance for free ale pass him by and was therefore diligent in the office—had had chance to taste and pass it as meeting all the rules regarding ale for sale. Not that Bess had ever brewed a bad lot of ale in her life, but law was law and every brewing had to be approved as good before sold—though there was justice in Bess saying as she'd paid down her two pence that, "I'm still ahead in the matter. He always drinks down six pence worth when he comes a-tasting," and Philip Green's flush and the onlookers' laughter had agreed with her.

Now Father Henry turned from noting her fine to the list of other matters to be dealt with today and said, reading ahead, "One more minor matter and then the four main ones before we're done."

Master Naylor looked to Simon with silent question of whether they should pause a while or go on.

Prior Byfield was held by two lords, part of the manor belonging to Lord Lovell, part to St. Frideswide's nunnery, so that some of the villagers held their land of Lord Lovell, others from the nunnery, and some—though not

Simon himself, thank the saints—from both. Therefore
the rights and customs under which some of the villagers
lived differed from the rights and customs ruling others,
and whoever held from both Lord Lovell and the nunnery
had to deal with both sets of rights and customs, according
to which of their holdings was in the matter. Mind, Simon
knew of villages owned by three and even more lords,
and the tangle there must be nigh to unholy sometimes.
The saints knew it could be bad enough here, but all but
the worst of confusions were usually avoided because the
nunnery's steward and the village's reeve had long since
taken to holding the manors' courts together, seeing to
things all at once instead of separately. Not that that
couldn't cause troubles upon occasion; and if, as had
sometimes happened in the past, either steward or reeve
were unreasonable men it did not work at all, but Master
Naylor and Simon had worked together for five years
now, and for the most part it went well. They were both
men who could see two sides of a problem at once, even
when one of the sides wasn't his own, and they both preferred fairness to greed in settling problems, so they did
well enough together on most things, and Simon now nodded agreement without need for Master Naylor to ask it
aloud that they should go straight on with the court rather
than pause a while, because they both knew a pause would
give their six jurors a chance to wander off. Then they
would have to be gathered in again and time wasted doing
it, whereas if they pressed straight on, things might be
finished in time for Simon to finish weeding his last furlong in Shaldewell Field today.

Master Naylor passed his nod on to Father Edmund,
who said in his clear priest's voice, "Hal Millwarde,
miller, come before the court."

Simon made a silent, inward sigh and settled himself
as his cousin swaggered out from the mingled gathering
of onlookers to stand before him and Master Naylor, giving a sideways frown at the jurors on their two benches,

a distrustful glower at the priest with his poised pen, and a deeper glower at Simon whose fault he held this all to be because the windmill on the rise west of the village, where the village's and nunnery's grain was ground, was Lord Lovell's and its jurisdiction therefore under Simon. It was a thing Simon could not change nor Hal forgive him, despite they went through this every few courts. Summoned at least once a year for taking excessive toll for grinding of someone's grain, Hal always protested he'd done nothing wrong; everyone ignored his protest because it wasn't true; he was fined and he paid and went away grumbling that he'd been wronged yet again, though he and everyone else knew he hadn't been, and that his family would starve, though they never did.

But Hal was ever one who loved a good grumble, and come next chance they met at the alehouse, Simon would buy him an ale, listen to his complaints, agree he had a hard life, and afterwards their friendship would be back to where it had comfortably been since childhood until the next time Hal came before the court.

It went the usual way this time. Charged with taking a larger portion of the flour he had ground than he should have for his fee from three different folk in the village just before Easter, Hal protested they had all under-judged how much grain they had brought him. Called out to testify, all three swore they had taken care to measure their grain in Father Edmund's presence before going to the mill because everyone knew that Lent was the time of year Hal Millwarde tended most to be greedy. Father Edmund agreed he had witnessed their measuring and that it had been as they said. The jurors, knowing the miller, knowing their neighbors, and trusting the priest, found Hal guilty and, annoyed because everyone had already been going more short of food than usual this Lent after last year's poor harvest, making Hal doubly in the wrong to take such advantage of his place, fined him three pence instead of the usual two.

Outraged, Hal swung from them to Simon, demanding, "You're not agreeing to that, are you? Three pence? Three pence instead of two? Where's the justice in that?"

"I don't know," Simon said. "If it was me, I'd have said justice would have been better served in charging you four pence for it." Then added while Hal gaped at him, "Or maybe I would have made it five."

Offended past words, Hal snapped his mouth shut and swung toward the priest, plunging hand in pouch to fumble out the needed coins and throw them on the table before stalking away in perfected fury, leaving Simon to suppose it would take at least two bowls of ale to bring him around the next time they met.

To hand next was the more troublesome matter of Jenet atte Forge and Hamon Otale, and Simon was glad they were both the nunnery's villeins and so Master Naylor's problem, not his. As all of Prior Byfield knew, Jenet had loaned Hamon—and why she had ever thought he could repay it, Hamon being, even by the most generous estimate, hardly competent to do anything more on his own than tie up his hosen—three shillings last autumn, to be repaid at Whitsuntide. Whitsuntide being past and no sign of her money coming home, Jenet had brought plea against him.

Master Naylor, with his usual intent attention, listened to Hamon's shuffle-footed admitting that he hadn't the money anymore or anything even close to it. "I meant to buy a cart and do some carting," he said. "Only the cart broke down at midwinter, see. Past fixing, it was, and nothing I could do about, so there I am, aren't I?"

There he was indeed, Master Naylor agreed, forbearing to point out what everyone in the village knew—that the cart had been almost past use even when Hamon had first brought it back from Banbury. But Hamon was not someone who learned from anything he ever did or anything he was ever told, and Master Naylor merely asked Father Edmund to read out, for the jurors to hear, the indenture drawn up between Jenet and Hamon last autumn. It was among the first things Father Edmund had done when he first came to be priest here. After the rather under-learned and under-devoted priest they had had for a while between Father Clement's death and him, his clerkly skills were almost as welcome as his churchly ones. He had laid out the indenture simply and clearly, and the jurors nodded easy understanding at its end and asked Hamon's sureties, Walter Hopper and Dick Blakeman, to come forward.

Because manor law required everyone who held property in Prior Byfield manor to attend all manor courts, Walter and Dick were inevitably there, even if they had not known this was coming, and came elbowing out from among the other holders to acknowledge that those were their sign manuals, yes, they had agreed to stand surety for Hamon repaying Jenet her three shillings, and since he could not, yes, they agreed—Dick very unhappily—that they were responsible to Jenet for her money.

"And since I talked Dick into it, when he would rather have not," Walter said, "I'll take the whole of it on myself, please you, Master Naylor."

Dick and Master Naylor and everyone else fixed surprised looks on Walter.

"You've the money to hand to pay her?" Master Naylor asked, ready money in that quantity not easily come by for most folk, even someone who made the best of his holding and something more on the side with leather work the way Walter did, and it was no surprise he answered, "Nay." But he went on, "But I've a cow in milk that I'll turn over to Jenet's use until I can repay her, if she will. Though likely that won't be until after Michaelmas," he added apologetically.

"It's your brown-spotted cow you mean?" Jenet asked. "With the cracked horn?" There was as little about each other's livestock as about each other's lives the villagers didn't know, and if that was the cow Walter was offering, it was a good offer indeed.

"Aye, that's her," Walter said.

"Done," Jenet answered and looked toward the jurors for confirmation. "Yes? You agree it's fair?"

If Jenet thought a thing was fair, there was unlikely to be anyone foolish enough to disagree with her. Six heads nodded ready agreement and she nodded back, saying, "Good, then. Father Edmund, put it down."

Simon was not altogether sure he saw a twitch that might have been a smile in a more open man at the corner of Master Naylor's mouth, but there were smiles enough among the onlookers, and Dick Blakeman was shaking Walter Hopper's hand with gratitude at being saved responsibility for three shillings he could ill afford just now, what with his wife being near to birthing their fourth child and Dick needing to hire the help she wouldn't be able to give him in their fields this summer.

The question was, for Simon, why either man had agreed to stand surety for someone as hapless as Hamon Otale. Or, more to the point, why Walter had been willing to stand surety and talked Dick into it. But maybe Dick would hire Hamon for the summer and then Hamon would be able to pay Walter something back.

For the time being anyway, everyone seemed satisfied on all sides and that was better than the next matter was likely to turn out, Simon thought uncomfortably as Father Edmund called Tomkin Goddard and John Gregory forward.

Probably sharing Simon's certainty of trouble coming and knowing the brunt of the decision and the displeasures that would fall on them afterward, the jurors shifted on their benches, while the onlookers roused to smothered laughter and elbowing among themselves as Tomkin and John shoved out from opposite sides of the crowd into the open in front of Simon and Master Naylor, sending each other angry looks and keeping what distance between them they could. Even as boys, the two of them had never been able to abide each other, and that wasn't helped by

their messuages—their houses and garths—being side by
each at the green's lower end, making it easy for them to
be forever able to find ways of offending one another.
Nor did it help that Tomkin Goddard was Lord Lovell's
villein while John Gregory was the nunnery's, and each
expected reeve or steward to back whatever they did
against the other, no matter what it was.

Unhappily for them, neither Simon nor Master Naylor
chose to see matters that simply. More often than not,
Tomkin and John found themselves at the displeasure of
both men, and today was one of those times. Master Naylor, with no sign of the discomfort Simon and the jurors
were sharing, fixed a hard stare first on them both, then
looked at the jurors and asked, "May I question?"

The jurors nodded readily. There were more ways than
one to handle court matters but inevitably someone would
have to question, and very openly every juror preferred it
to be someone else this time. In truth, so did Simon, and
when Master Naylor looked to him for his permission, he
gave it readily. Questioning Tomkin and John too often
turned into a shouting match between them and against
whoever was trying to determine where right and wrong
might lie in the matter, and even now both men had their
mouths open, ready to speak, but finding themselves suddenly in Master Naylor's care, they snapped their mouths
shut, wary, because they had been dealt with by Master
Naylor before this and had not enjoyed it.

Nor did they now, as Master Naylor tersely asked at
Tomkin, "It was your goat went through John Gregory's
fence and ate three young cabbages and a dozen onions
in his garden?"

"Aye. But she wouldn't have been in there if he kept
the fence mended . . ."

Master Naylor silenced him with a slightly raised hand
and asked at John, "It was your fence that let through
Tomkin Goddard's goat?"

"No 'let' about it," John answered, surly with his

wrongs. "The beast shoved right through, broke a hole . . ."

"Whereupon you threw stones at the goat?" Master Naylor asked.

"Aye! And I'd do it again. That . . ."

"Whereupon you, Tomkin, then threw a stone at John, yes?" Master Naylor asked.

"Only because . . ." Tomkin started.

"And then you threw a stone at him?" Master Naylor asked John.

"Aye. The . . ."

"Whereupon your wives, having more sense than either of you, stopped you both from doing more. Yes?"

John and Tomkin shuffled for answer while from the edges of the onlookers their wives nodded vigorous agreement.

Master Naylor turned to the jurors. "You've heard them both admit to assault on one another. I suggest you should find them both in mercy for it and . . ."

"Here now!" John protested. "That's not . . ."

". . . fine them accordingly," Master Naylor finished.

"What about my fence? That goat made a great hole . . ."

"There was hole there already! That's how she . . ."

"We'll deal with fence and goat next," Master Naylor said quellingly. "Sirs?"

The jurors' heads went together, their talk low but brisk and brief before one of them, Martin whose messuage was at the bottom of the village not far from Tomkin's and John's, stood up to say formally, "We find them both in mercy for assault, to be fined one pence each for the fault."

He and the rest of the jurors seemed to think that ended it, though he was carefully not looking at Tomkin and John's furious faces, but Simon asked, "And their weapons?" because any weapon used against someone was supposed to be seized, to be sold or recovered by way of fine, for the lord's profit.

Martin cast him a perturbed glance, but Tod Denton on the rear bench tugged at Martin's tunic hem, bringing him down to whisper in his ear, the other jurors leaning to listen and all of them nodding agreement before Martin straightened to say for all of them, holding in a grin, "The weapons they used being stones, we leave it to you and Master Naylor to decide their worth and if you want them."

"Stones be damned!" John snarled. "What about my fence and garden that goat ruined?"

Martin added hastily at Master Naylor and Simon, "And we leave the matter of damage done to fence, garden, and goat to both of you, too," and sat down quickly.

"Not that there was any damage done that goat," Tod put in. "She's a hide like an ale cask. I went to see her and couldn't find even a bump."

"Damn the goat!" John yelled. "It's my garden and fence that took the hurt!"

"If you kept your fence mended . . ." Tomkin began at him.

Master Naylor suggested, without raised voice, "There can be fines for disrupting court, you know."

Both men shut up and Master Naylor asked Simon, "How would you say we should decide this goat and fence and garden, Perryn?"

Since Master Naylor had so tidily dealt with the worst part of the problem, Simon took this share of it willingly. "I'd say it only right that Tomkin replace what the goat ate in the garden. Three cabbage plants and a dozen young onions."

"Ha!" John exclaimed triumphantly while Tomkin went red-faced and Simon went on, "And John must repair his fence and keep it in repair to the common good or be fined one pence again whenever there's trouble with it proved against him."

Now Tomkin went, "Ha!" and John red-faced, but their wives, knowing a good time to escape even if their husbands did not, came forward, each to take her own man by the arm and draw him off.

It had all gone far more simply than Simon had feared it would, but now they had to face the next matter, and despite it looked to be simpler, a mere shifting of a lease from one man to another, he knew there was going to be trouble not so easily gone around as Tomkin Goddard's and John Gregory's.

Father Edmund was summoning the men forward now and all the differences between them were unhappily plain to see. Matthew Woderove glanced from Simon to Master Naylor to the jurors, trying for confidence but his shoulders already beginning to huddle against what he feared was coming. Even his clothing betrayed him—tunic and hosen and shoes as worn and tired and past their best as he was—while Gilbey Dunn, taking place beside him, wore prosperity's certainty as easily and well as he wore his wide-cut, well-dyed, knee-length gown of finely woven dark russet wool, his hosen unpatched, his soft leather shoes so new they hadn't lost their shape yet. There could hardly be doubt whether or not the lease for Farnfield, a stretch of rough pasture land along the woodshore beyond the fields, should go to Gilbey, except for knowing how hard the loss would be for Matthew, much though he deserved it, having let the land go to waste while he held it.

Still, the decision would have been easier, Simon thought, if he could have disliked Matthew. It should not have been difficult; the man had no skill at anything, failed at everything, including his marriage to Simon's sister, though Simon had several opinions—not all of them to Matthew's fault—about where the failure lay there, and he had long since stopped asking himself how Mary had ever come to marry so hapless a man, there hardly ever being answer to what drew such ill-suited folk to one another, though between Matthew and Mary, Simon knew it had had much to do with Matthew being the handsomest boy in the village in his time and bidding fair to be one of the richest men if he kept on with what his father had begun. But he hadn't. Nor was he handsome anymore, being one of those men who left their best looks behind them well before they were thirty. Not that Simon felt he had much to his own credit on that side, but at least he'd had the sense to marry Anne and not some shallow-wit like his sister who couldn't do more for a man than make his life miserable when she didn't have all she wanted . . .

Simon made a hasty prayer of penance for the thought's unkindness and set himself to what had to be done here and now, regardless of how he wished things were for Matthew. Though Gilbey Dunn and Matthew were both Lord Lovell's villeins, the land and lease in question belonged to St. Frideswide's, and so it was to Master Naylor that Gilbey was stating his desire to take over the lease on Farnfield since it had come to its end at Midsummer yesterday.

By form, Master Naylor asked, "And you, Matthew Woderove, are you desirous of giving it up?"

Although he had to have known the question was coming, Matthew hesitated as if surprised at being asked, said, "No," uncertainly, then tried for firmer. "No. No, not at all. It was held by my father and then by me for twenty years now. I want to renew the lease."

Simon inwardly sighed. He had known it was unlikely that Matthew would simply let it go but he had hoped it anyway. What made despising Matthew difficult was that he tried so hard, meant so well in everything he did, even if it was all to such little avail. Over and over again he had failed where he should have succeeded, ignored where he should have paid heed, and now, because he had ignored the Farnfield land for so long, he was about to fail in his bid to keep it, and failure to keep land was nigh to the worst failure a man could have. He would still have his main holding and the land that went with it, inherited from his father, but leased land was the lord's to take back and give elsewhere if need be, and Matthew had let it become necessary.

With his face and voice seemingly disinterested in the matter though surely he was having much the same thought, Master Naylor said to Matthew, "You understand that twenty years make changes in things and the lease can't be renewed under the old terms. What terms do you offer in their stead?"

"I . . ." Matthew fumbled to a stop, looked around for help that wasn't there, gathered himself, and said, blinking rapidly, "I offer the old terms and . . . and three pence more rent a year."

It was not much of an offer but more than he probably should make, considering he had probably been losing money on the land instead of making it, with the waste he'd made of it these past five years.

Master Naylor looked to Gilbey. "And you offer?"

"A shilling and a half rent a year and a tithe of whatever profit I make from the land above that," Gilbey said evenly. Half again as much the ready money Matthew presently paid, plus a tithe that was no part of the present lease. Discontented murmurs ran among the onlookers at such a hopeless outbidding of Matthew. There was little liking in the village for Gilbey Dunn.

Master Naylor leaned a little forward to ask Gilbey with open curiosity, "What is it you plan to do that makes the land worth that much to you?"

Gilbey made a small shrug as if it hardly mattered. "Pasturing, I think. I've a mind to run a few more milch cows and maybe some beef, once it's cleared to use again."

He said it simply but Simon doubted that was the whole of it. Gilbey and money found their way to each other too often and too seemingly easily for anything to

be that simple. And here was Gilbey, sure enough, beginning to bargain, saying, "But I'd not expect to pay above
half-rent this year, what with the cost of clearing it and
me not able to use it until that's done."

"But still answer for the tithe," Master Naylor returned,
knowing Gilbey as well as Simon did, "supposing you
should make something from it this year after all."

"Aye, I'll still answer for the tithe," Gilbey agreed,
with a shade of grudging behind the words.

Master Naylor looked to Matthew. "Can you better
what he offers?"

Matthew sent an angry look Gilbey's way before saying sullenly at the ground in front of himself, "No."

Master Naylor looked to Simon, asking as he had to,
for form's sake, despite they already knew what Simon
must needs answer, "What say you, Perryn? Would I do
well to give the lease to Gilbey Dunn or not?" Wanting
Simon's yea or nay in the matter because Simon was Lord
Lovell's reeve and Gilbey and Matthew were Lord Lovell's villeins.

And Simon answered strongly, refusing to be a coward
at it, "All considered, I see no reason he shouldn't have
it for what he's offered."

He looked at Matthew then, trying to let him see that
he was sorry, but an outraged exclaim behind Matthew
had already jerked his head around toward his wife shoving out from among the onlookers. A dull, deep flush
swept up Matthew's face as he moved to stop her; and
Simon's own wife, Anne, was behind her, trying, as
Simon had asked her, to hold Mary back and talk her into
quietness, but Mary was having none of either Anne or
Matthew. Leaving Anne behind and passing Matthew
with a sideways swipe that shoved his reaching hand
away, she closed on Gilbey, to say fiercely, thrusting a
pointing finger at his face, "You'll put your nose into
other people's lives once too often, Gilbey Dunn. That's
our land you're taking! You mind what I say!"

"Mary, please," Matthew pleaded from behind her. "It's done. Come away. Please."

"*Our* land!" she insisted at Gilbey who was making no move to answer her, only standing there, and now Anne was there, too, taking her by the arm, trying to make her heed but being as ignored as Matthew was.

It was Father Edmund saying from the table with his quiet priestly authority, "Mary. That's enough," that stopped her. She pulled up short, threw him a glance hot with anger, threw other glances at Simon and Master Naylor no less angry, then let herself be drawn away by Anne, with Matthew following close on her other side; and as Anne circled her away around the onlookers, Mary turned her anger and thrusting finger on him instead, making Simon glad not to hear what she was saying while they went.

Beside him Master Naylor took up as if undisturbed by any of it and said, "Then, Gilbey Dunn, let the lease on Farnfield be yours on these terms. To run for ten years, from Midsummer to Midsummer, at a shilling and a half rent a year and a tithe of your profit above that, with the rent to be one shilling for this first year because of the land being much in waste. Agreed?"

Gilbey opened his mouth as if to protest the change to what he had offered, then changed his mind and said, "Agreed."

He and Master Naylor and Simon all looked to the jurors, their decision not needed in a matter like this but their witness wanted against later disagreement, should it come. They all nodded understanding of what had passed, and Master Naylor said, "Let it be so noted," to Father Edmund, who nodded in return without looking up from his pen scratching across paper.

Gilbey bowed to Master Naylor and to Simon and withdrew, leaving Simon glad to be finished with both him and the lease despite knowing there would be listening to Mary over it later. Their father had always called her his 'little bird' because she had been—and was—so small built and lively, pretty in her childhood and pretty enough now, for that matter, he supposed, but the word for her that always came to Simon's mind was "shrew," and as good a question as to why she'd married Matthew Woderove was why had Matthew had married her.

Still, to each their own and, "There's only the dividing of William Bonde's land between Alson and young William still to do today," he said.

"And that should be no trouble?" Master Naylor asked in his ear as Alson Bonde hobbled forward on her son's arm. Her husband had been St. Frideswide's villein and therefore how his property would go between his widow and only son was Master Naylor's concern, but he freely depended on Simon's knowledge of the village and its folk in such matters, just as Simon depended on his in others, and Simon whispered back, "No trouble. They're well agreed, the last I knew."

Father Edmund rose to bring his own stool for old Alson sit on although it meant he'd have to stand to write and was thanked by her smile as she sat down gratefully.

Master Naylor inquired what the custom was concerning the Bonde holding, and Alson, whose legs might be old but whose wits were well with her, said the custom was for half of it to go the widow for her life, the other half to the eldest son. "And that part is easy enough," she added, "there being only young William," patting her son's hand where it rested on her shoulder as he stood beside her.

Young William was somewhere past thirty years old, having been born toward the end of the king-before-last's reign, and though he was married and had three sons of his own, none of them were named William, and he was likely to stay 'young William' all his life, however old he came to be.

"You say the same?" Master Naylor asked him.

"I do." His certainty was easy and unhesitant. There

were few complications in young William. A fondness for too much ale on a Sunday afternoon or holiday, followed by a desire to sing more loudly than anyone so constantly far off key should ever do, was the worst that could be said about him. He was good to his wife, good to his children, good to his mother, and even if he seemed never to have a thought of his own about how things should be done, he followed other folks' ways and how things had always been done without making trouble over it. There was no reason Simon knew that he shouldn't have his share of his father's holding, nor did the jurors, when Master Naylor asked them, "What say you? Is this dividing evenly between widow and eldest son the custom as you know it for the Bonde holding?"

The jurors had been ready for the question. They bent toward each other in busy comment only briefly before Tod Denton, as the oldest, said for them all, "Aye, that's the way it's been since any of us remember. The holding divided 'tween widow and eldest son, with her share going back to the son when she dies. God keep you in possession of it a long while yet, Alson," he added.

"Thank you, Tod, and the same to you with yours," she answered.

"Then let it be put down as such," Master Naylor said, closing the matter.

And what pity it couldn't all be that easy, Simon was thinking soon afterwards, when he and Master Naylor were still sitting on the oak tree's bench but at ease, bowls of ale in hand and everyone gone away to other business, except for Simon's sons, Adam and Colyn, sitting side by side on one of the oak's upheaved roots, waiting fairly patiently for their father to have done and come away to his other business this afternoon which wasn't to be weeding that furlong in Shaldewell Field after all; he had forgotten his promise to take them fishing after manor court until he had turned from thanking Father Edmund for his help and found the two of them waiting behind him, smiling, each with a bowl of ale in one hand and fishing pole in the other.

"Mother said you might forget," Adam had said cheerfully, "and said we should bring you these to help sweeten your remembering."

So he and Master Naylor were having a drink and a friendly word before they went their ways, partly because it didn't hurt to stay friendly with a man you had so often to work with but mostly because Simon simply liked him. Steward though he was and strong hand though he kept over all the nunnery properties, letting nothing go by that was St. Frideswide's due, Master Naylor was a fair man who had never, to Simon's knowledge, misused his place or power.

Simon tried to be the same himself, and it pleased him when they could talk together almost as friends, though "almost" was as near as Master Naylor ever came with anybody, Simon thought. Still, "almost" was better than "not at all," and Simon made bold to ask, as he and Master Naylor rose to their feet, ready to part company, and Adam and Colyn leaped up to come take the empty bowls back to the alehouse, "How goes it at the nunnery then? All still well with your new prioress?"

"All's well, so far as I can tell, with both her and the nunnery," Master Naylor said. "There's nothing to complain of there."

And even if there had been, he would likely never have said so, Simon thought, idle talk not being Master Naylor's way.

But there was never harm in asking.

# Chapter 2

The warm days of June were drifted into the warm days of July, with the early haying done, the shearing and its noise of sheep finished, and the weather still holding fair, giving hope for the late haying and, God willing, harvest. Though for now, Frevisse told herself, it should be enough that this year of our Lord's grace 1440 had, thus far, gone so quietly in every way.

She was come out from the cloister into St. Frideswide nunnery's walled garden to sit on the turf bench in the sun-speckled shade of the chestnut tree through this quiet while of the afternoon with one of the nunnery's account rolls, intending to bring the kitchen accounts to date, but somehow very little of them was being done because now

that she was here it seemed enough merely to sit, letting
the day happen around her. The garden, with its high
walls and single gate, its herb-edged flower beds and careful paths, the vine-shadowed arbor, the turfed seats along
the wall, their grass grown with small daisies, was a place
unto itself. All of summer seemed held here, touched by
no more of the world beyond its walls than came in with
the busyness of the bees and sometimes birdsong.

Across the garden Dame Perpetua sat on another of the
turf benches, a small box with awl, thick needle, and
heavy thread beside her and a breviary in need of mending
on her lap, though she seemed working on it only slightly
more than Frevisse was on her accounts. And if Dame
Claire's excuse for being here was because, as infirmarian
and responsible for the nunnery's health, she needed to
see to the herbs here in the garden that she used in her
medicines, she *looked* to be doing no more than drifting
from one plant to another, plucking an occasional leaf to
smell with what looked more like idle pleasure than purpose. At least Dame Juliana was truly at work, diligently
weeding one of the corner beds where something unde
sirable had apparently been creeping in among the gilly-
flowers; but then, the garden here and in the cloister garth
were her delights and a chance to work in them were all
the pleasure she could ask of any day.

On the other hand, Sister Johane and Sister Cecely
were making no pretense of doing anything. Their em-
broidery was left on a bench, not a stitch done, while they
walked together in the arbor, their black gowns and black
veils dappled with sunlight among the leaf-shadows, talking despite it was still the silent time of the day, when no
one should talk except at need. They were the youngest
of the nuns and cousins to each other and in St. Frideswide's more by their families' wishes than their own in-
clinations, by all that Frevisse had ever noted about them.

She caught herself on the thought and made a quick,
small prayer of contrition. However true, it was a petty

thought, and for a while afterwards she set herself to the kitchen accounts . . .

*Die sabbati proximo ante festum Pentecostes:*
*Item in piscibus*—for fish, one shilling ten pence.
*Item in farina avenarum*—for ground meal, nine and a half pence.
*Item in pipero*—for pepper, three pence.

And another pence to the carrier for having bought and brought it by particular request from Banbury, she remembered and penned in.

*Item in piscibus et fabis*—for fish and beans . . . Why had she put them together in the account? she wondered.

. . . and found she was looking not at the page in front of her anymore but at the bees in the blue-flowered spires of the bellflowers across the path, their hum and bumble far more interesting than *Item in primis in pane*—for bread, one shilling twelve pence—that had been when the priory's oven had needed repairing and they had had to buy from the village instead of baking their own—and told herself with in-kept laughter that after all it was only right she take an interest in the bees. The past years' hard weather had made for a death of bees and thereby a dearth of honey and none knew better than she did, as the priory's cellarer, that if the priory's hives failed to thrive this summer, there would be need to buy honey come the autumn and there was presently small money in St. Frideswide's for buying anything, even necessities, which honey was because certainly they could not afford sugar and without even honey it would be an unsweet winter.

The trouble had come with their last prioress who, one way and another, had made a waste of the priory's properties and taken them deep into debts—as well as into other troubles. Domina Elisabeth, their present prioress, was slowly bringing matters around, St. Benedict keep her. She had brought peace and prayers back into the nunnery, there was good hope for the harvest, Master Naylor had bargained a better-than-expected price for the wool clip, and Domina Elisabeth's plan to bring in a little ready money toward settling some of their debts by setting the nuns to copying books to sell had actually begun to pay. In fact, today was a little holiday because of their latest success at it; yesterday had seen the finish of a psalter ordered for an anchorite in Northampton by her family as a gift for when she took her final vows of enclosure on St. Mary Magdalen's day. It was a plain work, no one in St. Frideswide's having skill at illumination, but that was all the better for an anchorite in her plain life. What mattered was that the script had been well written, clear and even and an almost unvarying black—Dame Perpetua had an excellent receipt for ink—with only the faintest differences to show how many hands had worked at it.

St. Frideswide's was a small priory, unable to spare anyone from their other duties to do only scribework, and among the ten nuns, only Domina Elisabeth, Dame Perpetua, Dame Juliana, Sister Johane, and Frevisse had proved skilled enough to do it at all and all of them had offices or other duties that took up much of their time aside from scribing.

Or else their scribing took them away from their offices and so Frevisse was behind in the kitchen accounts and should be paying better heed to them now while she had the chance, she thought, and tried again to take an interest in *Item in candelis*—for candles, two pence. As cellarer she was responsible for the nunnery's worldly needs within the cloister—what they ate or wore or used; what they were in need of; whether what they had would do or if, St. Zita forbid, something had to be bought. Besides that, she was also kitchener, overseeing everything that was done, everything that was used, in the priory's kitchens, both in the cloister and in the guesthalls. What time those duties did not take up, the account keeping for them did, it seemed, so that between all that and the scribework and the eight daily Offices of prayers in the church, time merely to sit had been slight.

Dame Claire and Dame Juliana were now talking together over one of the lavender-bordered middle beds, and Frevisse noted sadly that although Domina Elisabeth had made some attempt to restore the rule—lost under their last prioress—that silence should be kept except at certain times and places in St. Frideswide's, no one held to it very much, even the older nuns, except herself sometimes, when she was able, and Sister Thomasine always, when she was allowed.

But then Sister Thomasine had never lost her quiet, even in the worst days under Domina Alys, and if she had no other duty to hold her, she was probably praying in the church even now.

The garden's gate opening turned everyone to look, even Sister Johane and Sister Cecely pausing in their chatter to see who was come, despite the gate led only to the cloister and no one more unfamiliar than another nun or cloister servants was likely; and indeed it was only Sister Emma and everyone went back to what they had been doing, except Frevisse because Sister Emma, after a moment's hesitation to look around the garden, came purposefully toward her, and regretfully Frevisse rolled closed the accounts. Today Sister Emma was taking turn to attend on Domina Elisabeth, and if she was seeking Frevisse, it was on Domina Elisabeth's behalf rather than her own. Indeed she called while still bustling along the path, before she reached where Frevisse sat, "My lady says you're to come. She needs you in her parlor right away, please you."

Tucking the account roll under one arm and picking up the pen and ink, Frevisse asked, "To what purpose?"

Reaching her, Sister Emma dropped her voice to almost a whisper, as if somehow it must be kept a secret, "There's a Master Spencer come to see her."

Frevisse did not see why that needed whispering, but

she asked as she rose and started back toward the gate with Sister Emma, "She's there alone with him?"

"Oh, no!" Sister Emma indulged in being scandalized at the thought that she might have left their prioress in private with a man. "Sister Amicia is there." Sister Amicia presently being hosteler, in charge of the guesthalls and therefore of any guests to the nunnery, which Frevisse presumed this Master Spencer was. "And Master Naylor has been sent for," Sister Emma added, a little breathless though Frevisse had been trying to hold in her quicker walk to Sister Emma's bustling one.

Hand out to open the garden's gate, Frevisse paused to look at her. "Master Naylor?"

Sister Emma nodded, catching her breath and eager to tell more. "This Master Spencer gave Domina Elisabeth a letter and added, right then and there before Sister Amicia could leave, that it might be well if she were to send for Master Naylor to come to answer in the matter."

Frevisse went out the gate and along the way to the slype, the narrow passage into the cloister walk, Sister Emma still happily saying behind her—because almost anything out of the way of the cloister's ordinary day was delight to Sister Emma, and with the rule of silence slackened, there was little to hold her back from her best pastime of talk—"So Domina Elisabeth bade Sister Amicia wait a moment and she read the letter, only there wasn't much of it . . ."

Frevisse supposed probably nothing more than "I pray you pay heed to the bearer of this letter. He knows what I wish said to you," with signature and seal to identify the sender, and who that was Sister Emma surely did not know or she would have said.

". . . and then she said I was to find someone to go for Master Naylor and then I was to find you and bid you come, please you, and Sister Amicia could stay with her." More breathless now, talking to have it all said as she and Frevisse went around the cloister walk toward the stairs up to Domina Elisabeth's rooms, she added, "What do you suppose it's about?"

"I couldn't guess," Frevisse said, leaving speculation to Sister Emma who was enjoying it so much.

As they passed the short passage from the cloister walk to the outer door, Master Naylor was coming in and paused to let them pass, bowing to them while they did. He was never given to much talk; nor had he ever, Frevisse knew, found it easy to take direction from women, even St. Frideswide's prioresses, but through one thing and another, something like respect had grown between him and her over the years, and she bent her head in answer to his bow, then led up the stairs to Domina Elisabeth's parlor, Sister Emma panting behind her, Master Naylor following after.

The parlor door stood open but Frevisse paused to knock lightly and receive Domina Elisabeth's *"Benedicite"* before she entered. Because among her duties St. Frideswide's prioress had to receive important guests and conduct such nunnery business as needed more privity than the daily chapter meeting involving all the nuns, her parlor was more richly furnished than the rest of the nunnery, with not only a fireplace and glass in the three tall windows overlooking the courtyard but brightly embroidered cushions on the window seat and a Spanish woven carpet over a table set with a silver ewer and bowl and two chairs, one of them high-backed and elaborately carved, rather than the usual stools for sitting. For Domina Elisabeth, a scribe's slant-topped desk had been added, set beside the window for best light, where she could work at the copying tasks she shared with her nuns, and beside the hearth there was a cushioned basket where her cat occasionally slept between whiles of trying out various beds in the nuns' dormitory, usually preferring Dame Claire's, who did not like the beast, while scorning Sister Johane's endless attempts to win its affections.

As she entered, Frevisse took in Domina Elisabeth

standing beside her desk, one hand out to rest on a letter lying open there—the message she had lately received, Frevisse supposed—and a man—Master Spencer, surely—standing nearby, facing her, and Sister Amicia keeping watch beside the door for propriety's sake, in the moment before lowering her eyes properly toward the floor in an unknown man's presence while she crossed to make deep curtsy to Domina Elisabeth, then stepped aside for Master Naylor to make his bow while Sister Emma announced the obvious with, "I've brought them, my lady," and added brightly, "Good company makes short miles!"

Sister Emma used proverbs far more often than she understood them, and even though this one was somewhat more apt that Sister Emma's often were, Domina Elisabeth paused, distracted, said, "Yes. Well." And, "Thank you." Then, "You and Sister Amicia may go."

It took a brief pause for Sister Emma and Sister Amicia to realize they were being sent away without having heard anything worth telling anyone, but they recovered, made hasty curtsies to Domina Elisabeth, and left in a swish of long black skirts, and only when they were gone did Frevisse realize Domina Elisabeth had given no order for food or drink to be brought for whoever this man was, a failure of courtesy that roused a warning in her even as Domina Elisabeth said somewhat crisply, "Master Naylor, you and Master Spencer are acquainted, I believe?"

"We've worked together, yes," Master Naylor answered, and then, as if he had been asked for an explanation, "He's Lord Lovell's bailiff for Prior Byfield."

Seemingly introducing her to Master Spencer was another courtesy being bypassed, and Frevisse raised her head to see what passed between the men as Master Naylor nodded greeting to the other man with, "Master Spencer. I hadn't thought to see you again before Michaelmas."

Master Spencer returned the nod but only barely and looked away to Domina Elisabeth who said as if doing a thing she did not want to, "He's come from Lord Lovell with a problem concerning you, Master Naylor."

Master Naylor looked between the two of them with a trace of surprise on his usually unrevealing face. "A problem?"

"It seems Lord Lovell has had report that possibly you're a villein of his," Domina Elisabeth said.

In the sudden gap of silence then, Frevisse was aware of the soft cooing of doves around the well in the courtyard below the open window, the warm shift of air across her face as a corner of the day's light wind found its way into the room, the distant clop of horses being led across cobbles in the outer yard, until slowly, as if finding his way to the words, Master Naylor said, "What am I to answer to that except to say it isn't true?"

"You could, if it's true, admit it," Domina Elisabeth said, as carefully as he'd asked it, "because clearly you've had far more than your fugitive year from him and are free, even if you were born bond."

Master Naylor looked at Master Spencer. "In this case, that wouldn't serve, would it? Lord Lovell always pursues his rights to any villein that flees."

"He would have entered his claim to you into the courts when you first fled, yes," Master Spencer agreed. And under law, that gave Lord Lovell right to claim his property no matter how long a time had passed.

"Except I was never his villein," Master Naylor said.

"That will have to be proven." Master Spencer turned from him to Domina Elisabeth. "You understand that with his skills and abilities, Naylor is valuable enough for my lord to pursue this in hope of having him back."

Frevisse noted that Master Spencer had already reduced Master Naylor to only Naylor, as without title as he would be without freedom if Lord Lovell's claim were proved true.

"And there are his wife and children, too," Master Spencer went on.

Frevisse saw Master Naylor's hands clench into fists at his sides, his first overt sign of anger and not for himself but for his family, threatened because a person's freedom or unfreedom were determined not only by their parentage but by their birthplace. If Master Naylor was proved to have been born unfree, then even if his wife was freeborn, their children would be unfree like their father, Lord Lovell's property along with him, unless it was shown they had been born on freehold land, and Frevisse knew for certain that at least some of them had been born here in St. Frideswide's priory that was not freehold. So if Master Naylor were proved villein born and his children born here, they could only be free if their mother was freeborn and not married to their father. But that would leave them bastards.

Tense with in-held anger, Master Naylor said, "My wife is freeborn. And my children. And me."

Not looking at him but somewhere into the air over Domina Elisabeth's shoulder, Master Spencer answered, "I promise you I'm no more pleased with this than you are, Naylor, but we both have to see it through, that's all."

"Then," said Domina Elisabeth curtly, "you might begin by continuing to call him *Master* Naylor until it's proven otherwise against him. Who made this accusation?"

"That isn't something I'm free to say," Master Spencer answered. "Someone saw him and recognized . . ."

"*Thought* they recognized," Frevisse put in with a curtness that matched Domina Elisabeth's.

"Thought they recognized him," Master Spencer said stiffly, giving her a sharp, resenting glance, "and rightly sent word to Lord Lovell of it."

By St. Benedict's Rule, the nunnery was required to take in as guests any travellers who asked for hospitality. It could have been anyone among those who had stayed in the guesthalls, here for only a night or two in passing, through the past few weeks, who had seen Master Naylor and thought they knew him and felt duty bound to tell Lord Lovell. Unless Master Spencer chose to tell them, they had no way of guessing who it had been, and likely who it had been did not really matter. The hurt was done and would have to be dealt with, whoever had caused it, Frevisse thought, while Master Spencer went on, "What I've come for, besides to tell you of it, is to insure he doesn't have chance to run again while this is sorted out."

"I can't run 'again,'" Master Naylor said grimly, "not having ever run at all."

Except for a sideways flinch of his eyes, Master Spencer ignored that. "Because he's potentially so valuable to his grace, I'm here to take him into my keeping, to see him to Minster Lovell, where he can be held safe, since bringing it to court will take time."

"No," Domina Elisabeth said with flat certainty.

Momentarily off-balanced by so utter a refusal, Master Spencer stared at her, then recovered his place and dignity, drew himself up, and started, "I fear I have to insist . . ."

"No," Domina Elisabeth repeated, her certainty unabated. "You will not take Master Naylor into your keeping or anywhere away from here. Considering how much it is in Lord Lovell's interest to find him unfree, I can't think it advisable to put him in your power."

"Madam!" Master Spencer rose to outrage. "I promise you his grace . . ."

"Is Lord Lovell bound by promises you make in his name?" Domina Elisabeth asked.

Master Spencer paused, tried, "If Naylor . . ."

Domina Elisabeth raised a hand in warning to him.

He colored. "If *Master* Naylor should run . . ."

"St. Frideswide's will undertake that he will not," Domina Elisabeth said.

But Master Spencer had found what looked to him to be firm ground. "If it's proven, madam, that he's Lord Lovell's villein and in the meantime you've let him flee,

I pray you consider that the priory will be liable for Lord Lovell's loss of him. Would St. Frideswide's be able to make good the loss and pay the penalties for it?"

Knowing as full well as Frevisse did that the answer to that was no, Domina Elisabeth skirted direct response with, "He won't be left free to run. I'll see to his being kept in his own house under watch while this is sorted out."

"Watched by whom?" Master Spencer asked. "They're all men who've worked under him. How good a watch can they be trusted to keep?"

Domina Elisabeth smiled at him pleasantly. "You're welcome, of course, to leave men of your own here to watch as well." And added before he could answer that, "I'll of course also be writing to Abbot Gilberd of St. Bartholomew's in Northampton for advice."

As only a priory, St. Frideswide's affairs were perforce overseen by an abbey that by right had final say in all its business but in practice mostly left the nuns to manage themselves. Only the disaster their last prioress had made of things had brought Abbot Gilberd directly into their affairs and allowed him to appoint their new prioress, rather than let them elect their own as was usual. He had chosen his sister, and now she invoked him as a reminder to Master Spencer that he had not only her to deal with, a "mere" woman, supposing he harbored any such fool's notion regarding women, which he shouldn't from what Frevisse knew of Lady Lovell, and it was with a touch of caution that he ventured in answer, "I see no reason why, under guard, Master Naylor can't stay here. With men of mine to guard him along with yours."

"And Lord Lovell paying for their keep, of course, since they're here in his service, not as our guests," Domina Elisabeth said.

Grudgingly Master Spencer agreed but added, "But I want Naylor's—Master Naylor's—elder son removed . . ." Master Naylor began a sharp movement toward him and

Master Spencer finished hurriedly, ". . . from the priory and given into the keeping of our reeve in the village. As surety he'll make no escape."

That was clever of him, Frevisse granted. From everything Frevisse knew of Master Naylor, he was most unlikely ever to leave his family behind while seeing to his own safety. Domina Elisabeth looked to him and asked, "Would you trust your boy to this reeve?"

"To Simon Perryn? Yes."

Domina Elisabeth looked back to Master Spencer. "Then we accept your request."

Master Spencer opened his mouth, probably to protest that it had been a demand, not a request, but seemingly thought better of it.

Domina Elisabeth smiled on him. "Is there aught else we need to deal with just now?"

"I think not, madam," he answered stiffly.

"We can speak more about it on the morrow if we find it necessary," she said and turned to Master Naylor. "Perhaps you'd best go and see to your son being taken to Simon Perryn and settling who'll be your guards this while."

Master Naylor bowed his acceptance, his long, lined face unreadable, but Master Spencer, very readable with indignation and disbelief, burst out, "Madam, he can't be allowed to choose his own guards!"

Domina Elisabeth's smile at him was hard edged with waning patience. "This is hardly a time of year, with so much to be done, both before and for the harvest, that we can afford to waste men standing about doing nothing. Who but Master Naylor knows best which men can be spared and when and for how long from their work?"

"But madam!"

Domina Elisabeth continued her smile at him. "You, of course, may arrange the matter of your own guards to your own satisfaction."

"But, madam!"

"Yes?" Her graciousness did not falter but, ever so slightly, her smile hardened, and Master Spencer pulled back from whatever else he had wanted to say. "Then we're finished for now, I think," Domina Elisabeth said pleasantly. "I trust you'll accept our hospitality for to-night?"

Looking as if he would rather chew raw nettles but the day too far along to leave him other choice unless he and his men were going to sleep on the roadside, Master Spencer said, managing to somewhat match her graciousness, "Yes. Thank you, madam."

"And Master Naylor," she said, turning to him again.

"My lady?"

"Be assured we'll pursue this matter to the end."

Master Naylor bowed. "My lady."

She dismissed them both with, "You may go," and they went, Master Spencer making a final bow and "Madam" to her.

Frevisse, undismissed, went on standing where she had stood all this while, not far into the room, her head bowed again while she listened to their feet going down the stairs, the brief silence, and then the hinge-squeal and thudding shut of the door that told they had left the cloister.

Across the room, looking out the window and down at them as they crossed the courtyard toward the gate-way, Domina Elisabeth said, annoyed and mocking, " 'Madam.' " The graciousness she had wielded against Master Spencer was abruptly gone. She turned away from the window. "Dame Frevisse, what do you make of this?"

One of the few things that made Frevisse uneasy with Domina Elisabeth was that the prioress was given to asking her opinion too often on things not strictly Frevisse's concern. It came, Frevisse feared, from Domina Elisabeth knowing, by way of Abbot Gilberd, too much about her, but there was no way to refuse being drawn into her pri-oress's confidence, and now she said cautiously, "I've never known Master Naylor to tell a lie or been given cause to think he's other than he seems."

"What do you know of him besides his duties here?"

"Nothing," Frevisse said in surprise. There had never been reason to know more of Master Naylor than that he did his work well.

"Nor do I."

"I'd have him write down all there is to know of where he was born," Frevisse said slowly, considering the matter. "Where and when and who are his family and who he thinks can confirm what he says."

Domina Elisabeth nodded agreement and said, carrying the thought exactly where Frevisse had been taking it, "And send that to my brother so he can send someone to prove Master Naylor's claims and bring us evidence enough to satisfy Lord Lovell so that maybe this won't have to go to any court." Which would be expensive. "That's the most we can do there. The other part of this trouble will be yours, I'm afraid."

Careful to keep wariness out of her voice, Frevisse asked, "The other part, my lady?"

Domina Elisabeth crossed her parlor to sit down in her high-backed chair. "I wanted you here for more than merely listening. I gathered from Lord Lovell's letter before ever Master Spencer spoke that we were in some manner of trouble concerning Master Naylor. We've protected him as best we can for now, but I doubt he'll be cleared of this foolishness so soon as we would like. Not soon enough with harvest so near, that's certain, and that isn't good, considering how many field and village matters have to be seen to in these next few weeks if they're going to be worth seeing to at all. I want you to take his place."

Under her vow of obedience, flat refusal was impossible, and while Frevisse marshalled all the reasons there were she could not possibly do this thing, Domina Elisabeth went on, "You're already cellarer. Taking Master

Naylor's place follows readily from what you already do."

Hiding desperation, Frevisse said, "Any one of the men who work under him will know better what's to be done than I possibly can."

"Assuredly, but they don't have the authority."

"Give it to them."

"I'd rather deal with you than with someone I don't know as well as I know Master Naylor, and it will serve as notice that we don't expect to be long without Master Naylor's services."

"I don't know enough," Frevisse insisted.

"You'll talk with Master Naylor whenever and however much you need to. Besides, I know you're able to make decisions on your own and give needed orders without waste of time when there's no time to waste."

"One of the other nuns," Frevisse tried, knowing that was the last and weakest of her hopes.

"None of the others is as able as you are to deal between men. None of us has been as much in the world as you've been."

"I won't be able to carry out my duties as cellarer and kitchener as fully as I should."

"Sister Johane can help you with the cellarer's less demanding matters. Sister Emma can take over as kitchener."

"Sister Emma in the kitchen . . ." Frevisse broke off, unsure which of Sister Emma's many kitchen failures was best to tell.

Domina Elisabeth, not experienced yet in what could happen in a kitchen if Sister Emma was not closely watched, said with unruffled certainty, "She'll learn best by doing."

She hasn't yet, Frevisse held back from saying.

The cloister bell began to ring Vespers' prayers, calling the nuns from whatever they were doing, from wherever they were, to the church. The priory's days were woven around the eight Offices of prayer, beginning with Matins and Lauds at midnight. Vespers marked the afternoon's end, with supper following it, and an hour's recreation before Compline's prayers, then bed.

"Of course you'll be excused the Offices whenever necessary while this lasts," Domina Elisabeth said, rising and coming toward the door in answer to the bell's summons.

Frevisse stopped in the midst of stepping aside and curtsying to her to ask blankly, "What?"

Already past her, Domina Elisabeth said back over her shoulder, "When you're in the village and out about the fields, you can't be forever running back here whenever it's time for prayers. You're excused them for this while, whenever necessary."

Frevisse found, following Domina Elisabeth down the stairs and into the cloister walk, that she was angry. Not even so much at being forced into Master Naylor's place when she very much did not want to be but at the way Domina Elisabeth was so easily dismissing her from prayers that were supposed to be the heart of everything they did within St. Frideswide's. But Domina Elisabeth was going on, "And there's the question of who should go with you." Because no nun was supposed to leave the nunnery unaccompanied by another nun. "I think Sister Thomasine would be best."

Frevisse lost stride, literally stumbling over that. Of the few nuns there were in St. Frideswide's, Sister Thomasine would have been, from simply a practical point of view, Frevisse's last choice.

"She prays so much of the time, I doubt it's good for her," Domina Elisabeth continued, going along the cloister walk toward the church now, some nuns already waiting at the door there, others still coming from elsewhere around the cloister. "She needs to be more in the world, I think, if only for a little while. Because how can she pray well for what she doesn't understand?"

The sense in that was counterbalanced, Frevisse feared,

by the reality of Sister Thomasine. She had desired nunhood and the cloistered life since she was a child, had
shunned men to the point of fear in her first years in St.
Frideswide's. Frevisse could not remember when last Sister Thomasine had been out of the cloister but didn't think
she had been past the priory's gates to the outside world
since coming in them eleven years or more ago, and behind her prioress' back, Frevisse prayed soundlessly and
from the heart, *"Ad Dominum, cum tribularer, clamavi et
exaudivit me. Kyrie, eleison. Christe, eleison . . ."* To the
Lord, when I was troubled, I cried out and he heard me.
Lord, have mercy. Christ, have mercy . . . On her as well
as Sister Thomasine.

# Chapter 3

imon's thought when word came from the priory was that it was bad news all the way around—first of what was toward with Master Naylor and then that a nun was taking his place. Simon's grandam had always said—far more often than anyone wanted to hear it—that you could always judge someone by how they took news of another's troubles, and the news of Master Naylor's troubles had proved her right again, as she would have declared to any who'd listen if she hadn't been dead these fifteen years.

Some had been simply glad to have something different to talk about. It hardly mattered who was in trouble so long as they could run off their tongues about it, shake their heads, and tut-tut over how the world went, you never knew, did you?

Then there were those—and not just those who might have had quarrel with Master Naylor one time or another but even some with reason to be grateful to him for justice or mercy given—who made glee he was come to grief and might come to worse before it was done. They were the sort who always felt that another man's going down somehow meant they were going up, as if everything were a seesaw, when to Simon's mind Fortune's wheel was still showed best the way the world went, taking you around and up and around and down and around and up again, and the best you could hope was that the being down went faster, ended sooner, than the being up, but the only thing certain was that Fortune was always turning that wheel. As his grandam, God keep her soul, had likewise been wont to say, Fortune's wheel and a fool's tongue were the two things never still.

For himself, Simon was sorry to hear of Master Naylor's trouble, whatever the rights or wrongs of it, and wished him well. It was when he found he had to deal with a nun in Master Naylor's place that he had turned sorry for himself, too.

"How'm I to deal with a nun?" he'd complained to Anne. "What's she to know of aught? Likely she can't even tell handle from prongs on a hayfork, let be what field should be grazed and which one plowed and what to do when Ralph Denton's hell-bound cow has been impounded again."

"So long as she knows she doesn't know and follows where you lead, it'll be well enough," Anne had answered and thumped the bread dough over on its board and gone on kneading it. "It's if she thinks she knows and doesn't that you'll have trouble right enough."

Simon had been wanting pity, not reason, and tried again. "With having to go back and forth to the nunnery whenever there's need to talk to her, there's good hours wasted every day."

"You can be to the nunnery by the field path in less time than it takes you to down a bowl of ale on a hot day," Anne had answered, "and you'll save the cost of the ale in the bargain."

Simon had given up. She'd find out soon enough what he was trying to make her understand, that this dealing with a nun was going to be trouble and more trouble, nothing but trouble.

So he was surprised to be sitting here on the bench by his own front door in the pear tree's shade, talking with this Dame Frevisse about what fieldwork needed to be done before Lammastide and starting to be at ease with her. Partly that was because she listened more than she talked, though he was finding there was a sharpness to the way she listened, as if she were hearing more than he said, that kept him careful of his words, but it boded well she'd come to the village, had sought him out instead of sending for him, and it boded better she'd brought a short, penned message from Master Naylor that she had his trust in taking his place this while. With that to start from, Simon had settled down to make the best of it, and they had agreed, right off, that neither of them was happy with Master Naylor's trouble and never thought, either of them, that he was villein-born and had run from it and lied about it. "I think his tongue would turn to wood if ever he tried to lie, he's that stiff-necked a man over truth," Simon had said, and Dame Frevisse had laughed, agreeing. Then he had set to telling her what things she'd need to know in Master Naylor's place: how far along the crops were, which fields were still in need of weeding before second haying came next week, who was caught up on their workdays, who was behind and why, and that he didn't know yet if there'd be need to hire out of the village for the harvest or not.

"It looks we'll likely need more men if we're to have

it done as fast as I'd like," Simon said, "but money is
short to hand after these past bad years and if we can do
without hiring it'd be to the good."

"But if we put off hiring for too long," Dame Frevisse
said, "there might be no one left to hire if after all there's
need."

"Aye, because likely everyone else is in the same case
as we are, and we're short a man already as it is, with
Matthew Woderove gone."

"Gone?" Dame Frevisse asked. "Dead?"

"Nay. Run off and stolen a horse into the bargain, too,
the fool."

"One of ours or one of Lord Lovell's?"

"Gilbey Dunn's, and he's not happy about it, right
enough."

"Not the horse. This Matthew Woderove. Is he the priory's or Lord Lovell's villein?"

"Oh. Lord Lovell's." And so Simon's problem and not
hers, worse luck.

"Warrant has been put out for him?"

"I sent word to Master Spencer. That's all I know about
it but I suppose so." His lordship was tight that way, he
didn't add aloud.

"Was this just lately?"

"Just past Midsummer."

"Odd he'd leave before harvest could give him money
to run on."

"He'd had bad luck of late," Simon said, easy enough
with her now to tell her the thing at length. "He lost his
bid on some leased land last manor court to Gilbey Dunn,
then quarreled with his wife over it and next thing anyone
knew, he was gone and so was Gilbey's horse."

And hadn't Mary been furious over it? She'd screamed
and thrown things, and what Matthew hadn't taken with
him in the way of clothing she'd dumped into the pigsty
and told the pigs they were welcome to it. Anne said it
was because it was one thing not to be able to bear a man,

the way Mary had long been swearing she couldn't bear Matthew, but another to find out he couldn't bear you. Simon had said it was past his understanding how anybody could bear Mary, and Anne had looked at him with pitying patience and said that was because he was Mary's brother; there were others saw her differently. Tom Hulcote for one. Knowing more than he wanted to about Mary and Tom Hulcote and the less said the better, Simon had dropped the matter, and Anne had let him.

"What's to be done about his land if he doesn't come back?" Dame Frevisse asked, bypassing the idle side of talk in favor of the heart of the problem of Matthew's going.

"His wife will run it for a time, until it's sure he's not coming back. Then it will come to manor court at Michaelmas to be decided who'll have it in his place."

"Will it go to her?"

"Nay, she'd not be able to manage it on her own. The land and messuage will go forfeit back to Lord Lovell, and likely whatever else there is that isn't all hers will be sold to pay Gilbey for the horse."

"A bad business all around. But nothing I need deal with?"

"It will be all mine when the time comes," Simon said regretfully. But it was not so bad as it might be. Mary had land of her own from their father and she'd be able to make do with that. But not happily, and Simon was already hearing about it from her, though what he was supposed to do, he didn't know.

Pushing that aside, he went on to matters at hand. "There's Alson Bonde, though. She and her son are priory villeins and there's something come up between them you maybe should know."

Dame Frevisse bent her head in the way that Simon was coming to recognize meant she was ready to listen. A woman more keeping of her words he'd never met; it threw him off pace but he gathered himself and said, "Old

Alson, after her husband died, was given half the holding
for life, and that was well enough with young William,
her son, but now she's wanting to let her land to Martin
Fisher for ten years and young William is flat against it."

"Why? Why does she want to lease it and why is he
against it?"

"She wants to lease it because it's too much for him
to work alone. It was well enough when it was him and
old William, but it's too much for just him, and his three
boys are too small yet to be of much use. Alson wants to
lease her share to Martin Fisher, who could use more land
than he has, and give the money to young William, except
for what she needs to live on, so he can hire help and
save him working himself to death before his boys are
grown."

"That seems well thought on. Why is young William
against it?"

"He just keeps saying his father wouldn't have done
it. He's not quick of his wits, is young William. A good
man but not quick. Lease or no lease, I think to him it's
like the land will be out of the family and he knows his
father would never have wanted that and so he can't want
it either."

Simon hesitated over saying more but, "Yes?" Dame
Frevisse asked.

Close-mouthed and sharp-eyed. Someone was blessed
she'd become a nun instead of a wife, Simon thought, but
only said, "The thing is, Gilbey Dunn's been nosing in
about it. Just a little, his mind not made up to offer for
it, but if he does . . ." Simon paused; but if Master Naylor's trouble went on for long, these were all things she'd
learn anyway, and he said, "Gilbey has a strong eye and
a sure hand to his own ends, and since he married a few
years ago and has sons now, he seems more set than ever
on being even better off than he is. Some say as how it's
his wife that's pushing him, she being out of Banbury and
freeborn and on the young side for old Gilbey . . ." That

was astray from what needed saying and Simon shifted ground to, "The thing is, if he decides to offer for the Bonde lease, he'll likely offer more than Alson can bear to let pass by and then there'll be a falling out indeed between her and young William like I don't want to see."

"But there'll be a falling out if she settles with Martin Fisher, too, won't there?"

"Not so bad, likely. Martin's a good man."

"And Gilbey isn't?"

"It's not that Gilbey's bad," Simon allowed slowly. "Naught the priest should see to."

"But?"

"He's not much liked in the village," Simon said, then added, to be as fair as might be, "It's not so much what he does." Though that wasn't strictly to the truth. What Gilbey did was be richer than anyone else and not mind who knew it or care what anyone thought of it. "He just doesn't set well with folks. It's how he is."

"So, all around, it would be better something was decided and settled with Martin Fisher and soon, rather than have Gilbey Dunn come in on it, and you've some thought on how to do that."

Simon had, and said more readily than he would have to her an hour ago, "Martin has a half-grown girl and young William has sons. I've thought that if, along with the lease, there was agreement made for Martin's daughter to marry young William's oldest boy when they're old enough, then young William wouldn't mind the lease, the land still being in the family, like. Only I didn't want to say aught to them about it until I knew the priory would favor the lease to start with."

Dame Frevisse thought on that in silence for a moment, then said, "I don't see there'd be objection to it from the priory's side."

"Gilbey Dunn would offer better money, if he comes to it."

"It's better to have peace in a family than money,"

Dame Frevisse said, then added after a small pause, "so long as there's enough to eat."

Simon, bypassing whether she'd meant that as a jest or no, went on to, "There's only the bylaws, then. Seems we might want a new one, saying no one is to take hire outside the village if he can find work here for . . . well, we're trying to decide how many pence a day to allow, times and need being what they are. And the rest of the bylaws need to be read out in church next Sunday or so, for those as like to forget them from one year to the next."

Dame Frevisse nodded her understanding of that. "There are always those will tether their horses in the wheat stubble before Michaelmas no matter what, unless they're told straight to their face and in front of everyone that they're not to."

Simon was about to agree to that with a laugh when his man Watt came at a hurry into sight along the street and by the plank bridge over the ditch into the yard. He stopped short as he caught sight of Simon and Dame Frevisse, then came on, to bow to her without quite taking his eyes from her, because although the priory was just across East Field from Prior Byfield, the nuns were nonetheless an uncommon sight, and said to Simon, "There's some men ridden in. They're at the alehouse and want to talk to the reeve."

Forebearing to ask what Watt had been doing at the alehouse, Simon stood up and made bow to Dame Frevisse, asking, "By your leave?"

# Chapter 4

Frevisse gave Simon Perryn leave to go without hesitation, agreed to wait to finish with the by-laws and hear some questions he had for Master Naylor about the second haying, and watched him leave, a sure-striding, square-built man of middle years and middle height in a dark blue tunic of well-woven cloth, un-mended heavy green hosen, and leathern boots that had had good wear and would last for more. There was nothing shabby about his servant either, even rough-dressed as he was for fieldwork, and that spoke as well of master as of man. In truth, everything Frevisse had so far seen of Perryn and his holding spoke well of him, everything well kept and prospering. Here in his foreyard, between the house and the shallow ditch that separated the mes-suage from the street and village green, the garden was laid out in neatly bordered beds with narrow paths between and crowded full of herbs and summer vegetables—garden peas and beans, summer squash, lettuce and other greens, rhubarb—for fresh eating after all the months there had been only kept food to hand. Along one side of the yard a low withy fence separated the yard from a neighbor's, while on the other side there was a long byre, right-angled to the house because none but the poorest peasant shared house-space with their animals. Whatever cows Perryn had were long since out to pasture this morning after milking, but there were chickens scattered around the dusty stretch of yard in front of it, questing for what they could find in the way of dropped grain or roused insects; and because messuages were usually narrow-fronted to the street and long to the back, behind the house there were likely a barn, maybe another byre, sheds, probably a sty with pigs and piglets for winter pork and bacon, possibly more garden, and maybe other fruit trees besides the pear tree here and, across the yard, beyond the garden, an apple tree with branches beginning to bend to the weight of its apples, its shade sheltering a patch of grass and another bench.

That was where Sister Thomasine had betaken herself, to sit alone at her prayers while Frevisse talked with Perryn and where she was now but no longer alone or at her prayers. A while ago a small girl-child in a loose, knee-long smock had toddled out from the house, stood for a time staring at Perryn and Frevisse, then trotted off across the yard to Sister Thomasine and was there now, leaning against her knees, listening to Sister Thomasine who seemed to be explaining about the string of rosary beads she held.

That Sister Thomasine might be good with children had never occurred to Frevisse. But neither had she thought Sister Thomasine would be so little disturbed at being out in the world. She had taken their prioress' order with bowed head and a quiet "Yes, my lady" and nothing

more, and when the time had come this morning to go
out the gateway from the priory's inner yard as she had
not gone since entering as a novice, she had done nothing
more than pause, bow her head to murmur a brief prayer
and make the sign of the cross over her breast, before she
went on, her hands tucked into her opposite sleeves and her
head down, showing as little as possible of herself and seeing as little of the world as might be while she and Frevisse
crossed the priory's outer yard with its clutter of stables,
barns, byres, workshops, storage sheds and folk—mostly
men—busy at their work.

Time had been, in Sister Thomasine's young days, that
even the sound of men's voices had been enough to
shrivel her with fear but thankfully she was grown past
that depth of simplicity. In truth, Frevisse had come to
see that in the ways of prayer and the spirit, Sister Thomasine was very far from simple, whatever lack of interest
she had in going out into the world beyond priory walls,
although today as they had walked along the road sunken
between low-cropped hedges toward the village, she had
stopped once to bend down and touch an herb Robert's
red petals bright in the wayside grass, another time had
paused, head lifted, to heed a chaffinch making merry on
an upthrust hedge branch, and once, where a low field
gate let them see beyond the hedges, she had stopped to
watch the long grass in an unmown hayfield bend and
sway with the warm wind, then turned to Frevisse and
said in her soft, near-whispering voice, "It's very beautiful, God's world."

Frevisse had nodded silent agreement, Sister Thomasine had watched the wind-brushed hayfield for another
moment, and they had gone on, Sister Thomasine withdrawing into herself again when they entered the village,
leaving questioning of where the reeve lived to Frevisse
and, when they had found him, taking herself aside to sit
under the apple tree with her prayers.

Frevisse stirred out of her thoughts, considering she

might after all not wait for Perryn to return. If they left now, she and Sister Thomasine might be in time for None, and she could come back tomorrow after talking over what small matters she needed to with Master Naylor about the bylaws. But before she could do more than stir, a woman said beside her, "My lady, would you and the other sister care for something to drink?"

Frevisse turned to look up at the woman in the doorway with a green-glazed pitcher in one hand, two green-glazed cups in the other. Simon Perryn's wife, she guessed, because although, as with most women of middle years, the wimple and veil made it difficult to judge her age, she was assuredly no servant. Though her gown was simply cut, shaped to her but loose enough for working in, it was of well-dyed, good linen, her wimple and veil of equal quality, the veil lightly starched, the wimple falling in soft folds over her throat and shoulders, only marred on the breast by a somewhat grubby handprint of a size to have come from the little girl across the yard; and though she likely had never had a nun at her doorstep before now, she was at ease, smiling, as she held out the pitcher and cups.

Frevisse smiled back at her. "You'll have to ask Sister Thomasine if she does but, if you'll join me, I'll gladly thank you for some."

Perryn's wife made her a smiling curtsy and crossed the yard to where Sister Thomasine and the child were still busy together, spoke with them and was coming back when a burst of boys appeared from between house and byre. There momentarily seemed to be a great many of them but as they skidded to a halt, bumping into one another, at sight of her, Frevisse saw there were only three, the oldest maybe twelve, the youngest maybe eight, the other somewhere in between, but all of them wet and muddy. Staring at her, they jostled elbows into each other, made awkward boy-bows, and headed away along one of the paths through the garden toward Perryn's wife, who met them where their way crossed the garden's wide middle path and said sternly, albeit around laughter, "Nay, keep your distance. I don't need you dripping on me nor you're not going inside like that either."

"But Mum . . ." the middle one began in protest.

She pointed toward a shadowed corner beside the byre. "You just take yourselves over there and dry for a while before you even think of coming inside. Cisily will bring you something to eat and drink," she added.

Promise of food diverted them and they went, laughing and loud, where their mother had pointed while she came on, to set the jug and cups on the bench and lean through the houseplace doorway to call, "Cisily! Starving boys by the byre. Milk and buttered bread, please," and sat down on the bench where her husband had been. Still smiling, she said, "They've been to the stream," and took up the jug to pour a pale ale into one of the cups with, "Sister Thomasine wanted none but I hope you do?"

She held the cup out to Frevisse who took it with thanks and, "You'll join me, I pray you?"

"Thank you, my lady," she said and added while she poured for herself, "I'm Anne, the reeve's wife."

Frevisse acknowledged that with a slight bow of her head and, "I'm Dame Frevisse."

They talked a little of Master Naylor's trouble, then moved on to how grateful they were for the good weather. An older woman in simple servant's garb and apron came out of the house bearing a tray with a plain pottery jug and wooden cups and half a loaf of sliced buttered bread. Brisk and cheerful, she crossed the yard toward the boys who leaped to their feet, the tallest taking the tray from her. She told them, "Mind you bring it in when you're done, not just leave it sitting here," and for what it might be worth they nodded agreement, mouths already crammed with bread. On her way back to the house she took the chance for a thorough look at Frevisse while making a quick-bobbed curtsy to her and her mistress, and was just gone inside when Anne stood quickly up, calling, "Lucy, no," and moved to head off the little girl now making a toddle-legged run along the straightest garden path toward the boys—or, more probably, toward their food.

Anne caught her where the garden paths crossed, saying as she scooped her up, "There now, if you get dirty with them you'll have to be washed now and at bedtime, too, and you don't want that, do you?"

"Food!" Lucy declared, her determination undeterred by being carried toward the house tucked under her mother's arm like a kindling bundle.

Setting her down on the houseplace's door sill, Anne said, "Cisily will give you your own bread and milk inside," straightened the child's gown and gave her a gentle push. Lucy, as biddable as her brothers if food was promised, went in and Anne sat down again with a great sigh and an apology.

"She's a pretty child," Frevisse ventured, that usually something safe to say to a parent and this time true.

"Pretty is as pretty does, and sometimes she's none too pretty, I promise you," Anne returned, smiling. "We named her for my husband's grandmother and she looks like to be as set to her ways as she was." Anne did not add "more's the pity," but it was there in her rueful tone.

"And you've Master Naylor's son on your hands, too," Frevisse remembered somewhat belatedly. "How does he?"

"Dickon? Very well." Anne nodded across the yard toward the boys, sitting with their backs to the byre wall now, each with a cup in one hand and a large slice of bread in the other, the two older boys kicking lazily at each other's bare feet lest things be too peaceful. "He's the brown-haired one." The other two were fair-haired like their sister and younger than Dickon, guessing by their look. "It helps he was already friends with most of the village boys before this trouble and here as often as not, so nothing is strange to him."

"Is he bothered by what's happening?"

"If he is, he keeps it to himself. He says he doesn't mind being away from his sisters and baby brother because, according to him, they all stink. Mind you, when someone—not Adam or Colyn, they know better—teased him the other day over his father being a villein instead of a free man, Dickon took him down, rubbed his face in the dirt, and told him, 'My father never lies and if he says he's not a villein, then he's not a villein, there!' "

Anne told it laughingly but her laughter stopped and her face clouded as she looked away toward the street and a woman coming along it, a napkin-covered plate in her hands. "Gilbey Dunn's wife," she said, not welcomingly, but brought up a smile and rose to greet her as the woman started across the plank bridge into the yard.

Frevisse stayed seated, watching the woman come. She had had brief dealing with Gilbey Dunn years ago and was curious as to what sort of woman had married him. She was younger than Anne and, Frevisse was startled to see, lovely out of the ordinary. Her face was heart-shaped from wide forehead to perfect chin, and she was so fair skinned and pale browed she was surely golden-haired beneath her veil and wimple. Beyond that, her rose-colored dress was of a finer sort than most village women would have, better even than Anne's for cut and cloth, but it was the way she wore it, with a light-hipped grace, that made the greatest difference.

By then, Anne had met her, was bringing her back toward the bench with a creditable display of welcome, saying, "Dame Frevisse, this is Elena, Gilbey Dunn's wife. Elena, Dame Frevisse is doing what can be done to take Master Naylor's place this while."

Elena curtsyed deeply, with practiced grace, Frevisse slightly bowed her head, and they briefly exchanged comments on Master Naylor before Elena turned to Anne, taking the napkin from the plate to show small cakes and said, "They're honey-raisin, new-baked, that I thought the boys might like. And Lucy, too," she added to the little girl come to stand in the doorway staring at her and bent to hold the plate out to her.

"Only one," Anne said.

"There's enough for two apiece," Elena said.

"Two," Anne said. "And say thank you."

Lucy, a cake in either hand, said clearly, loudly, "Thank you," and disappeared inside again.

Meanwhile, the boys had begun to sidle across the yard as soon as the plate had been uncovered, coming faster when they saw Lucy claiming cakes, and now the taller of the fair-haired boys, with his brother and Dickon Naylor crowded close at his back, said, "Thank you, too," with earnest hope behind Elena, and she turned and held the plate out to them all. Hands flashed and with chorused thanks the boys retreated toward the byre as Elena turned back to Anne and Frevisse, holding the plate out to them, too, laughing silently.

Frevisse said thanks but shook her head. Anne said, "Keep mine a moment while I bring a cup for you and see to a pot I left on the fire. Please, sit."

She gestured to the bench and left them, and Elena sat, holding the plate toward Frevisse again, asking, "You're sure?"

Frevisse assured her she was. Elena looked briefly across the yard to Sister Thomasine beneath the apple tree, her head bowed over the rosary in her hands and made no offer that way but settled with the plate and its remaining cakes on her lap. "It's a warm day," she observed.

"You wanted to talk to me?" Frevisse said in return.

The neat arch of Elena's eyebrows curved higher and her smile suddenly warmed past mere good manners. "Yes, I do indeed, if you please, my lady. About my husband."

How had so well-spoken a woman come to be a villein's wife in Prior Byfield, Frevisse wondered. But only asked cautiously, "Yes?" Because from what she knew of Gilbey Dunn, caution seemed best.

"You'll be talked to about him this while that village matters are in your hands. I wanted to talk to you about him first."

That it was already so widely known that she was taking Master Naylor's place came as no surprise to Frevisse, knowledgeable of village ways. To show she, too, knew more than might be expected of her, she said, "I understand he's interested in acquiring more land."

"That's not a fault," Elena said quickly, a little too carefully.

"It's not a fault," Frevisse agreed. "Most men want to better themselves." She hesitated, then added, deliberately to see Elena's response, "The fault only comes if they do it with harm to others."

"Gilbey has harmed no one."

That might be strictly true, if harm direct was meant, but there was harm indirect, and she asked, "Didn't he lately bid a lease away from a man who's now run off because of it?"

"It's more likely Matthew Woderove left because of his wife than because of Gilbey," Elena answered calmly. And raised herself in Frevisse's opinion by saying nothing else of Matthew Woderove's wife, though surely there was more that could have been. Instead she said, "He's a good man, my husband. He does well by all he holds, whether from Lord Lovell or your priory, and pays well for it, too. Better than most could or would. Any of the accounts you look at will show you that. There's some who hold it against him that he does so well, but that's all they have to hold against him. What I've come to ask is that you don't, that's all."

Frevisse could hear Anne inside, telling Cisily what to do with the stew on the fire and moving toward the door while she did, and quickly she asked Elena, "Why does your husband pay the fine to keep from ever being reeve here?"

Elena paused at the shift of direction, then answered openly enough, "He isn't liked."

"That isn't needed for the office," Frevisse returned. Years and experience and a degree of wealth grown out of both were what were looked for, whether the office was appointed by the lord, as in Prior Byfield, or elected, as in other places. By that, Gilbey was as likely to the office as Simon Perryn was. "There's money to be made in it," she added bluntly.

"There's better ways to make money without having to daily deal with people who dislike you," Elena returned as bluntly. And laughed as if suddenly, truly pleased. "My husband said I'd likely find talking with you more challenge than I'd expect."

It was one thing for her to remember Gilbey Dunn and another to find that he remembered her, Frevisse found. Somewhat discomfited, she asked, "Why did he say that?"

"Because unlike most women, he said, you see further than the flutter of your veil."

And so did his wife, Frevisse judged; but Anne came out then, with a cup for Elena and a stool for herself. As she poured Elena ale after Frevisse refused more, she said, "So. You've kept in talk?"

"I was about to set to persuading Dame Frevisse that she should put in good word for my husband when the matter of Matthew Woderove's holding comes up," Elena said easily.

"Matthew might still come back," Anne answered, a little stiffly.

"He might," Elena allowed. "But if he doesn't . . ."

"I think your husband has done Matthew enough harm without being the one to take his holding, too," Anne said, more stiffly.

"The only person who's harmed Matthew Woderove is

himself," Elena said, unangrily but giving no ground.

Anne began an answer but Lucy called from inside and instead she rose with, "I pray you excuse me."

When she was inside, Elena rose, too, not outwardly bothered, and said smilingly to Frevisse, "I'll go, too, I think. By your leave." What could have been regret tinged her smile and voice as she added, "Anne will be more comfortable if I'm not here."

To Frevisse's granting she could go, she made a low curtsy of farewell and went, leaving the plate and the remaining cakes on the bench. Anne was in time, coming out, to see her leaving and could have called farewell, or Elena might have looked back and waved, but neither did, and Anne, sitting down on the bench again, said while watching her out of sight, "I'll say for her she never overstays her welcome."

Frevisse almost asked how much welcome Elena had ever had but changed to, "Is she freeborn? Your husband said she's from Banbury." The nearest market town.

"Aye, she's freeborn. Her father is a baker there, with property and a likelihood of being mayor. What she was thinking of, to marry Gilbey and come here, I don't know." Anne broke off a corner of one of the cakes and crumbled it between her fingers. "She's too young for him by far and . . . well, you've seen her. Men can't help but look at her, and they want to do more than look, too, that's sure. That Tom Hulcote that works for Gilbey, for one. Gilbey'd do well to watch him." It sounded a well-worn theme, with more to be said about it, just as with Matthew Woderove's wife, but Anne broke off, turning a little pink across the cheeks, probably at such tale-telling to a nun, and changed course with, "It's that Gilbey's not given to doing fool things. It was years since his first wife and their daughter died, and he seemed content enough. Then, next thing we knew, he'd married her and built a bigger house and started a family all over again. At his age! What was either of them thinking?"

"There's children then?"

"Oh, yes. Two sweet little boys."

"Are they villein or free?"

"Free. When she nears her birthing time, Elena goes to Gilbey's sister. She bought herself free years ago and married and lives in Banbury. Both boys were born there."

And so were free, like their mother, instead of villein like their father.

"Gilbey isn't well liked, is he?" Frevisse asked.

Anne sniffed. "He's too lucky, making money at everything he turns his hand to, and keeps what he has to himself, no fear, while letting you know he has it." She waxed openly indignant. "You know he bought a lease away from Matthew Woderove this past Midsummer's court? It's for a stretch of rough pasturage gone to scrub and not worth the bother of clearing it again, everyone thought, but he's bought half a dozen cows in milk from somewhere and turned them out on it, hired two girls and set them to be his milkmaids, making cheese as fast as can be to sell in Banbury, and the word is that come autumn, he won't try to overwinter the cows but slaughter them and salt the beef down to sell. You see how he goes about things?"

What Frevisse saw was that Gilbey Dunn had a skill for turning money into more money and, covering her interest, asked, "Why didn't Matthew Woderove use it that way?"

"Matthew has only the one cow and no skill at making money enough to have more. He never had the chance, did he?"

But he had had the land and let it waste. Gilbey had seen its possibility and taken it, able to because of what he had not wasted through the years in the way of money and other chances, Frevisse guessed.

"For all he's so clever, though," Anne said, nibbling crumbs from one of the cakes as if grudging they tasted so good but unable to help herself, "I'd keep an eye on

Elena and that Tom Hulcote together if I were him."

Perryn came into sight at that moment, long-striding up the street, his hand raised in greeting and an apology started as he crossed the plank bridge into the yard. Frevisse and Anne stood up and moved to meet him, but the boys were quicker, tumbling up like a rout of puppies from a game they had been scratching in the dust beside the byre, to pelt across the yard with happy shouts and cluster around him, jostling each other to be the first to tell him something while he tousled their hair and told them, "You wait on a moment. I'll hear it all later. Right now there's strangers by the alehouse if you want to go and have a stare at them."

They did, and in a flurry of bare legs and yells they dashed away, leaving Perryn abruptly deserted and sharing a smile warm with affection with his wife as she came toward him. It was a smile full of so many things understood between them past the need of saying that Frevisse understood far more about them both—beginning with how glad they were of each other and how much they loved their sons—than words would have sufficed for.

But Perryn was already saying, "I pray your pardon, my lady. It was something more than I thought it would be. There's men of the crowner come with questions about a body."

"Here?" Frevisse asked, unlikely though that was. The village would know of any body before the crowner would, surely.

"Nay. Over Wroxton way. Seems there's been one found near there, with no one knowing who he was. The crowner's sent these men out on rounds with some of what was found with him in hopes someone can say who he was after all."

"Poor man," Anne said.

"The trouble is," Perryn went on, "they don't want to spend long over it, so I've had to send to bring everyone in from the fields, and when they're done, I'll have to see to them all going out again or they'll likely stand about talking the rest of the day away."

"And you'd rather I came back tomorrow to finish our business," Frevisse said.

"If it'd not be too much trouble, my lady."

"None. Or not compared to what you have on your hands now." Not that it would not have mattered if it had been too much trouble, because the crowner and his men were charged, as officers of the king, with looking into any uncertain deaths, to find if there was guilt or only happenstance involved, and whether or no the matter should be given over to the county sheriff. Therefore their business had precedence over hers. But then, neither did she mind the excuse it gave her to have done with manor business for today.

While she thanked Anne for her hospitality and beckoned for Sister Thomasine to join her, Perryn left them, returning down the street toward the alehouse, where Frevisse could now see the five horsemen waiting near a widespread oak on the green. A scattering of village folk not out to the fields today for one reason or another were already gathering to them and, grateful she needed have no part in it, she turned with Sister Thomasine to go the other way, back to St. Frideswide's.

# Chapter 5

hen, next day, the nuns came out of
the church into the cloister walk after
the midmorning Office of Terce, the
day was already far warmer than other days had been of
late, and Sister Amicia, slipping a finger inside her wimple to loosen it and let in a little air, murmured, "It's going
to be hot before it's done," while Dame Juliana looked
up from the cloister garth's garden of herbs and flowers
to the narrowness of blue sky, naked of clouds, that was
all that could be seen of the world from there and said,
"We need rain." Domina Elisabeth, having led the way
out of the church, was already well away, headed back
toward her rooms and whatever work awaited her there.
Dame Perpetua and Sister Johane were returning to their
scribe's desks, set against the church wall here along the

walk for best light on their copying. There were no com-
missions in hand just now, but Domina Elisabeth had set
them to the *Revelations of St. Birgitta* on the expectation
that something so popular could be sold to someone when
it was finished. The other nuns, and now Sister Amicia
and Dame Juliana, were straying their various ways away
along the cloister walk, in no haste to be back to what
they had been doing before the bell called them to Terce,
while Frevisse stood undecided between going to her own
scribal work, as she would have to do sometime today,
or else to talk with Master Naylor since she had not yesterday.

The question was resolved by a guesthall servant coming into the cloister walk from the passage to the outer
door and guesthall yard. Frevisse, having been hosteler,
in charge of St. Frideswide's guesthalls more than once
through the years, knew her and started toward her, saying, "Ela," and the woman turned her way with a relieved
smile, making a quick curtsy as they met at the corner of
the cloister walk and saying, "There's someone come as
wants to see you, my lady. Can you come out to him?"

"Who?"

"Simon Perryn, the reeve."

"Where is he?" Frevisse asked, already on her way to
the outer door.

"By the well in the yard," Ela answered, following her,
but in the yard veered away, back toward the guesthall,
as Perryn rose from where he had sat down on one of the
well's steps, hood in hand and looking uncertain whether
he should be here, but he bowed and said, "Good day,
my lady. I hope it's no trouble I've come without asking
leave but I didn't know when you'd be back and there's
something happened I thought you ought to know as soon
as might be."

"When there's need, better you come than not. What's
happened?"

"That body up Wroxton way that those men came about yesterday, you remember?"

She nodded that she did, though after saying a prayer for the fellow's soul on her way back to St. Frideswide's, she had not thought of him again until now.

"Seems, by what the crowner's man brought, it's Matthew Woderove."

"The man who ran off a few weeks ago?"

"Aye. His wife knew his shirt and says the bit of hair they'd brought along matches his. I'd say the same," Perryn added unhappily. "She's my sister, see, and taking it hard."

"Do they know how he died?"

"There wasn't much left to tell by from the body, what there was of it. By the look of it, he's been dead most of the time he's been gone and was lying out in a ditch the while."

And the weather had been warm, and birds and other things would have been at him.

"But it's sure his skull was broken," Perryn went on, "and it looks like he was stabbed twice at least. There were knife-scrapes on his ribs."

Probably killed for the horse he'd stolen, then robbed of whatever little else he'd had and left to rot, Frevisse supposed and shook her head against the waste and ugliness of it.

"It's Wroxton folk are in trouble," Perryn said. "They knew the body was there but said naught about it to anyone since he wasn't one of their own."

By law, any untimely deaths had to be reported to crowner or sheriff, but those who reported such a death were then burdened with legal duties because of it, whether they had aught to do with the death or not, and sometimes, especially when the death had nothing to do with anyone they knew, folk would ignore the law, in hope the trouble would pass unnoticed. That would have been Wroxton's hope and they would be paying in fines and penalties for it.

"How did it come to be known?" Frevisse asked.

"Someone who'd seen talked of it in Banbury, and the crowner heard about it."

"You'll have the body brought back here for burying?"

"Oh, aye. Among his own folk and all. But it's other than that I've come about. Now it's sure he's dead, his holding is open, no mistake, and there's a quarrel already shaping over it."

"Over who's to have it? There're no children to inherit? Doesn't his wife have right in it?"

"When he and Mary married, our father settled a toft and some land on her for a marriage portion, the thought being that instead of some of Matthew's land being given over for her widow's dower, it would all go to their children. Only they never had children, and there's no one going to make the mistake of thinking Mary can manage the holding on her own. She's clever enough, all in all, but not that way, if you see what I mean."

Frevisse saw and acknowledged Perryn's careful way of saying his sister was no fool but not given to what was needed for the running of a holding. "So, now it's known that Woderove is dead and won't ever be back," Frevisse said, "she's lost all rights to the holding and there are others interested."

Perryn gave a glooming nod. "Gilbey Dunn, for one. Last night, almost as soon as it was known Matthew was dead, he told me he'd take it over and see to the harvest and Mary having a fair share of it this year for compensation, though what Gilbey thinks is a fair share is anyone's guess."

"If the 'fair share' is settled on and agreed to beforehand, it sounds a reasonable offer," Frevisse said slowly, looking for reasons it was not but finding none except that Gilbey Dunn maybe had enough already and didn't need more.

"Gilbey'd do better by the holding than ever Matthew did, that's sure," Perryn said, "so there's no problem with that. The trouble lies in that Tom Hulcote's offered for it, too, and almost as fast as Gilbey did."

Frevisse searched and found she knew Hulcote's name from Anne Perryn's talk yesterday and said, "He works for Gilbey Dunn."

"He did but quit of late, just ere Gilbey would have turned him off anyway. He holds a toft and not much else and works for other men to make his way. Lately mostly for Gilbey."

With talk of there being something more than work between him and Gilbey's wife, Frevisse recalled but only said, "Now he wants to better himself by taking over the Woderove holding?"

"Just so."

"Would he do well by it?"

"He might. Aye. Maybe." Perryn's uncertainty was plain before he settled for saying, "He's not steady about doing what he says he'll do, is the trouble. He's not always someone who takes the orders he's given. The thing is, his offer betters Gilbey's because he's offered to marry the widow . . ."

"Your sister."

"Aye. He says he'll marry her to have the holding."

There was nothing uncommon in that. When a woman could not run a holding by herself and there was a man willing to take both it and her, it settled two problems at once. At its best, neither woman nor man lost, the woman keeping her place instead of losing it, the man gaining what he would not have been able to have any other way. It worked more often than not, and Frevisse asked, "What does your sister say to it?"

"She says she's willing."

"But you're not."

Perryn frowned at his feet, thinking before he said slowly, "The thing is, Hulcote is the priory's villein, so it's not my choice only. I'd hoped to speak with Master Naylor on it, but they're not letting anyone near him, seems."

"That will be Master Spencer's doing." In return for leaving Master Naylor at the priory, Lord Lovell's steward had left orders with his guards to keep him strictly confined and let nearly no one in to see him. "I meant to go to him today," Frevisse said. "I'll go now."

"There's one thing more," Perryn said. "It's in manor court the final word on this will have to be and there's not one due until Michaelmas, but if we're agreed, we can call it sooner and it'd likely be best to have this settled soon, what with harvest so near to hand and all. Ask Master Naylor what he says to that, too, would you?"

"Assuredly. How soon would it suit you to have answer?"

They were going toward the gateway to the outer yard now, Perryn walking respectfully well aside but not behind her as if he were a servant, while he consideringly answered, "Notice has to be given and all, so not sooner than two days but as little longer than that as may be. Mary is going on . . ." He broke off, probably because it was a family thing, with no need Frevisse know of it; said instead, "Is there any new word about Master Naylor, one way or other?"

"Nothing yet. We hope to have some word from Abbot Gilberd no later than tomorrow of what he'll do to help. Has Master Naylor ever said anything to you about where he's from, his family?" There had been a nephew at the priory for a while, a few years back, but he was gone, and Lord Lovell could claim family testimony to Master Naylor's birth was useless anyway because their own free birth might be called into question if his was proved false.

"He's never talked much about himself," Perryn said, "and never about where he came from to me."

They were nearing the outer gateway where their ways would part. With what she trusted was reasonably good hope, Frevisse said, "Abbot Gilberd will find those enough who can swear Master Naylor is freeborn."

"And before too long," Perryn said, matching her hope.

They made their farewells and he went his way, out the gateway to the road, while she turned aside. There were three houses built side to each here, close inside the priory's main gateway, their front doors opening directly into the priory's outer yard, their backs to the inside of the priory wall but set forward from it with space enough for gardens at their rear. The porter, with keeping of the gateway, lived in the one nearest the gate. Beside his was Master Naylor's while he was steward of St. Frideswide's, and the third would have been for the priory's bailiff if ever St. Frideswide's had grown enough to need another man to oversee its properties and lands, but the widow who had founded it near to a hundred years ago had died before endowing it as fully as she had meant to, and there had never been a flourish of prosperity afterwards to bring it much more than she had left it, so the third house served for keeping such of the priory's records as did not need to be directly in Domina Elisabeth's hands or in Frevisse's as cellarer.

The two guards presently on duty at Master Naylor's door stood up from their bench when she came their way. She spoke to the priory man, nodded with distant politeness at Lord Lovell's, and said to him mildly, "It would make matters easier if the reeve were allowed to talk with Master Naylor directly."

"It would, wouldn't it, my lady?" the priory man said, his glance at the man beside him thick with disgust.

The other man came not quite to shuffling with unease as he said more to the dusty ground than Frevisse, "It's orders, my lady."

She knew the orders Master Spencer had left: she could see Master Naylor and talk with him as much as she wanted; anyone else, in need of his immediate answer about some minor thing here inside the priory, could pass in a question by way of the priory guard and have the answer back the same way but never talk to him directly. It was cumbersome and annoying, and she hoped whoever Abbot Gilberd sent would have authority to do something about it, but she could not and settled now for knocking at the house door standing open in the day's warmth.

Mistress Naylor came shortly from somewhere inside with floured hands and apron, unwimpled because of the heat, only a veil pinned over her dark hair. She was a small-boned woman from whom Frevisse had never had more than ten words together, with "my lady" invariably two of them. Now, to Frevisse's greeting and request to see Master Naylor, she made a low curtsy and said, "Through here, my lady, if you please," and led back the way she had come.

The house was much as Frevisse supposed its two neighbors must be, with two narrow ground-story rooms, the front one facing the yard, the other opening into the garden at the back, with between them a staircase hardly wider than a man's shoulders going steeply up to whatever narrow rooms there were above. The front room served for general living, the back one as the kitchen, with today as small a fire as possible burning on the hearth under a trivet-set pot, with a griddle heating beside it for whatever Mistress Naylor was making toward dinner. Even so small a fire made the room too hot and Frevisse was glad go on, out the rear door into the garden where Master Naylor was sitting with his children in the shade of a young peach tree. The girls had been sewing what looked might be a red dress when they were done but rose to their feet as their mother and Frevisse came into the garden. They were younger than their brother Dickon and small-boned like their mother, but the boy standing beside their father was younger still, past toddling stage but not by much, and when Master Naylor stood up to bow to Frevisse, he wrapped both arms around his father's leg and slid around behind him, to peek at Frevisse from that sure safety as Master Naylor said, "My lady," and the girls curtsyed.

"Master Naylor," Frevisse returned, bending her head to him and them in return. "Are you free to talk?"

"As you will, my lady," he answered. He was never a man much given to words or any outward warmth that Frevisse had ever seen, but when he stooped to draw his son around to in front of him and pry him loose from his leg, he did it gently enough and lifted him up to tell him, "You go to your mother for a time."

"No," the child said positively.

"If you stay out here," Master Naylor said seriously, "you'll try to help your sisters with their sewing. Then they'll end up sticking needles into you. I don't want all that yelling, so you have to go with your mother."

"We'll make patty-cakes," Mistress Naylor promised, sufficient compensation, it seemed, because when Master Naylor handed him away, he wrapped his arms around her neck in place of his father's leg and let himself be carried off without complaint.

The girls were beginning to gather their sewing to go, too, but Master Naylor said, "Stay. No need," took up the joint stool where he had been sitting and with, "By your leave, my lady," led Frevisse away to the garden's far end.

It was a larger garden than it might have been. A high wicker fence stood between it and the porter's yard, but because the third house was unused, the fence there had been taken down and its garden added to the steward's; and while the beds along the narrow paths near to his rear door were filled with herbs and some flowers, the rest was table vegetables much like at the Perryns', with the addition of a well-strawed strawberry bed and, at the far end, green beans trellised up and over a rough-built arbor to make a shaded place to sit. That was where Master Naylor led her, setting down the joint stool and waiting until she was seated and had nodded her permission to him before he sat on the one already there.

There being no particular point, beyond mere manners' sake, in asking how he did since he seemed to be doing as well as might be—and there being nothing she could change even if he were not—Frevisse told him directly all that Perryn had told her concerning Matthew Woderove's death and the two bids already made to have his holding. Master Naylor listened without sign or comment and sat silent for a while when she had finished, apparently absorbed in watching a bean tendril, before finally looking at her to say, "I agree about the court. It should be as soon as might be. Friday, if it can be managed. Else on Saturday. About the Woderove holding, it's Perryn's final say, the holding being Lord Lovell's."

"He wants your thought on it, Hulcote being the priory's villein."

Master Naylor held silent again, not so much as if considering his answer as not wanting to give it, before he finally said, "I'd favor Tom Hulcote's bid."

His hesitation over it made Frevisse ask, "Why?"

"Because I've found him a good worker when he works for himself. He deserves the chance if that's what he wants."

That was not all. Something hung unsaid. "And?" Frevisse pressed.

Distaste twinged at Master Naylor's mouth and he breathed down heavily through his nose before he brought himself to say, "It would also serve to settle what's between him and Mary Woderove."

"And that is?" Frevisse asked although fairly certain, from his disapproval, what he meant.

Curtly, not liking to say it, Master Naylor answered, "He's been giving her a green gown and everyone in the village knows it."

Meaning that Tom Hulcote and Mary Woderove had been together in ways they should not have been.

"Did her husband know?" Frevisse asked.

"There's no saying. Since he wasn't the sort who could have stopped her even if he did, my thought is he didn't let himself know."

"But from something someone said in the village," Frevisse said, slowly and not for the sake of tale-telling but because there could be trouble coming another way if it were true, "this Tom Hulcote is suspected with Gilbey Dunn's wife."

"Gilbey's wife is forever being suspected with one man or another, ever since she came to the village," Master Naylor said, "but so far as I know it's never been more than other people's talk. It only happens to be Tom Hulcote this time. Next week it will be someone else."

It would not be the first time Frevisse knew of someone's reputation being made for them out of what other people thought they might do rather than what they actually did. She could likewise see how Elena, simply being as she was and Gilbey Dunn's wife, would draw suspicion.

"Nor is Gilbey Dunn so pure of soul," Master Naylor added, "as not to watch out for his wife better than to be made cuckold."

"But this between Hulcote and Mary Woderove is sure?"

"There's nothing 'suspected' there," Master Naylor said baldly. "It's sure, and now Matthew isn't there for folk to be sorry for, Simon will probably have leyrwite from her." The fine put on a woman for unlawful coupling. "It's to the best that Hulcote have the holding and marry her and make an end of it."

"But?" Frevisse asked, again to something unsaid behind the words.

"The other side has to be looked at. That Gilbey will do well by the holding if he's given it. He does well by everything that's his. With Tom, I think he will but can't be certain, and what I have to ask is whether I'm favoring him because I think he ought to have the chance at it or because I don't like Gilbey Dunn."

Unhappily Frevisse did not like Gilbey Dunn either. But then neither had she heard much to Tom Hulcote's good, so that hardly helped, except Master Naylor knew more of him than she did and, carefully thinking her way to it while she spoke, she said, "Leaving liking and un-liking out of it, and granting you think Tom Hulcote would do well by the holding, maybe it comes down to asking why should Gilbey Dunn have more of what he already has in plenty, when Tom Hulcote has so next to nothing. Would that make the answering easier?"

"Put that way, it somewhat does." Master Naylor made the small twist of his mouth that served him for a smile. "Tell Perryn, if you like, that on my side there's no ob-jection to Tom having the holding at the price he's of-fered. Perryn will have to decide from there, and that's probably to the good, since he knows the village and his sister best."

## Chapter 6

wo days later there was a soft rain falling
from a low gray sky as Frevisse came with
Sister Thomasine and Father Henry, the nun-
nery's priest, by the road from the priory into the village.
Simon Perryn had sent word the manor court would be
held in the church, rather than on the green, but they
would have been able to tell it anyway by the scattered
drift of villagers into the churchyard.

"Too wet to work in the fields," Father Henry said; and
therefore most of the village would be free to come to the
court and probably would, since Perryn's hope to forestall
trouble by having it soon had been vain. He had likewise
sent word there had been a shouting match between Gilbey Dunn and Tom Hulcote at the alehouse last night

that had not come to blows only because various neighbors had stopped them, but then others, including Perryn,
had had to stop the fight that had threatened to flare up
then and there between the few who backed Gilbey—
more out of dislike for Tom Hulcote than liking for Gilbey, Frevisse gathered—and those who favored Tom,
probably for the reverse reason. Therefore Frevisse had
asked Father Henry's company, because when the village
had sometimes been without a priest in the past years,
Father Henry had seen to the villagers' needs as well as
to the nunnery's and knew the folk maybe better than
Father Edmund yet could, being there less than a year.
Her hope was that between them the two priests would
force order if tempers flared but, all else failing, Father
Henry's size would be of use because except for his tonsure, almost hidden by unruly yellow curls, and his plain
dark priest's gown, he had more the burly look of someone ready to swing a scythe to good purpose than use
chalice and paten in the Mass, especially set beside Father
Edmund who, with his dark hair smoothly combed to his
well-shaped head around a neatly kept tonsure and his
priest's gown of finer cloth than any Father Henry had
ever worn, ever looked better suited to a bishop's household than a village church.

But he reportedly did his duties well and just now he
was waiting under the pentice that roofed the churchyard
gateway, greeting everyone with a smile and quiet words,
doing what he could to forestall trouble, Frevisse judged.
He welcomed the three of them with open relief, and
when Frevisse thanked him for having agreed court could
be held in the church, he smilingly said, "With the rain,
the choice lay between here and the alehouse, and here
seemed better."

"You think it's likely, then, that there'll be trouble?"
Father Henry asked.

"If there is, it will be more Tom Hulcote's fault than
Gilbey Dunn's, I fear," Father Edmund said. "Tom has
been talking too big at the alehouse and around the green

about how if he doesn't have Mary Woderove and the holding, it's because Gilbey Dunn is willing to beggar everyone else to make himself more wealthy than he already is."

"And those who like trouble for trouble's sake are listening to him?" Father Henry said.

"Even so."

Four women were approaching in haste and probably fear of having missed their chance at a good place in the church. Frevisse left Father Edmund to them, leaving the gateway's shelter with Father Henry and Sister Thomasine to cross the churchyard through the warm rain to the church porch and into the church where, as she had expected, there was a full crowding of folk, even given that St. Chad's was small, its nave hardly larger than a good-sized byre, its chancel even less. It was a plain space, unaisled, with a simple timber roof and everything open to the wooden shingles, but over the years its people and priests had done well by it. Father Clement in his day had paid for the chancel window to be glassed, and though the glass was unpainted, greened and slightly bubbled, it was the only glass in the village and so the light that fell through it onto the altar was strange, adding to the mysteries made there by the priest at Mass. It also meant that with the nave's few, small windows kept closed except when there were services, there was no longer a constant fight with the sparrows to keep them from nesting in the rafters and atop the rood screen.

The rood screen itself, between nave and chancel, had been carved in an open fretwork of black walnut maybe fifty years ago and its red paint and yellow stars had been kept fresh, redone whenever need be by whoever in the village had the best hand for it at the time. The other paintings in the church went untouched because no one dared say they had the skill. So far back that no one had any notion of when, the nave walls had been painted with Bible scenes in strong reds, greens, and blue-greens, with here and there a touch of yellow to be the gold of a king's crown or an angel's halo. Flanking the chancel arch were St. Chad himself and St. Peter, their robes falling in rigid, beautiful folds about their lean, long, tall-beyond-mortal-men's bodies as they stared solemnly with wide ovaled eyes into an eternity somewhere above and far beyond the worshipers' heads, while beyond them in the chancel Christ sat enthroned in majesty, as oval-eyed and formal as his saints, one hand raised in benediction, the other resting on the book of God's word that all men should heed, with Matthew, Mark, Luke, and John arrayed around him in their aspects of Lion, Man, Ox, and Eagle borne on clouds to show they were in heaven with him.

Rushes covered the nave floor for cleanliness and, in the winter, for warmth and besides what the priest and altar needed, there were no furnishings except the baptismal font and a few benches for those who came early enough to services, with no need for a pew because no lord lived in the village to warrant one. Today, the shutters open to give what light there was from the overcast day, the benches had been shifted end-on to the rood screen to serve the court and everyone else was left to stand and the villagers, not much damp from the softly falling rain, were gathered in clumps and clusters of family and friends, busy in talk, though heads turned and the hum of voices fell as Frevisse, Sister Thomasine, and Father Henry entered, only to take up again, a little lower and maybe faster, to have all said before they had to stop when court began.

Sister Thomasine, wordless since leaving St. Frides-wide's, her eyes lowered, her hands tucked into her habit's opposite sleeves, went silently across the little width of the church to the corner beyond the baptismal font, raised on its single stone step, where no one else was, withdrawing as much as might be from everything and everyone around her. Frevisse, with people shifting, bowing, curtsying out of her way, went to the front of the nave, Father Henry following more slowly, pausing to speak to various folk. Simon Perryn and six men Frevisse took to be the jurors were waiting beside the benches. They bowed to her as she joined them, no need to remove their hoods or hats that were already off in God's house, and she bent her head to them in return, no one bothering with giving names because Father Edmund entered then and passed up the nave with smiles and words to various folk, to take a seat at a table set ready with paper, ink, pens, and several closed scrolls behind the jurors' bench.

"By your leave, we'll begin then?" Perryn asked her, and Frevisse agreed with a slight nod. To be to the fore of so many people, all of them looking at her, was not something she liked, but Perryn, seeming to have no mind of it at all, said easily to the jurors, "We'll start then," and bowed her to a place on the bench facing the jurors on theirs across the space between them left for the court's business to be done but angled enough to the nave that she could watch the people watching her.

While Perryn, the jurors, and Father Edmund took their places, she noticed Father Henry had shifted away to the nave's north wall, from where he could come readily into the midst of things if there was need, though thus far there was no sign there would be, only the expected shift and shuffle of people making themselves comfortable on their feet. She glimpsed Anne well back and near the door, Dickon Naylor and her sons beside her. Of little Lucy there was no sign but there were other children in plenty, including a baby carried on its mother's hip, fretfully rubbing its eyes and trying to burrow its head into the side of its mother's neck while she talked with the women around her. Frevisse thought the woman with a face like a wizened apple might be Ada Bychurch, Prior Byfield's midwife, but it had been years since Frevisse had seen her and she was not certain and none of the others were familiar at all, save Elena, Gilbey's wife, standing to the side and fore of the crowd not far from the jurors, her

hands folded quietly into each other at the waist of her
rose-colored gown, her fair loveliness encircled by soft
wimple and starched veil shiningly white in the nave's
gray shadows. Graceful even in her quietness, she looked
what she was, a wealthy villein's wife who had servants
to see to such things as having her veil starched and
smooth-pressed when she went out. Standing squarely beside her, his thumbs hooked into his wide, finely wrought
leather belt, Gilbey was no balder than when Frevisse had
seen him last —how many years ago was that?—with only
a little more flesh on his stocky frame and nothing softened in his blunt face. To Frevisse's eye he looked like
what he was, too—someone bound to the world by the
gold and silver circles of coins and—unless he was
greatly changed from when Frevisse had last encountered
him—by the lusts of the flesh.

The rest of the upwards of two score other folk
crowded into the nave were only faces to her. Young faces
fresh-fleshed and little touched by living yet. Older faces
marked, less and more, by their years and their lives' hap
penings and, especially for the men, by weather lived in
day in, day out, no matter what it was. Old faces seamed
and etched by all their years of living. Worried faces,
wondering how much trouble there would be. Dull faces
here to stare at whatever happened because they'd stare
at anything. Faces eager with wanting trouble, a few faces
angry, meaning to make it. They all lived through their
days a scant half-mile, if that much, from where she lived
her own, year in, year out, and she knew no more of them
than they did of her and she was come here to help make
decisions that would shape some of their lives and, that
done, would go back to her own and leave them to theirs
as utterly as she had left them to it until now.

Heart-felt and unbidden, the prayer that began so many
of the daily Offices came to her. *Deus, in adjutorium
meum intende.* God, come to my aid. And then the anti-
phon that was part of today's Terce. *Excita, Domine, po-*

*tentiam tuam, ut salvos facias nos.* Rouse, Lord, your power, that you make us safe.

And suddenly she was sure which of the men standing to the fore of the crowd was Tom Hulcote. His uneasiness, different from the men's around him, gave him away as, restless-footed in the rushes, with both smothered anger and deep unease shadowing his face, he kept shifting his look toward and away from Gilbey who never bothered with so much as a glance his way.

Or it was maybe Elena, Gilbey's wife, he was looking at? From where she sat, Frevisse could not tell.

He was younger than Frevisse had thought he would be. Not beyond his twenties. Why had she thought he would be older? Because Simon Perryn was of middle years and therefore likely his sister was, too, and so would be the man she was sinning with? But he was not, nor was he the surly, heavy-built bully with a rough face and rougher ways that had somehow been in her mind. Except for the in-held anger and open unease, he was simply a young man with nothing particular about him, plainly dressed in what was surely his best—though they were none too good—tunic and hosen and hood, with his brown hair trimmed and clean.

And now Frevisse noted the woman standing close behind him, her hand laid on his forearm as she rose on her toes to whisper in his ear. Mary Woderove, surely. A small-boned, child-pretty woman whose head came hardly to her lover's shoulder, though he was not over-tall, until she tiptoed. She looked all the younger for the black veil she wore in token of her widowhood instead of the married woman's usual white one, but the veil seemed to be all she gave to her widowhood, Frevisse thought uncharitably, watching as Mary leaned nearer, pressing her breasts against Tom Hulcote's back while she went on whispering to him, smiling up at him until as Simon Perryn gave word to the jurors for the court to start, Tom Hulcote frowned, shook his head, and urged her away with a small twitch of his arm. Mary whispered something else, still smiling, and drew back, leaving her lover with a dark flush reddening his face.

Along with word of where court would be and warning there might be trouble, Perryn had asked if another matter besides the Wodcrove holding could be seen to, too. Frevisse had sent back word it could and now settled to listen while Alson Bonde and Martin Fisher were called forward. There was a stirring through the crowd, with whispering between those who knew what it was about and those who did not, but it seemed that Perryn had dealt in the matter as he had purposed, because agreement on the lease between them was smoothly made and written into the court records, and a man who must be Alson's son was waiting at the crowd's fore-edge, to lay an arm around her shoulders when it was done and nod friendliwise to Martin Fisher, too, who nodded back the same, as Perryn said low in Frevisse's ear, "The betrothal's agreed on and everybody happy . . ."

He was interrupted by a bull-shouldered youth shoving out into the court's open space, pulling an older man after him by a hard grip on his sleeve, and Perryn stood up and demanded, "Hamon? Walter? What is this?"

"It's him," the younger man said, jerking his head back at the other man. "He won't leave off bothering me. I want the court to tell him to leave off, he's got no right."

"Walter?" Perryn asked, not seeming greatly disturbed.

The older man twitched his sleeve from Hamon's hold and answered, equally calm, "He's on about how I've told him he's to work for me, to pay back what he cost me on that surety."

"There was naught said about paying back!" Hamon protested.

"There was, while Father Edmund was writing out the agreement, and there were those heard you say it," Walter said.

"But it weren't in the agreement! I never signed naught that said I'd have to pay back!"

"But you gave your word to it. Before witnesses," Walter said.

"But I never swore . . ." The younger man's voice was rising.

"Steady, Hamon," Perryn said.

Hamon tucked in his chin, like a bull baffled by baiting. "I never . . ." he stubbornly began again.

"Hamon," Perryn said warningly.

Hamon dropped to sullen silence.

"Now," Perryn said, "we'll tell Dame Frevisse what's toward here, you both being priory villeins and in her rule."

None so happy to hear that, Frevisse sat up straighter, to pay closer heed as Perryn detailed a loan made to Hamon by Jenet atte Forge—a broad woman in a yellow dress took a step forward from the women around Ada Bychurch to make curtsy to the court—with Walter Hopper here and Dick Blakeman—a narrow-framed man moved forward a step from the north wall, made a quick, awkward bow, and stepped hurriedly back beside a wide-hipped, sweet-faced woman holding a swaddled baby—as surety it be repaid, which it hadn't been, and Walter had seen to Jenet atte Forge being satisfied with use of one of his cows in milk for the summer, in place of him and Dick paying outright money, which they did not have.

"And now?" Frevisse asked at Walter.

He bowed with more assurance than Dick Blakeman had and said to her, "Now I've been telling Hamon here that he owes me work until I'm paid back for paying off his debt."

"And I say I don't! I never signed to any such thing and I'm off two days hence to work over Bloxham way where they'll be paying me something and you say you won't!"

"I'm not going to pay you because you're working to

pay me back what you owe me," Walter said as if it were something he had already said more than a few times before.

"I don't owe you aught!"

"Hamon," Perryn said, "hush."

Hamon hushed. Perryn looked to Frevisse who realized he was giving the problem over to her and gathered her wits to say to Walter, "You said there were witnesses heard him agree to pay you back."

"Aye."

Perryn put up a hand, stopping Hamon from saying anything to that, and Frevisse asked of Walter, "Who?"

"Father Edmund, for one."

Frevisse looked to the priest.

He met her look. "It's even as Walter says. He said to Hamon, 'If I have to pay this in your place, you'll work it out on my land for me, yes?' And Hamon said, 'Surely.' "

"But I didn't . . ." Hamon started.

"Hamon," Perryn said.

Hamon huffed and held quiet.

"Who else?" Frevisse asked.

Walter named two other men, one of them a juror, the other raising his hand from the far end of the nave to show he was there. To Frevisse's question, they both agreed that Walter and Hamon had said what Father Edmund said they had said. "Walter even asked Hamon twice," the juror said. "Twice he said it, and twice Hamon answered he would."

Both the other man and Father Edmund agreed to that, and Frevisse looked to Hamon. He looked down at his feet. He was not as young as he had seemed to her at first sight, and she thought now it was not lack of years but lack of good sense that made his face so soft as she said with curbed impatience, "Well, Hamon? Three men besides Walter Hopper say they heard you say you'd work for him if you failed the debt. Have you answer to that?"

Hamon started to scuff his right foot at the floor without looking up. "I might have said it. I was that glad he was going surety for me, I'd likely have said anything. But I never signed . . ."

"But you said it," Frevisse interrupted.

Hamon tucked his chin down more sullenly. "I said it," he granted.

"Before witnesses."

"Aye." Grudgingly.

"Then it would seem to me it's an agreement you must keep." From the side of her eye she saw by a small nod of Perryn's head that he agreed with that. She looked to the jurors. "Yes?"

They equally agreed, and while Father Edmund wrote it into the record, Walter clapped a hand on Hamon's shoulder, saying, "There now. That's done and it'll be none so bad, you'll see. Come on. I'll stand you a drink when we're done here," drawing him away into the crowd.

Perryn turned to the jurors and said, "It's Woderove's holding we have to deal with now," and if he regretted that as much as Frevisse did, he gave no sign of it. Ignoring both the jurors' uneasy shifting on their bench and the ripple of talk and movement through the crowd, he looked to Father Edmund. "You have the records for it ready?"

Father Edmund laid a hand on the scrolls on the table in front of him. "Here."

"Then read them aloud, if you please, Father."

Mary Woderove stepped forward past Tom Hulcote, into the space between jurors and crowd and said angrily at her brother, "You know full well what they say! Everyone knows. That the holding goes to the firstborn son and down the line of sons, and if there are no sons, then to the daughters. You know that and that Matthew and I had nobody, no sons or daughters either, and now you want to take what's mine away from me because of it and everyone knows that, too!"

Steadily, looking straightly back at her, Perryn said, "If that's the right of it, that the custom and law is for the Woderove holding to go by blood from heir to heir, and you say it is, then you say, too, that there being no heir by blood, the holding is in Lord Lovell's hands for the while, yes?"

"No!" Mary cried. "It naught matters what your foul custom says! The holding's mine! Matthew meant for me to have it!"

Steadily, as if repeating a thing that he had said before and known he would have to say again to no better end, Perryn said with heavy patience, "If Matthew had, as he sometimes talked of doing, given up the holding to Lord Lovell and taken it back on lease and in the lease given reversion of the holding to you at his death, then, yes, the holding would be yours. But Matthew never did that, and so the holding is not yours."

"But it can be," Mary said sharply. "It's for you to say who has it. You're the reeve. You can give it to me."

"I'm the reeve," Perryn agreed, "but last say in this is Master Spencer's, or else even Master Holt's." Lord Lovell's high steward.

"But the *first* say is yours," Mary flung back, her pretty face all taut with anger, "and they listen to you!"

"And since they listen to me, I cannot say to them that you should have the holding, because the holding is too much for you to manage on your own."

"You gave Avice Millwarde her widow's holding two years ago. Why not me now?"

"Because Avice Millwarde can run a holding and everyone knows it. Everyone likewise knows that you could not."

Mary took a step toward her brother and pointed an angry finger up toward his face. "What everybody knows is that I'm your sister and you hate me!"

Perryn looked down at her with no outward feeling, answering after a moment, "Are you going to let Father Edmund read the custom concerning the holding or not?"

Mary's face worked, unlovely for the moment, toward answering that, but before she found it, Father Edmund said quietly from behind his table, "Mary."

She jerked her head toward him, looking as ready to snap at him as at her brother.

Unheeding her anger, Father Edmund said with simple quietness, "Let things go on as you know they have to, Mary. All will be well, I promise you."

Mary opened her mouth to say something. Father Edmund cocked his head at her, more in question than rebuke, and she seemed to think better of whatever she had been about to say, closed her mouth, made him a curt curtsy that pointedly ignored her brother, crossed her arms tightly across herself below her breasts, and bowed her head to stare at the floor in a fierce silence that gave up nothing except words.

Perryn looked near to telling her to step back among the onlookers, but Father Edmund warned him off that with a small shake of his head and, before anything else could happen, began to read from the scroll he had been holding partly unrolled this while. What he read said much the same as what had passed between Mary and her brother concerning the Woderove holding, and when Father Edmund had finished, Perryn looked to the jurors and asked, "Is that how you remember it being in time past?"

They agreed that it was.

"Does anyone remember otherwise?" he asked of the onlookers at large.

No one said they did.

"Then the Woderove holding is in Lord Lovell's hands, to be kept or given as is seen fit," Perryn said. "Yes?"

The jurors nodded silent agreement, but Mary said sullenly at the floor, "Then you can give it to me."

Ignoring he had heard her, though he must have, Perryn said, "Is there anyone here makes bid to have the holding?"

Tom Hulcote was stepping forward even as he said it, with an angry glance across to Gilbey Dunn. "I do. I bid for it at the terms Woderove held it and another workday to the lord into the bargain." He put an arm around Mary's shoulders. "And I'll marry the widow with it for good measure."

"Is she willing to that?" Perryn asked formally.

Mary jerked her head up. "Yes. Very willing. And you damnably well know it."

Tom Hulcote tightened his arm around her, drawing her to him.

"Is there any other offer?" Perryn asked, not looking at Gilbey Dunn.

Gilbey took a measured pace forward, and when Perryn acknowledged him with a nod, said, bold with self-assurance, "I offer to take the holding on lease for twenty years, at six shillings a year, or whatever else may be agreed on between Lord Lovell's steward and me."

Mary Woderove swung out from Tom's hold and around on Gilbey. "And what becomes of *me* if you take it all?" she demanded fiercely.

Gilbey turned a cold look on her. "You have a toft and some land, and he has something." He made an equally cold look at Tom Hulcote. "Let you marry, if that's what you want, and live as you can with what you have."

Tom laid a hand on Mary's shoulder. "I want better than that for her!"

"Then you should be a better man," Gilbey said coldly back.

Tom made a threatening step forward. "I'm as good as you and likely better!"

"Then pity you don't show it," Gilbey returned, holding his ground, older than Tom by some not-few years but with no apparent doubt that he'd be his match if their quarrel came to more than words.

Mary shifted away from them, back toward the onlookers. Elena took a step forward—toward her husband
or toward Tom Hulcote, Frevisse wondered—but before
more happened, Perryn said, "That's enough. From both
of you. Think on you're in the church."

"Let *him* think . . ." Tom Hulcote began.

"You'll be fined if you keep on like this," Perryn
warned.

"Fined!" Tom cried. "You'd do it, too! Me but not him,
because all you're for is to keep the poor down and folk
like him and you up, and don't think we don't know it!
Them that has, keeps and always has, and now for bad
measure you want to take what the rest of us have, too!"

There were answering grumbles and shifting among
some of the onlookers. Father Henry eased away from the
wall and in amongst the largest clot of them, beginning
to lay hands weightily on various shoulders and saying
things into various ears as Father Edmund rose to his feet
behind the table to say in his clear, carrying priest's voice,
"Remember, all of you, where you are and what will come
of violence done here."

Tom Hulcote turned to him with suddenly a desperate
plea instead of anger. "Help me in this," he begged, and
pointed at Gilbey. "He has land enough, more than
enough. Tell him to let this bit go to someone as needs
it!"

"Tom, that isn't where the issue lies," Father Edmund
began.

"It is!" Tom's anger flared up again. "Tell him, priest—
tell yourself, come to that—what's said in the Bible about
rich men and heaven! You've preached it often enough!"

"Tom!" Perryn warned sharply. "Don't make me have
to judge against you!"

"Judge against me?" He swung toward Perryn now,
voice rising. "You're the one who'd best watch out for
judgment. You and him!"

He pointed viciously at Gilbey, and Frevisse stood up

abruptly, rapping out with bridled anger, "Enough!"

She had been still long enough to be forgotten, and her suddenness brought heads around toward her and a brief, startled silence into which she said at Tom, "You're the priory's villein and my say has been asked in this matter on that account. My say is that angers are too high and hot now for decision to be made. By your reeve's leave and yours—" with a nod to the jurors and in a quieter voice "—I say we should have a half hour's pause before we finish." Long enough to talk Tom Hulcote down and around, she hoped, and give Father Henry more chance at settling the other men.

"A good thought," Perryn said quickly. And to the jurors, "Yes?" and to a man, they nodded in matching, swift agreement.

# Chapter 7

The church emptied by fits and starts, in clots of people talking as they crowded out the door into the churchyard or else in little groups around the nave while waiting for the doorway to clear and their own chance to leave.

Frevisse, in no hurry to be anywhere else, stayed where she was and noted Gilbey and his wife did, too, drawn together aside and turned away from everyone else, Elena's hand resting on his arm as she said something to him too low for Frevisse to hear. No one approached them, but the several men coming Tom Hulcote's way were headed off by Father Henry who, with his arms laid across several shoulders and a hand stretched to grip someone's tunic, turned them aside and toward the door, talking cheerily at them while Father Edmund closed on Tom.

Mary was there first, holding on to her lover's arm, standing on tiptoe to say something in his ear. Frevisse, unable to hear past Perryn talking with the jurors, watched as Father Edmund said something to them both that made Tom go sullen, tuck in his chin, and glower at the priest while Mary faced Father Edmund with her chin up and her little mouth in an angry pout, bringing Frevisse to the uncharitable thought that she had better make the most of her prettiness while it lasted, because there looked to be little else to recommend her.

But then, from what was said of her, making the most of her prettiness was exactly what she had been doing with Tom Hulcote.

That thought decided Frevisse that she had best do something else than stand here being unkind about Mary Woderove. Sister Thomasine was still standing against the wall beyond the font with lowered eyes and hands folded into her opposite sleeves while the last of the onlookers crowded out the door, and Frevisse moved to go to her but saw Father Henry turn from herding his men out the door, whatever grievance they had been going to share with Tom Hulcote forgotten for now because they were grinning as they went out, and cross toward Sister Thomasine. Not needed there, Frevisse joined Perryn, just finished with the jurors. Gilbey and Elena were going away down the nave toward the door, the jurors trailing after them, and Frevisse and Perryn followed, leaving Father Edmund still in talk with Tom and Mary, saying to them with patient insistence, "Consider. One reason for not making threats is that now, if anything happens in the least way to Simon or Gilbey, you'll be the first one men will look to for the trouble."

Beside her, Perryn made a soft snorting sound that told he had overheard, too, and quietly, for only the two of them to hear, Frevisse asked, "What do you think you'll decide about the holding when all's said and done?"

"All's as said and done as I need for it to be," Perryn answered, a tight edge of anger under his words, and for the first time Frevisse realized that, for all that the reeve kept a quiet outside, he would rouse if there was cause enough. "Unless you've strong word against it, the jurors and I agree the holding should be kept in Lord Lovell's hands for now, with Master Spencer's leave when he's been advised of how things stand. It means I'll have to see to the hire of men to work it for the while and that's not to the good but better than otherwise at present."

From the little liking she had for Mary or Tom or Gilbey, Frevisse had nothing to say against that, but, "Mayhap someone else will offer for it."

Perryn shook his head regretfully. "Not so long as it's a quarreling point 'tween Gilbey and Tom. There's none wants to be caught there."

Frevisse could see why. She little liked being there herself, even knowing that in a while she would walk away from it. "But Mary will have the profit from the crops this year?"

"Oh, aye. She'll not be done out of what's rightfully hers, though that won't be the way she tells it."

They were to the church door now. Past Father Henry and Sister Thomasine going out ahead of them, Frevisse could see the small rain had finished while they were inside and the sun was making a watery-yellow attempt to burn through the clouds.

"Uh," said Perryn as a moist, heavy heat met them beyond the church porch, and Frevisse felt the same, on the instant too aware of her layers of clothing and close-fitted wimple. Already among the village women scattered across the churchyard in talk and with an eye to their children playing among the grave mounds some had slipped off their wimples and were settling their veils or kerchiefs over their hair as loosely as when they worked in the fields.

"Good for the last of the haying, though," Perryn said.

And if they could be at it tomorrow, they might well finish soon enough to have a rest between haying's hard, long labor and the harder, longer one of harvest.

Frevisse made a small prayer for God's blessing and to St. Dorothy for abundance, then asked, "What was that about between Walter Hopper and Hamon whatever-his-name?"

Perryn rumbled a deep, brief laugh. "That was thinking ahead on Walter's part, that was. The thing is, he holds land enough that his workdays to the priory add up, and most years he has to hire a man or more to work some of them for him while he sees to his own land. In this dealing with Hamon, he gambled last autumn that the bad weather would change this year, knowing that if it did, there'd be out-of-the-ordinary high wages to be paid for anyone he needed to hire."

"Ah," Frevisse said, understanding. "He therefore stood surety for this Hamon's debt, certain he'd not be able to repay, and now will have him to work for no wages at all."

"Instead of having to bargain for others at rising prices, aye. Mind you, it's no great cheat for Hamon, all considered. Walter will feed him along the way and Walter feeds well, and Hamon will be no shorter of money at the end than he would have been if he was hiring out on his own since he spends whatever he gets as fast as he gets it, at the alehouse here and on worse in Banbury."

"He's a troublemaker?" Frevisse asked.

"Hamon? Nay, except what he makes for himself. He's not yet learned and never will, I doubt, that it's not play that holds life together but work. That makes him fair useless here, where most everything is work. Eh, well, that's what the rest of us are here for, I sometimes think. To see to such as can't see to themselves."

One of the jurors came up on his other side then, wanting to speak with him. Perryn asked her pardon and drew aside and, glad of the chance to gather herself and her thoughts, Frevisse looked away, over the low church wall at the field beyond it, flowing away in waist-high green grain toward the distant woodshore's darker band of forest. It was one of the three great fields around the village, each laid out in its own patterning of strips ploughed this way and that with how the land lay and planted or left fallow or set to hay turn and turn and turn about, year by year by year. They stretched out on all sides of the village, laced through with paths for workers going out and coming in and with wider ways for hay wains and harvest carts, with sometimes a tree left standing in a grassy balk, its shade somewhere for folk to sit through the midmorning and afternoon rest times and almost inevitably the tree was large—save here and there where some past giant had gone down with age or in a storm and been replaced by a stripling now no more than maybe half a century old— thick-trunked, the crowns of leaves widespread, their shade familiar to uncounted and mostly forgotten—even their graves in the churchyard replaced by newer ones— generations of Prior Byfield folk.

No one held all of any but almost everyone in the village held some of each, and there was meadow, too, for grazing cattle along the stream in the low places that too often flooded with the spring and autumn rains to be worth planting; and rough pasture beyond the fields, poorer soil cleared by men in want of more land before the Great Death of almost a hundred years ago had made such a dearth of people that there was, even now, no longer need to plough or plant those acres anymore. And of course on a green hillock well out of the village the windmill for grinding of the village's grain spread its sailed arms against the sky. And downstream was the marsh with its rushes for so many uses, and here and there a hedgerow, and the road that ran through the village and away to north and south and places for the most part too far away to be bothered over by Prior Byfield folk. But it

was the fields that were Prior Byfield's life. If there was
to be food in the village, then month in, month out, the
fields had to be ploughed, harrowed, seeded, tended, har-
vested, ploughed again, harrowed again, seeded, tended
. . . year around to year, no end to it, come what may, if
Prior Byfield was to live.

Knowing that, Frevisse could only wonder how had it
been for Simon Perryn and the others these past three
years of ill weather. To watch their hoped-for harvests rot
in the fields and then live with the hunger that came afterwards, and everything to do again—the ploughing, har-
rowing, seeding—days into weeks into months of work
with no surety that the next year would be any better.

The field of grain beyond the churchyard wall, only
weeks away from ripeness, gave evidence of their courage
and hope that they would win their gamble this year at
least.

Domina Elisabeth had had the right of it, Frevisse
thought—and not about Sister Thomasine alone. Her own
prayers would hereafter have a different weight to them,
now that the village folk had names and faces for her.

She looked for Sister Thomasine and found her drawn
aside into the lee of the church porch, alone again and in
no seeming distress. When Frevisse approached her, she
looked up calmly enough, and asked, "Is it settled?"

"The reeve and jurors have decided to keep the holding
in Lord Lovell's hands for the time being, rather than give
it to either man," Frevisse answered; and then did not
resist asking, "What do you think of it all?"

"Of it all?" Sister Thomasine asked, puzzled.

Frevisse made a small gesture to the gathered clumps
of people scattered around the churchyard. "Of all this.
Of everyone."

With the slightest of thoughtful frowns, Sister Thomasine looked around at the clusters of men and women,
all of them busy in talk, and the children everywhere,
most of the older ones playing at some kind of walking-

tag among their elders, just short of running so no one could say at them, "Don't run," but managing to annoy their elders with it anyway while the younger ones were mostly, oddly enough, keeping with their mothers, sitting on the grass beside them or leaning against them, their mothers' hands absently resting on heads or shoulders or patting at fretful ones wanting to be heeded or go home. Frevisse only wished someone would take Mary Wode-rove home. She was near the wall beside the gateway pentice, being talked to by Anne, Perryn's wife, and three other women, and though she seemed quieted out of her anger, she was standing with her head down, refusing to look at them. Anne's younger boy was there, too, pushing restlessly against his mother, scratching behind one ear at some idle itch, although his brother and Dickon had found a perch further along the wall with some other boys who were listening wide-eared to Father Edmund and Father Henry talking again with Tom Hulcote and some other men. Faced with both priests, they were all subdued enough, though Tom kept shaking his head again and again against whatever was being said at him.

Sister Thomasine sighed and turned her mild gaze back to Frevisse, the slight frown softened to puzzlement as she said gently, "I don't see why so many choose to make such trouble for themselves, to care so much for worldly things that at the end all come to nothing. Why care so much for things that always end, when there's God in-stead?"

It was what a nun, a bride of Christ, should say, but Frevisse knew Sister Thomasine well enough to know that the should and ought that guarded and guided most people's tongues had nothing to do with her answer. She truly did not see what there was in the World that could pos-sibly be preferred to God.

Frevisse had made the same choice, had given her life over to God and prayer, but knew she had carried with her into her nun's life an understanding of the other

choices and why people made them. She was unsure—
and unsettled by her unsurety—whether Sister Thomasine's lack of that understanding was a weakness or a
strength.

The clot of men around Tom Hulcote was breaking up,
dispersing at the priests' urging, Frevisse guessed, with
Father Edmund keeping a hand on Tom's shoulder and
going with him toward Mary, still among the women,
while Father Henry came toward Frevisse and Sister Thomasine with half his heed still on Tom's friends, watching
to be sure they wandered off rather than clustered into
talk again. As he joined them, Frevisse asked, "Did you
talk him out of his anger?"

"I don't know. Our best hope is that the worst of it is
past. But Tom is as much hurt as angered over it, and the
sore of the hurt will keep rubbing the anger awake, I'm
afraid. He wants very much to have Mary Woderove to
wife."

"They could marry, even without the holding," Frevisse said.

"They neither of them want to live that poorly, I fear,"
Father Henry said gravely.

Frevisse was saved from struggling to hold back from
her answer to that by a shout, "Hai! Look!" from one of
the boys atop the wall that turned heads first toward him
and then where he was pointing, away toward a rider lead-
ing a packhorse just coming into view from the Banbury
road beyond the priest's house.

There was no mistaking Otes, the Banbury carrier.
Frevisse had had dealings with him when she was hosteler
and again lately as the priory's cellarer, because he came
this way every few weeks on his rounds, carrying letters
sometimes, and bringing things ordered by those lacking
time or else the wish to go all the way to Banbury market
for something not to be had otherwise—needles, say, or
spices—and taking orders for things to be brought next
time he came. Old Bet, the dun mare he rode, and Splotch,

his strong-backed, brown-and-white spotted packhorse, were as well known as he was, and children were tearing off handfuls of the rich churchyard grass before running to meet him. His usual place was likely the village ale-house or else the oak tree on the green, but since most of the village looked to be gathered here, he turned church-ward, to draw rein at the gateway, returning greetings but not so cheerfully as Frevisse was used to seeing him, his eyes running among the folk gathering to him until he found out Mary Woderove and said to her over the heads between them, with a twitch of his head toward his pack-horse, burdened with the usual packs and hampers on ei-ther side but between them this time a wooden box maybe two feet long, barely a foot wide or deep, "It's your hus-band, Mary. I've brought him home."

Frevisse understood immediately and started a prayer. It was a moment longer before Mary, understanding at last, cried out shrilly and flung her hands over her face as Anne and the other women closed on her and Tom Hul-cote drew hurriedly back with the look on his face of most men confronted by a crying woman and almost everyone else looked merely uncertain what to do, except the horses, who were reaching soft-lipped for the children's offerings of fresh grasses, mouthing them carefully out of one small hand after another while the children stared at their parents and everyone else behaving suddenly so strangely. Father Edmund made the sign of the cross in the air toward what was earthly left of Matthew Woderove as he and Father Henry both began to pray aloud for the man's soul. Sister Thomasine bent her head, joining Frev-isse in the Office of the Dead: *Requiem aeternam dona eis, Domine. Et lux perpetua luceat eis*. Give eternal rest to them, Lord. And perpetual light shine on them . . . *A porte inferi Erue, Domine, animas eorum*. From the gate of hell Rescue, Lord, their souls. But Frevisse was also watching Mary sobbing in Anne's arms, and Tom Hulcote caught awkwardly apart, alone, looking uneasily from

Mary to the wooden box with her husband's bones to Mary again; and at Gilbey and Elena Dunn even more apart from everyone than Tom Hulcote but close to each other.

Four ambitious people, Frevisse thought. All with hope for gain because of Matthew Wodecrove's death.

And there was Matthew Woderove, dead.

She pushed the thought away. It was prayers for the man's soul that were needed—*Delicta juventutis meae et ignorantias meas ne memineris, Domine.* The offenses of my youth and my weaknesses do not think on, Lord . . .

Still on Old Bet and looking faintly embarrassed by all he had unleashed, Otes said pleadingly to Father Edmund, "What should I be doing with him, eh?"

The priest ended a prayer and crossed himself, the gesture echoed by everyone, even the children, before he said, "Take him to his house, I suppose. That's where the wake . . ."

Mary cried out and jerked back from Anne. "No!" She flailed a hand toward the box. "No! I won't have it in my house! It can stay in the church! I don't want it near me! Leave it here."

"Mary, dear," Anne protested, trying to cover scandal with pity. "It's Matthew. You have to . . ."

"It isn't Matthew!" Mary cried at her, shoving Anne and another woman's hands away from her. "Whatever is in there, it isn't Matthew and I don't want it in my house!"

"Mary," Perryn said with plain disgust and no pity at all. "Don't be more of a fool than you are. It's in his own house Matthew should be tonight."

"Matthew is *dead,* and it's *my* house until you throw me out of it and I don't want that . . . that . . ." Driven past words with passion, Mary gestured again at the box.

Her brother began again, "Mary," but she cried out at him, flung away from Anne and the other women and everyone else into Tom Hulcote's arms, sobbing shrilly through wild tears, "Don't let him make me, Tom! Don't let him make me!"

Tom caught her, held her, his arms as tightly around her, saying down to the top of her head, "No, sweeting, no. I won't let him, no." Kissing the top of her head, then glaring over her at Perryn, all his anger came back, the more fierce for being for Mary's sake instead of his own. "You let her be, Simon Perryn. You've done enough to break her heart. You let her be with this."

Equally angry, Perryn returned, "Look you here, Tom Hulcote, it's Matthew whose heart was broken and by her, and he went off to his death because of it. Now he'll have his last right, to lie in his own house the last night his body is on earth instead of under it, and she's going to have to live with that."

"I'll not!" Mary wrenched around in Tom's arms to face her brother, her rage equal to either man's. "He cheated me every way while he was alive. He's not going to cheat me out of a little peace now he's dead! That box isn't coming into my house except over my own dead bones!"

"It's not your house, Mary Woderove!" Perryn returned. "It's forfeit to the lord and you're there on sufferance and my sufferance has near to worn out. If Matthew doesn't lie there tonight, neither will you, ever again!"

He meant it, and as reeve, he could make it happen. Even Mary in her extremity of anger saw he would if she pushed him farther and froze halfway to another shout at him, her angry blood draining out of her face to leave her pale. Her breast heaved twice with great breaths as she struggled to hold herself back. Then she turned in the circle of Tom's arms, pulled back against his hold for room enough between them to grab his tunic's front, and cried up at him, "They hate us, Tom! *He* hates us! He hates *you*! He'd rather we both died in a ditch than marry! Leave here or it'll be too late and they'll kill you, too!"

People were drawing back from her, even Anne. Only Father Edmund came forward, to put one hand on Tom's shoulder, the other on hers, saying gently, as if comforting a miserable child, "Mary. Mary. Stop this before you make yourself sick and your brother more angry. Mary, heed me."

With her face huddled down to hide its weeping ruin, she shook her head, denying his comfort; but after a look at Tom to ask permission that Tom gave with a small nod back at him, the priest took Mary by both shoulders and gently turned her toward him, saying, "All's in God's hands, whatever comes, Mary. Believe me. It's going to be well, one way or another."

Mary gave a hiccuping sob and crumpled into the priest's arms with the simple brokenheartedness of a small child wanting comfort. Holding her carefully while she cried against his shoulder, he patted her back, saying things into her ear, and from relief or because the best of the show seemed over, depending on how they saw it, people began to turn away, find somewhere else to look, something else to do. Father Henry went to talk to Otes still waiting outside the gate, and so did Perryn, but Anne came away toward Frevisse and Sister Thomasine, bringing her younger son with her and calling her other boy and Dickon down from the wall for the sake of asserting herself over something.

Sister Thomasine had returned to looking at the ground in front of her, so it was to Frevisse that Anne made a rueful shake of the head and said, "I don't know if Mary has ever understood the world isn't here simply to make her happy, or if she knows it and the problem is that she blackly resents it." She glanced back at her sister-in-law, now standing a little back from Father Edmund, gulping on the last of her sobs, her head hanging. "If only her bad temper was as little as she is, we'd all live the happier. And so would she. Colyn, stop that." Colyn had been scratching under his hair where it grew raggedly toward his tunic neck. Anne pulled his hand away. "Leave be, bad boy. You've been around John Upham's dogs again, and caught their fleas, haven't you?" She pushed his head forward so that she could part his hair to see his neck. "A good rubbing down with tansy when we get home is what you're going to . . ."

She broke off, staring at the back of his neck with something in the way she stood there that made Frevisse lean to see, too, but Colyn fidgeted, protesting, "Maaammm," and Anne let go his head to clamp her hands down on his shoulders, not with anger, Frevisse saw by her face, but in something near to . . . was it fear?

"What is it?" Frevisse asked sharply.

"I . . ." Anne was looking rapidly through the crowd for someone, not her husband, still in plain sight with Otes, but, "Mistress Margery!"

Her urgency drew people to look toward her and some began to come her way but a bone-thin woman in a faded green gown moved more quickly and with more purpose than the rest, to her before anyone else, Anne saying before she could ask anything, "Look," pushing Colyn's head forward again and his hair up from his neck. The boy squirmed but only from his hips down, knowing better than to make more protest while Mistress Margery bent to see. Frevisse shifted enough to see, too, and so did Sister Thomasine on the other side, come out of her withdrawal into curiosity.

"A rash," Mistress Margery said and pulled the boy's tunic away from his neck to see down inside. "It goes down his back, too."

"It itches," Colyn complained, squirming harder. Mistress Margery loosed him and he scratched at his chest. "Here, too."

"You look," Mistress Margery said over him to Sister Thomasine, and without hesitating Sister Thomasine did, putting his hand aside and opening his tunic's front at the neck. She worked more often than any of the other nuns

with Dame Claire in the infirmary, and now Frevisse realized why Mistress Margery seemed familiar to her. She
was the village's herbwife, who came sometimes to the
priory to exchange the herbs she gathered from the fields
and hedgerows and woods for ones Dame Claire grew in
the priory's gardens, and that would be how she and Sister
Thomasine were confident of one other.

"He has a rash here, too," Sister Thomasine said.

From among the little crowd gathering around them a
woman with a small girl beside her said, her voice scaling
up, "What kind of rash? *Plague* rash?" She was drawing
back even as she asked, shoving the little girl behind her
as she went. Nor was she alone. Everyone else was pulling
away, too. Only Anne, Mistress Margery, Sister Thomasine and Frevisse stayed where they were around Colyn—
Frevisse by plain force of will, not denying to herself her
sudden terror—and only Perryn, with his other son and
Dickon behind him, started toward them, but Anne cried
out, "Stay away, Simon! Don't come near! There's Adam
and Lucy will need you!" Because if it was plague, then
likely it was too late for Colyn or her, but if their father
lived, Adam and Lucy would still have someone. If they
lived.

Perryn broke stride, struggling between coming on and
staying where he was, but managed finally to catch himself back, taking firm hold not only on his feelings but on
both boys, to keep them where they were beside him.

Mistress Margery, seeming untouched by the fear
around her, said, "Take your tunic off, Colyn."

Colyn did and stood, naked to his breeks and staring
blindly at nothing in front of him, eyes huge with terror,
while the herbwife and Sister Thomasine looked at the
bright pink-to-red rash now easily seen all over his back
and chest and disappearing into the hair behind his ears.
There had been no outbreak of the Great Death in this
part of Oxfordshire for longer than Colyn had been alive,
but all save the very youngest children had heard the thing

talked of enough to know what its coming meant. Not simply death—death came often enough to any village to be familiar and accepted—but an ugly death that sometimes took so many in a village there were too few left alive to bury the dead.

Uncertainly Sister Thomasine said, "It doesn't look like what I've heard of the pestilence."

"Nay," Mistress Margery agreed, loudly enough to be heard across the churchyard. "This isn't plague rash."

Anne sobbed once, softly. Colyn's shoulders sagged. A shuddering sigh passed across the churchyard and hands moved in the sign of the cross with desperate thankfulness.

"See," Mistress Margery went on, still in a carrying voice. "It doesn't have the rosey rings. It isn't the plague."

"But then what is it?" Anne asked, after all only a little less desperate because whatever it was, her son had it.

Mistress Margery laid hand on Colyn's forehead. "He's hot." She meant by more than already came with the day. "Fevered hot. Feel."

Using the simplest, surest way to know if there was fever, Anne pressed her lips to Colyn's forehead in a kiss and drew back with a trembling nod of agreement. "He's dry-hot. He's fevered."

"Morbilli," Sister Thomasine said. Meaning the "little plague," rather than the great one.

"We call it mesels hereabouts," Mistress Margery said, "but aye, that's what it is, I think."

Anne caught Colyn tightly to her, as if that would be enough to keep him safe. Colyn, knowing as well as she did that it would not, began to cry.

# Chapter 8

Early as it was, the sunrise light still slanted honey-thick and golden across the goat-cropped grass of the village green, the morning was already heavy with heat, weighing down—along with the village's unnatural quiet at his back—on Simon as he trudged heavy-legged along his foreyard garden's path from the gateway to his housedoor. Wearily certain that going farther, even simply into the house, was too much trouble, he slumped down on the bench there with bowed head, hands hanging between his knees, listening to the quiet  no sounds from inside the house, no shifting of cows in the byre, no chickens busy around his feet—and told himself, wearily, not to mind it, that no one was dead, there was no need for mourning.

Yet.

That had been the worst of these four days since manor court—the waiting to see who would die.

Not *if* but who.

And how many.

Simon forced himself to straighten, dragging his back and then his head up against the tiredness that came from more than having been up all the night keeping watch by Colyn and Lucy and Adam in the church. There were eighteen children sick so far. One child or more from every family with small children in the village. No, twenty—he was forgetting Gilbey's two boys because they were being kept at home, not with the rest. Gilbey had even ridden to Banbury on Saturday and brought back a doctor to see his, at a fee Simon didn't care to think about. Sometimes Gilbey looked to have more money than sense, Simon thought bitterly. But then, with all Gilbey had, he could afford to take leave of his senses once in a while.

And sitting thinking about Gilbey was getting nothing done, Simon reminded himself, and there were things that desperately needed doing. Though for his very life Simon couldn't seem to think of any of them just now and scrubbed at his face with his hands, trying to be more awake, his stubble unfamiliarly harsh. There had been no Saturday bath and shaving this week. He had made do with a swim on Sunday, the stream warm enough for it, when he'd gone round the fields to see how things did, but shaving was too much trouble.

Or maybe it wasn't, he thought, finding he was scratching where the hairs prickled under his jawline.

Was it only Tuesday?

In those first terrible moments in the churchyard four days ago, mothers had begun to look to their children, harsh with fear as they felt foreheads and searched bodies for the telltale sign of rash. There had been the pink beginnings of it on only Adam and three others there, but

Mistress Margery had warned, "Spots are the surest sign but it can first show with no more than a running nose or a cough there's no reason for, or just in an ill temper because they don't feel well and don't yet know why."

Anne had whispered, "Lucy," left home with Cisily because she was fretful, and Simon had gone tight-throated with the same fear stark in his wife's eyes. The last time there had been mesels in the village, Adam had been newborn and not taken them—the very youngest babies never seemed to, Mistress Margery had said, nor those who had had it before—but their Jon, their firstborn, just turned three years old, had sickened, had burned up with fever and died, and Anne had nearly lost her milk with worry and then with grief, and almost they had lost her and Adam, too, and it had taken Mistress Margery more days to bring her back to health than Jon had taken to die.

"And it's going to spread," Mistress Margery had said in the churchyard. "Be sure of it. When it reaches one, it's like to reach all, it spreads so easy and fast, if they've been near each other at all of late," which they likely had been, always at play together at most days' ends when their work was done.

In the silence then, with the only sound the whimpering of Emma Millwarde's baby against her neck, everyone had stood staring at nothing or at their children, facing what was come on them with probably the same thought: How many children would it be this time who didn't live? Last time it had been three, all well on one day, all dead before a week was gone.

Into that stricken quiet, Sister Thomasine had said, "If so many are going to be ill and badly fevered, might it be well to keep them all together and in the church here in this hot weather?"

The few who heard her—Simon and Anne, Mistress Margery and Dame Frevisse—had momentarily stared blankly at her. Then understanding had bloomed in Mistress Margery's face and she'd said, "Yes! There'll be no place stay cooler than the church these hot days." With its stone walls and thickly thatched roof. "And if they're kept together, I can see to them far better, all at once, instead of running from village end to village end." And maybe coming too late, the way it had been during the throat-sickness three winters back, when Mistress Margery had been saving Martin Fisher's daughter, clearing her throat of the slime that was like to choke her, when word had come that John Gregory's boy was in like case at the village's other end but by the time she'd run the length of the village green to reach him, she was too late and he was dead, no fault of hers, just the way it was. She had saved others enough in her time for folk to know she knew her herbs and that there was power in her spells. She had even killed a man once with a spell, but only that once and only to save her own life, nor was she like some healers who only valued their skill for the money it brought them and cared naught about what they did or who they did it to. So folk had listened to her there in the churchyard while she told them why she wanted the sick children kept in the church, and the two nuns and Father Henry had explained to Father Edmund, to have his permission for it.

He'd given it readily, saying, "Where better for them to be than in here where we can best pray for them while we tend them?" and his willingness had helped talk around to it such as might have not seen the point, though even then Gilbey and his wife would have none of it. But there was none as missed them anyway and the nave was fair cramped as it was, with straw-stuffed mattresses brought from homes laid out in rows along both its sides for the children and barely space between for those who tended them to move and sit and sometimes lie down themselves.

How did the women take it, Simon wondered? The children's fevered restlessness and crying. The smells.

The men came and went, seeing how things were, giving what help they could, which never seemed to be much; and such women as didn't have sick children were in and out, bringing food and drink and taking fouled bedding away and bringing it back clean. That was what Cisily did when she wasn't helping nurse his three, but Anne and others never seemed to leave. Nor the nuns either. That was something Simon wouldn't have expected but there they were, the two of them, as tireless as the other women.

And today Colyn's fever had broken just ere dawn. Simon made the sign of the cross on himself at the thankful thought. The boy would better now, and Anne had been able to fall asleep beside him, leaving Cisily to watch over Adam and Lucy, still dangerously deep in their own fevers but somewhat quieted from some brew Mistress Margery had given them, and Simon had dragged himself up from the joint stool where he had sat most of the night and come home because things there could not be left to Watt and Dickon without he at least see how they did and do some of his share, too.

But nonetheless here he sat, doing nothing, and with a heavy sigh for his own weakness, he braced hands on knees, readying to force himself up and on with the day.

And found, in a little while, that he hadn't moved at all, was simply sitting with his eyes closed, nigh to drowsing.

He was that tired he couldn't trust himself, seemingly.

Or maybe he just didn't want to face everything there was to do because whenever he did that these past few days, he started to be afraid in different ways than simply for the children. There was the haying, first of all. The weather could not be better for it. Save for a little rain at early morning yesterday, there had only been hot, dry skies since manor court, even the nights bringing little ease from the heat and the dew drying fast off the grass in the mornings—but here they were, like to lose more of the last haying than they kept because with so many of the women seeing to the sick and others having to do double work at home because of it and Matthew gone, they were short of folk to go to the fields, even for the weeding that needed doing, let be the haying. And workdays owed the lord came before their own work so it would be his hay that was done first anyway and already it was less than two weeks to when Simon hoped to start the harvest. The first fine harvest there had looked to be after the string of bad years, and if they lost it, there would be dying in the village from more than mesels, and he was reeve, with it laid on him to make things come out well despite of everything, and he was afraid . . .

Simon slapped his hands down hard on his thighs, stinging himself to better wits. He was tired. That was all. Things were better than they had been for years, and they had seen their way through those and would through this.

And after all and come what may, none were dead yet.

Except poor old Matthew, who'd had naught but his burial after all, with Simon and some others digging a hasty hole—hardly big enough to be called a grave to Simon's mind—in a corner of the churchyard that same day he'd come home, and a few people—and Mary'd at least not grudged Matthew that much of her time—had gathered for Father Edmund's prayers over the box before the dirt had been shoveled back in. No wake or aught else, but Simon had vowed to buy his soul some Masses later, when there was time. But what in the name of St. Chad had Tom Hulcote been thinking of, coming up to him before they'd even cleaned the dirt off the shovels, to demand whether Simon was going to decide in his favor or not over the Woderove holding? Later, with time to think, Simon had reckoned it was Mary had put him up to it, but at the time all he had been was furious at him. Even now, Simon felt a hot shadow of that anger stir in him, along with the irk of knowing he was going to have to confess and do penance for it when confession time came round again.

Simon realized he had gone off on his thoughts again and pulled himself upright on the bench and then to his feet, to stand with fists planted on hips while he looked around the yard, trying to convince himself he was ready to get on with things. Thanks be to St. Roch that Dickon had been meseled years ago and so was safe from it this time and was doing all his share and more around the place with Watt.

But where were the two of them? Simon wondered, unable to bear the yard's quiet now he was full awake again. Lucy wasn't raising her voice somewhere around the place nor Cisily clattering a spoon against the morning porridge pot nor Anne telling someone to wash their hands if they thought they were going to eat at her table nor one of the boys teasing the other into mischief instead of to the morning milking. There was just this . . . terrible . . . quiet.

But it was past milking time, Simon told himself sternly, grabbing hold to something that didn't make misery course through him. That was why there was no stamping or lowing from the byre; Watt and Dickon had already done the milking and Dickon taken the cows to pasture while Watt carried the milk to Ienet Comber who was seeing to it for Anne in return for a tithe of it, which was better than letting it go to waste for lack of anyone doing anything with it at all. But had they done the mucking out yet? If not, he would. See to his own and then to rest, he reckoned and started for the barn, only to almost be run into by Dickon flinging at full run from around the house corner. The boy swerved and stumbled, and Simon reached out and caught him back to balance. In return, Dickon, gasping, caught hold on him, as Simon said, "Hai, hold up," and held him steady on his feet, seeing he was gray-faced under a sheen of sweat. "Are you gone daft, boy, running in this heat? You'll make yourself sick and then where'll we be, eh?"

Still clinging to him, Dickon panted out, "It's Tom Hulcote! You have to come!"

"Tom Hulcote be damned. You come over here and sit while I fetch you something to drink."

"He's up by Oxfall Field," Dickon gasped, desperate to say the words. "In the ditch there. Dead."

"Drunk, you mean," Simon said. "Or down with the heat, maybe."

*"Dead,"* Dickon sobbed. "All broken in. His head. All . . . all . . ." He couldn't make the words come fast enough around his need to breathe and his tears, now it was safe to cry. "His head . . . it's all . . . smashed in."

# Chapter 9

Frevisse returned to the priory in company with Ienet Comber bringing curded cheese to the nunnery kitchen. They parted in the kitchen yard with Ienet's promise that when her business with the curded cheese was done, she would wait there to keep Frevisse company back to the village, and Frevisse cut through the priory's side yard, meeting only servants, to a small gate into the inner yard, the shortest way to Master Naylor's house. She had intended no pause along the way but as she latched the small gate closed behind her the bell beyond the cloister walls began to ring to Sext and she stopped, her hand on the latch, her throat tightening with longing for the nunnery church's deep, familiar quiet, her own place in the choir stalls, the weaving of nun's voices through the Offices' prayers and psalms . . .

But that was all forbidden to her for this while. She could not even enter the cloister, and she bowed her head, whispering some of the words from today's Sext. . . . *Deus, Qui temperas rerum vices . . . Confer salutem corporum, Veramque pacem cordium . . .* God, Who governs time and fortune . . . Give health to the body, And true peace to the soul. Turning it from a prayer for herself into a prayer for others far more desperately in need than she was, she drew a deep, steadying breath and turned toward the gateway to the outer yard.

But to have been brought to this because of Sister Thomasine . . .

That day in the village churchyard, while Mistress Margery and Father Edmund and Father Henry were talking the women around to keeping the ill children together in the church, she and Sister Thomasine had been left in the lee of things, aside and quiet, on the verge of going home, Frevisse had thought until Sister Thomasine had said, "We'll have to send word to Domina Elisabeth we're staying."

Frevisse's immediate response was that no, they weren't, but years of nunhood had given her some governance over her tongue, making her hesitate, when this time she should not have, before saying carefully, "We'll have to ask her permission."

"Father Henry can ask for it when he goes back for Dame Claire," Sister Thomasine had said.

More to Frevisse's mind had been withdrawal to the nunnery themselves and a brief explanation to Domina Elisabeth followed by her refusal, but it hardly mattered and she had let it happen Sister Thomasine's way because Domina Elisabeth would never give permission for them to stay, however she was asked.

But from what Father Henry said when he returned, it seemed that their prioress had never had the mesels, nor had Dame Juliana or Sister Cecely, and so she had for-

bidden them to return for this while, in fear they would
bring the infection with them. Moreover, she had refused
Dame Claire to come, only given her leave to send all the
advice and herbs she would.

"But you," Frevisse had protested to Father Henry.
"You're not forbidden."

Father Henry had looked sheepish, as if something
were his fault. "I have to say the Mass." And therefore
the priory could not do without him, even at the danger.

But it meant Sister Johane was left with the duties of
cellarer for who knew how long. And with Sister Emma
as kitchener . . .

Her meals and Sister Thomasine's meals were brought
thrice daily from the nunnery kitchen, that their keep not
fall on the village, and Dame Claire sent medicines by
way of Father Henry, and Domina Elisabeth had sent
word that prayers were being said for the sick, and all that
was very well, Frevisse thought, walking through the brief
shade of the inner yard's gateway into the hot sunlight of
the priory's outer yard, but brought no end to the hours
of ill children and frightened parents and lack of prayers
there had been these four past days and were still to come.
Even with keeping the Offices as best they could in the
shortened form allowed when out of the nunnery, none of
them—not even Matins and Lauds at midnight—ever
went uninterrupted by a child or several waking restless
with fever and discomforts; and most of their mothers had
no servants at home and needed to go back and forth from
church to house and were tiring, needing Frevisse and
Sister Thomasine more and more through the days as well
as the nights. Some of the men tried to be of help with
at least their own child or children but most of them
hadn't the way of it. Why a man who mucked out byres
every day of his life should be put off by a small child's
dirtied napkin or anyone's vomit was more than Frevisse
understood. But she thought that, for many of them, the
trouble was they could not help letting their fears come

too much between them and what needed to be done; most of the women let nothing—fear least of all—come between them and their children's needs. In truth, for most of them the greater their fear, the fiercer they were in doing what needed to be done to keep their children alive, no matter the dirt or ugliness of it.

Interestingly, Father Henry in his own way was as fierce, though it had taken Frevisse a while to see it. Between his duties at the nunnery—and sometimes instead of his duties, she suspected—he was always with the children, two beds at a time if need be, holding hot, restless hands, telling stories and more stories, all kinds of stories, quieting children who needed something besides their own and others' misery to listen to, diverting mothers who needed the same. It was a pity that Father Edmund, as he admitted and anyone could easily see, was small use with children and less use the more ill they were, but he made up for it by being constantly out and about through the village, comforting people in their homes, lending a hand here and there as need was, or else praying at his own house since his church was no good to him at present, he smilingly said.

Unfortunately the case was much the same with Frevisse. She had never had nor ever wanted a way with children. But then neither had Sister Thomasine ever desired motherhood, devoted from girlhood to the cloister and prayers, but she had given herself over to the children's care far more wholeheartedly than Frevisse had, to Frevisse's shame. But then Sister Thomasine was also pleased beyond measure to be, all day and all night, in a church, uninterruptedly in sight of the altar except when she and Frevisse withdrew into the sacristy where mattresses had been brought for them to sleep in a little privacy. Though Sister Thomasine never stayed there long but after only brief sleep would rouse and slip back into the chancel to kneel and pray before the altar until she was needed again.

Frevisse suspected that, ill children or no, Sister Thomasine had rarely been more happy.

Unhappily, that did nearly nothing to improve Frevisse's struggle with her own ill humor, one admittedly greatly compounded of fear, because it frightened her to see how quickly a child could fall ill, frightened her more to see how quickly it could worsen, frightened her most of all to know how easily any one of them could die.

Behind her the cloister bell ceased ringing, telling her the other nuns were in church now, in their places in the choir beginning Sext, and she slipped one of the Office's antiphons over her uncalm thoughts. *Suscepisti me, Domine: et confirmasti me in conspectu tuo.* You have received me, Lord: and you have strengthened me in your sight. It loosened some of the knots in her with the comfort that, whatever happened, there was always the shelter of prayers and the certainty of Something Else beyond the burdens of everyday and the briefness of mortality.

But consideration of mortality brought her back to why she was come to see Master Naylor.

Beside the steward's door the two guards stood up, slow in the heat. For a moment Master Spencer's man looked as if he was about to challenge her but decided it was not worth the bother, while the priory guard, the same who had been here last time she came, knocked at the open door and asked, "Is it true what's said about Tom Hulcote? He's been found dead?"

"Yes," Frevisse said and nothing more. She had had enough talk of his death from Ienet Comber on their way here and the sun was cramming down hot on her head. What she wanted was to be in shade somewhere, not more talk to no purpose.

As before, Mistress Naylor came, wiping her hands on her apron but suddenly fear on her face as she saw Frevisse who said quickly, understanding, "Dickon is well."

Mistress Naylor gave a small gasp of relief, then hurriedly made belated curtsy, murmuring to her apron,

"Thank you, my lady. Come in, please you."

Grateful to be out of the sun even if inside were no cooler, Frevisse did, asking, "May I see your husband?"

Mistress Naylor, already edging past her to lead the way through the house, said, "Surely, my lady. How do the other children?"

"One of Simon Perryn's sons and a few others look to be past the worst. The rest are still very fevered."

"The Blessed Virgin keep them," Mistress Naylor said and led the way into the garden, where this time Master Naylor, his daughters and little son were in the bean-vine arbor, all their heads together over a boat he was carving from a piece of scrap wood, Frevisse saw as she came near, hearing him say before any of them knew she was there, ". . . and when I'm out of here, we'll all go sailing it down the stream."

"And Dickon, too?" the older girl asked.

"And Dickon, too." Then he saw his wife and Frevisse and stood up, tense for the moment he took to read by his wife's face that nothing was wrong. Then he was simply as Frevisse best knew him, briskly at business, giving the knife he had been using to the older girl and the half-made boat to his son, saying, "Here's Dame Frevisse come to see me. We'll finish the making this afternoon."

The younger girl started to protest, but her mother took her by the hand with, "Let's see what we can find to make a sail of," and they all went with her unprotestingly.

Master Naylor gestured Frevisse to sit. She gestured that he should, too, and when they both were, he asked, "Is it about Tom Hulcote?"

"You've heard already," Frevisse said ruefully.

"Word never trips when coming from village to here, that I've found," Master Naylor said. "The guard passed it in an hour ago."

"Did he also tell you it was Dickon found the body?"

"Dickon?" Master Naylor made to stand sharply up but caught himself back from the useless movement and demanded, "How did it come to be Dickon who found him?"

"He was coming back a long way around after seeing the cows out to pasture this morning. Something to do with setting snares, I think, but didn't ask closely." Because he should not have been setting snares.

Master Naylor understood that, too, and asked nothing about it, only, "How is he? Where is he now?"

"I haven't seen him. I gather he's with Bess the ale-wife."

Master Naylor nodded, satisfied with that. "He'll do well enough with her. Now, about Tom. What happened?"

As evenly as she could, Frevisse said, "From what Perryn tells me, he'd been stabbed in the back and the side of his head crushed in."

Master Naylor's mouth twisted on the ugliness of it, matching what she felt inside. "Where?" he asked harshly.

"He was found in the ditch above Oxfall Field."

"Found?" Master Naylor repeated. "You mean he wasn't killed there."

"Perryn says he looks to have been killed elsewhere. The only blood there was on him and there should have been more."

"Perryn says. You haven't seen for yourself?"

It was not so strange a question as it might have been. Over the years there had been other brutal deaths at St. Frideswide's and from them Master Naylor knew that Frevisse took more interest in the how and why and who of them than might be thought right to a woman. But this time she only answered, "No. Perryn and some other men had fetched the body in. I only knew about it afterwards."

But when he had come to her to tell her of it and say that Master Naylor should be told as soon as possible, she had taken the chance to ask him more, and now when Master Naylor said, "There was rain yestermorning at dawn. The blood might have washed away," she was able to say back, "Perryn says he can't have been lying out that long. Almost nothing had been at him in the night, and . . ." The thing was ugly enough to think without having to say it aloud. ". . . the birds had only just started on him."

Mistress Naylor came along a garden path, bringing two cups of water for which her husband and Frevisse thanked her, but Master Naylor waited until she was gone away again before saying, "He was moved last night, then. He was killed last night, too?"

"From the few men Perryn had had time to ask before he talked to me, nobody remembers seeing him since Saturday, likely."

"Saturday. And two more days since then," Master Naylor considered that. "He was maybe not dead all that while. He might have been away and been killed when coming back."

"Not . . . to judge by the smell." In weather as warm as this, something dead was very quickly something rotting and, "From what Perryn says about how far along the body is, he's been dead about that long."

"But not lying out anywhere. That means the reason no one saw him for those two days was that he was dead, that someone killed him on Saturday, maybe Sunday, but kept the body hidden until last night."

"Yes."

Master Naylor stood up, paced restlessly to the edge of the arbor's leaf-patterned shadows, stood with his back to her a moment, turned, returned, sat, and asked abruptly, "Two days at least since he was last seen, and no one missed him in that while?"

"It doesn't seem so."

"Not even Mary Woderove?" Master Naylor asked.

"I asked that of Perryn but he didn't know. He hadn't gone yet to tell her Tom was dead. I think he was hoping others would tell her first so he wouldn't have to face her first grief at it."

Master Naylor nodded grim understanding of that.

"But she started in at manor court," about which she

had long since sent word to Master Naylor by way of
Father Henry, "telling Tom he ought to leave here. I heard
her then, and Perryn says she was at it afterwards, too,
telling Tom and anyone else in hearing that he ought to
leave, make a start somewhere else, a new life for them
both where everyone wasn't against them. If she thought
he had . . ."

"Without telling her he was going to?" Master Naylor
asked.

"Or maybe he did tell her he was going to, and she
thought he was gone and didn't say anything, to give him
more time to be away. Only someone had killed him instead."

"Or else he wouldn't go, refused to go, and she killed
him," Master Naylor suggested.

Frevisse could see Mary Woderove working into
enough of a fury to want to kill even someone she was
supposed to love if he refused her what she wanted. But,
"I don't see that she could have killed him, hid his body,
and then moved it, all unheeded by anyone."

"She's over-small to have moved it," Master Naylor
agreed. "Or done the rest, I suppose," he added. "And
why would she, come to that?"

"From what I've seen of her, she's a woman who likes
to hold on to what she has," Frevisse said. "The threat of
someone leaving her might drive her into passion enough
to kill, but she was already telling Tom to go, so that
wouldn't be it."

"No," Master Naylor agreed.

"Was there anyone at all you know of might want him
dead?"

Master Naylor shook his head. "Tom was no worse a
trouble than some others are hereabouts. Less than some,
come to that, and not so often as others. Mostly he wasn't
even the kind of man who made men angry at him." Master Naylor stood up and paced again. Frevisse realized
with surprise that he was deeply angry. "The trouble was

that Tom didn't belong where he was. He couldn't fit quietly into his place here but didn't have the wits or skill to raise himself out of it on his own. He was no Gilbey Dunn. But given his chance . . ." Master Naylor stopped, staring down into his cup as if surprised to find he was still carrying it.

Reluctantly Frevisse asked, "That's why you thought he should have the Woderove holding and marry Mary?"

"Mary is sharp enough and Tom works . . . worked well enough when he could see there was something in it for him. With a little luck, they'd have made a go of it. Between the two of them, they would have had a chance."

And now they neither of them would. And Master Naylor, in his constrained way, was unhappy over that. Frevisse had long known that he was a skilled steward, with a keen eye to the priory's best interests. She had not known he also would take the trouble to see past someone's outward seeming to their possibilities, though perhaps she should have guessed it because it was a useful tool toward making him so good a steward. But all she said was, "And since he and Mary were already . . . linked, all they needed was for the holding to be given to them."

Master Naylor came back to sit again. "Yes."

Frevisse carefully set to one side of her mind that he had told her something of that when last they had talked but she had let it go and had a part in refusing them because of her ready, easy dislike for them both. She was at fault in that, she feared, and must needs take closer look at herself over it; but just now what mattered was that someone had killed Tom Hulcote, and slowly she said, "Mary Woderove's husband was killed away from here, luckily for them, since his death was so convenient to them."

"Or would have been convenient," Master Naylor said, "if things had fallen out for them afterwards the way they hoped."

"Tom's death isn't as obviously convenient to anyone."

"Particularly to Tom," Master Naylor said bitterly.

"But then the question is," Frevisse said, holding to where she was going, "for whom *was* Tom Hulcote's death convenient?"

# Chapter 10

aster Naylor had had no helpful answer to her question. From all he knew, Tom Hulcote had not mattered enough in anyone's life—except Mary Woderove's—for anyone to want him dead—and it was not dead that Mary wanted him. "He had no enemies I've ever heard of," Master Naylor had said. "Nor friends, come to that. He wasn't a man anyone cared that much about, either way." Except for Mary Woderove, he had not bothered to add.

"The men who were ready to make trouble at the manor court," Frevisse had said. "Weren't they friends?"

"From what Father Henry told me, they're just the usual lot who make trouble because they lack the wit to make anything else. They'd take up a sick dog's cause as fast as Tom Hulcote's, especially against Gilbey Dunn."

"What about Gilbey? He had no liking for Tom."

"Or Tom for him. If it was Gilbey found dead, it might be Tom I'd look to first, but for Gilbey to put himself to the trouble of killing anybody—you'd have to find good reason for it."

"The Woderove holding?"

"It was by far a greater matter to Tom than it was to Gilbey. It would be Gilbey I'd look for to be dead because of it, rather than Tom."

And that had been all the help he could give her. Nor had she found out much more than that in the two days since then, because she had returned to the village to find too many of the children worsening, and almost all the hours since then had been taken up with their necessities. Last night she had been so tired that when her turn came to sleep, she had barely been able to unpin her veil and set it aside before she fell onto her mattress and was still so tired when she awoke that her fingers had fumbled at pinning it on again. But St. Roch be thanked, since dawn this morning seven more children's fevers had broken, one after another in a welter of sweat and mothers' tears and the need for dry sheets or blankets and turned mattresses and urging, urging the children to drink just a little more barley water, just a little, before they sank into their first deeply quiet, blessedly cool sleeps in days, often with their spent mothers stretched out asleep beside them.

With all that, she had had little time to think of questions about Tom Hulcote, let alone ask them of anyone. She only knew, from undercurrents of talk among tired women and whoever of their family and friends came to help sometimes when other work was done that the uncertainty of Tom Hulcote's death was beginning to take its toll.

It was not that there had never been murder here before. Besides the several Frevisse knew too well it seemed, from what she half-heard and overheard, that

some while back one man had done for another with a
dagger in an alehouse quarrel, and ten years ago one of
the Gregorys had clouted someone over the head with a
shovel about a boundary stone, but those had been open
killings, seen by others, the why and how and guilt known
to everyone and the murderer seized while his victim's
body was still bleeding.

Tom Hulcote's death had happened secretly. No one
knew why or where or by whom he had been killed. The
only certainty was that his murderer was not a passing
stranger and long gone. A stranger would have killed him
and left, not chanced lingering for a day and more or
bothered with shifting the corpse. But if it had not been
a stranger, it had been someone here, and that meant there
was someone among them who was able to kill a man
and show no sign of it afterwards. Someone among them
was a murderer and they had no way of telling who, and
therefore, when there was chance, there were tight little
huddles of talk among the women and worry over more
than their children when presently their children were
more than enough worry; nor did Frevisse doubt there was
more talk in the village, and unsure looks and unspoken
wondering and distrusts and wariness growing, with no
cure for any of it so long as Tom Hulcote's murderer went
unknown.

Worse—and this she hoped no one else had thought
of—was that since no one knew why Tom had been
killed, there was no certainty that his death would be the
only one.

She straightened, sore-backed, from helping small Elyn
Denton drink her barley water and managed a smile down
at the child, who smiled sleepily back, rolled on her side,
and burrowed into her pillow, ready to nap, Frevisse
hoped, until her mother returned from seeing to her older
children still at home.

"Please you, my lady, Simon Perryn is asking if you'd

come out to him," Joane Goddard said in a low voice beside her.

"Me?" Frevisse said, looking where his children were bedded near the rood screen, Anne crouched between them, leaning over Lucy, whose fever was among those that had broken this morning.

Joane's voice dropped lower. "He doesn't want her to know, please you."

Frevisse feared she knew what that meant but had no way to refuse it. Mistress Margery was sleeping in the sacristy, in easy call if needed, and enough mothers were awake again and seeing to their children that Sister Thomasine was hardly being left alone to it, and when she spoke briefly to her on her way out, Sister Thomasine merely said without looking around from persuading Joane's boy Ralph, still fevered, to drink balm water, "Of course. Take as long as need be."

The rain that had been lightly falling since midday was drizzling to a stop, leaving behind it a thick, damp heat, but Frevisse paused inside the church porch to draw a deep breath of the heavy air with rather desperate relief. These past hot days, the church's stone walls and thatch had held coolness in as hoped, but with so many people so closely kept and the shutters not opened during the days to protect the meseled children's eyes from light nor after dark because of sick-making night vapors, the air was long since thickened with the smells there had to be among so many sick children as well as begun to warm, and she had not been outside since one brief time yesterday.

But Perryn was waiting at the churchyard gate, leaning against one of the pentice posts, looking as weary as she felt, but he straightened as she joined him, bowed, gave her greeting that she returned, then asked him with a nod at the last slow dripping of the rain off the edges of the pentice roof, "Will this set the haying back?"

"Most of the last cut was stacked before it started, and

what's left lying will dry without much hurt from this," he said. "It's what we couldn't cut today we won't make up." He nodded past her, toward the village green. "The crowner's come."

Frevisse turned to see two men in brown livery strolling across the green toward the alehouse. "When?" she asked, surprised no one had brought word of it into the church yet.

"About an hour ago."

"Who?" she asked.

"Master Montfort."

The way Perryn said it told her that, like her, he had dealt with the crowner before and felt no better about him than she did. That Montfort might not come himself was something she and Master Naylor had discussed, with her own hope being, "He might not. It being 'only' a villein's death, he might send one of his serjeants rather than come himself."

"We can but hope," Master Naylor had replied.

But hope had failed and he had come.

"He's at Father Edmund's," Perryn said, "and giving orders like no one had wit in the world but him."

"Has he called for the jurors yet?"

"Almost as soon as he was off his horse. They're there now."

Frevisse looked sharply away from the green to him. "Already? Why aren't you there? You were one of the finders of the body."

"He said I wasn't needed."

Frevisse saw now the hard set of Perryn's mouth, the rigidness behind his face's tired lines as he stared broodingly at the two men going into the alehouse, and she echoed with the beginning of alarm, "Not needed?"

The jury inquiring into a death was made of the men who first found the body because they were ones most likely to know the closest details concerning the death. Or if the matter were complicated enough, the jury was made of them and men from neighboring villages, and even though Montfort's usual way was to ask questions enough to have his mind made up before he had to deal with a jury, if this time he had already called a jury, then Perryn should have been on it, as one of the men who had brought in Tom Hulcote's body.

"He's sent for Dickon, though," Perryn said. "To witness. And ordered I wasn't to go far."

Worse, thought Frevisse. Montfort was moving as if he already had answers, and if he did, she did not like what she was seeing of the shape of them.

"It was to ask about Adam, though, I wanted to see you," Perryn said. "He's not bettering, is he?"

That had been the question Frevisse had feared and she tried to find another answer than the only one there was but had to say, "No. Not yet."

"Will he?" Perryn asked, his bluntness giving away more than Frevisse wanted to share of his fear. Colyn had bettered steadily since his fever had broken and Lucy had taken the mesels only lightly. But Adam . . .

This past day and more he seemed hardly to know even his mother and still his fever refused to break despite everything they did. If it did not break soon . . .

Low enough she hardly heard her own voice, Frevisse said, "We're praying for him."

Perryn stepped away from her, past her where she could not see his face, but not quite quickly enough she did not see the pain there. He knew as well as she did that the answers to prayers were not always the answers sought for. And although she believed that whatever came, came by God's will and therefore for a greater good than men could see, she had rarely found that to be much comfort against hurt or the harsh, present edge of grief, and for now she gave Perryn the only thing she could— her silence—looking the other way from him until behind her, he said tautly, "Here's trouble coming."

# Chapter 11

last few drops of the finished rain were falling off the thatch edge, sparkling in the thick sunlight, as Dame Frevisse drew aside and Simon stepped forward to meet the crowner's man in the gateway.

None too mannerly, the man asked, "You're the reeve, right?"

"I am, aye," Simon agreed.

"Master Montfort wants you."

There was no question but that he meant "now," and although Simon already knew the crowner's men followed their master's manners, he still gave way to a smoulder of anger at the rudeness, said, "Oh, aye," and would have added he'd be there just as soon as he had shifted a manure pile or two, but Dame Frevisse put in mildly, "Of course. Show us the way, why don't you, fellow?" with somehow an edge on "fellow" that made the man flick an uneasy glance toward her.

He had obviously had no order concerning a nun; nor had Simon had any thought but that she would go back to the church, but she stood staring, waiting for the man to go, and after a bare moment's hesitation, he gave her the slight bow he should have given earlier and turned away, back toward Father Edmund's.

Dame Frevisse followed, and Simon as he fell into stride beside her, asked low-voiced, "Is this something you should be doing?" Because if he had had choice, he would have stayed as far from Master Montfort as he could, not sought him out.

"This is manor business and therefore mine," she said, still seeming mildly but with more of an edge under the words and her wimple and veil making it hard to read her face from the side.

Nor was there time to pry more out of her, even if Simon had thought it possible. The priest's messuage was only the other side of the churchyard. If Simon had cared to, he could have shown the crowner's man the shorter way, through the narrow stile in the churchyard's low stone wall for the priest's use in going to the church and home again, but he was in no haste to come to Master Montfort. Around by the street and in through the fore-yard would be soon enough.

There wasn't even that much of a foreyard, since the priest's place had garden, byre and barns all to the back, though the barn was larger than most since whoever was priest in the village collected tithes in kind from all Lord Lovell's folk here and added church-gifts from the pri-ory's villeins to that for his services to them, all in all setting him up to rival Gilbey Dunn for wealth here and his profits going farther than most men's because he had nor kith nor kin to see to, only sometimes a housekeeper, unless he was a priest who failed to keep to his vows, but the last lax priest had been in Simon's grandam's young years and a hard time he must have had of it, according to her, with himself to support and a woman he called his wife and their six children, and "If ever a man perished by surfeit rather than the sword, it was him, sure," Simon's grandam had always said when telling the story. "He sowed thick, as they say, but reaped thin. There wasn't a brat worth breeding up in the lot."

Simon wished it was his grandam going to face Master Montfort, rather than him.

He likewise wished he thought some good were like to come of the crowner being here because the unease there had been ever since Tom's body was found was only worsening, too many folk uncertain of too many other folk and folk uncertain of them in return because someone among them was surely a murderer.

And from what he knew of Master Montfort he had small hope that things were going to better with him here. He had last had dealing with him six years back, when old Eva Mewes had slipped into the stream and drowned while doing Joane Goddard's laundry. That time Master Montfort had complained bitterly all the while he was here, it being a wet, chill March, over the weather and having to come to nowhere over nothing more than a villager's death, and had in the end ruled it an accident, as it had been, and taken the clothing old Eva had been washing as deodand—the cause of her death, and therefore taken to the king's profit. Master Montfort's complaints had been nothing to Joane Goddard's at having to buy her own clothing back to satisfy the fine, and she had at least had cause to complain, none of the trouble being of her own doing, while the crowner was there because it was his business to be there and why did he have to make it a misery for everyone?

This time he had not even been off his horse before he was demanding lodging and stabling as if they would have been denied him if he did not force the matter, though they were his by right of his being the king's officer and on the king's business. Nor did it matter that his needs that way had already been forethought and Father Edmund's house and yard and byre readied for him, his men, and horses.

At least he was wasting no time over what had brought him here. Simon would give him that. He'd still been stripping off his gloves when he demanded the jurors to be brought to him and said at Simon in the same breath, "Except you, reeve. I don't want you on the jury, but keep where I can find you when I want you."

He had added the same to Father Edmund, somewhat more graciously though not much, then asked, "The whelp who found the body. I want him here, too."

Simon had used that for reason to leave, found Dickon helping Watt hoe the onions at home, brought him back and given him over to one of the crowner's guards at Father Edmund's gateway, then gone off to the alehouse, looking for something else to do than think but found no company, everyone off to the fields for weeding while the rain delayed the haying. Even the old men who usually found naught to do but sit around with their talking had jounced off in Will Cufley's cart that morning, old Tod Denton saying he could hack a hoe well enough if he had to but don't expect him to do it often-like. There had only been Bess and she had gone on about Tom's death, the way everybody had been going on about it, one way or another, to no profit or useful end that Simon could see, since they knew what they knew and no more, no matter how much they talked, and what they knew was not enough. When he'd shown no interest in that, Bess had shifted to what might come of the crowner being here, another thing Simon had not wanted to think about, and he had put his halfpence on the table and gone out, with nowhere else to go but home, where Watt would only go on at him about the same things, so he'd gone to the church instead, wishing he could go to Anne, but that would have meant seeing Adam and he could not bear to see Adam.

Nor bear not knowing how he was, and he'd asked for Dame Frevisse to come out, for all the good that had done him.

God and the Blessed Virgin, but he wished all of this were over with.

Two of the crowner's men were sitting at ease on the bench beside the priest's housedoor, one of them whittling, a pile of wood chips growing between his feet, the other leaned back, arms crossed on his chest, looking ready to doze if there was a chance. They both cocked eyes toward their fellow bringing Simon and the nun but said nothing, letting him lead them inside.

The priest's main room was open to the rafters and ran long to right and left of the door and the full width of the house, with one end walled off into a second room that was even ceilinged and walled above to make a third with stairs up to it. Most folk in the village had only the one room on the ground, serving for kitchen and most other living, and a loft where the children slept and goods were stored, but then the priest's place was often used for lesser manor courts and village meetings and was where Lord Lovell's bailiff stayed when he was here and, for this while, Master Montfort, worse luck for Father Edmund.

The crowner was seated on the far side of the broad table set in the room's center, his beringed hands clasped on the polished tabletop, ignoring his guard's bow, going on speaking toward his clerk at the table's end, a drab-clad man on a stool, hunched over inkpot and papers, blinking owlishly behind thick glasses held on by loops of dark ribbon around his ears.

Simon took a quick look around, taking in Bert, Walter, John, and Hamon as jurors, crowded together on a bench to the left end of the room, and Dickon standing between them and the table, and Father Edmund at the room's other end beside his fireplace that Father Clement had had built, the first there had ever been in the village though of late Anne was pressing for one, too, since now Gilbey had one . . .

Simon caught himself back from trying to be somewhere else by not thinking about being here as Master Montfort swung around to dismiss the guard with a wave. The man bowed, moved aside, retreated, and Master Montfort fixed his small, hard eyes on Simon who made a quick, low bow in his turn, but when he straightened, Master Montfort was looking past him, eyes narrowed with displeasure.

"You, Dame?" he snapped. "On the gad again, are you?"

Dame Frevisse had fallen behind as they entered. Now she came forward to Simon's side, her eyes toward the floor, her hands tucked humbly nunwise into her opposite sleeves, and said hardly above a whisper, making a deep curtsy, "If it please you, sir."

"It doesn't," Master Montfort retorted.

"She's taken Master Naylor's place this while, sir," said Simon, to come between her and the crowner's open displeasure.

"Ah!" Satisfaction glowed suddenly on Master Montfort's face. He was a fox-haired man and florid-faced to match it, always in or about to be in ill humour, but Master Naylor's trouble brought him to an open smile. "Yes, that fool has finally come to grief, I hear, and none too soon, either. I've seen for years he was above his place, even if no one else could." And the worse fools, they, his tone said. "You're taking his place, is that it, Dame? Your prioress can't do better?"

"She's asked her brother's help," Dame Frevisse said so gently despite the roughness of his asking, that butter, as the saying went, would not have melted in her mouth, Simon thought. And then thought that if she had taken to talking to him that way, he would have been as wary as of the devil.

Master Montfort seemed to like it, though. He tapped rapid fingers on the tabletop and asked a little less balefully, "Your prioress' brother. He's the abbot of St. Bartholomew's, Northampton, yes?"

"If it please you, sir," Dame Frevisse agreed, her eyes still downward, as subdued a picture of womanhood as could be found.

Master Montfort tapped a little harder, thinking, then snapped, "Stay if you will, Dame. But it's a favor to your prioress. You're to stand aside and keep your mouth shut. You're allowed to listen, nothing more. You understand?"

For answer, Dame Frevisse made him another small curtsy and, head still bowed, drew well aside and back toward the wall beside the door. Master Montfort leaned to say something else, low-voiced again, to his clerk, who dipped pen tip in his inkpot, ducked low over a scrap of paper, and began to scribble. Simon used the chance to trade a nod with the priest and give Bert, Walter, John, and Hamon another look, not quite happy they were there and he was here. When he'd sought help to bring in Tom's body, he had simply taken the first four fit men he had found, routing John Rudyng and Bert Fleccher out of the alehouse where John was hiding out from his mother-in-law and Bert just lying low from life on the whole, then found Walter Hopper at his messuage and collected him and Hamon and a hurdle for carrying the body. Father Edmund, fetched by Dickon on Simon's order, had caught up to them as they'd left Walter's, and Dickon had shown the way to Tom's body. They were seen as they went by the field lane, of course, and followed by folk leaving their work to see what was toward, but they reached the body well ahead of anyone else, with time for Simon to see how Tom was lying all sprawled at the bottom of the ditch, looking like he'd rolled to where he was, his arms and legs loosely out. There was something over his face, something Dickon had said he'd put there before he left him, to keep the birds off, and it had, though there were five crows gathered to the body again, glossy black against the high-summer green of hedge and grassy ditch, and two of them had been trying to pluck the cloth away. Bert had yelled at them but Dickon, steadied down until then, had given a high, furious cry and grabbed up dirt clods from the field edge and rushed at them, throwing wildly after them as they rose on their wide black wings. They'd cawed offense at him and he'd yelled after them and been crying again, and Simon had gone and caught hold of him, turned him, and taken him well aside away from Tom's body that he'd seen more than enough of already, holding him while he sobbed it all out again.

It was never good, seeing a man's face that birds had been at, and worse when it was someone you'd known.

Meanwhile, the other men had seen to lifting Tom's body onto the hurdle. Father Edmund had covered it with a blanket he'd thought to bring, and then with Bert, Walter, John, and Hamon doing the carrying and Father Edmund the praying, they'd headed back, Simon and Dickon trailing behind, Simon's arm around Dickon's shoulders.

By then all those who should have been doing something better had caught up to them and seen them all the way back the village, to Tom's house, but when all was said and done, there were only the seven of them who had "found" it and brought it in; and with Dickon too young to be a juror and Father Edmund a priest, that had left Simon, Bert, Walter, John, and Hamon to be jurors when the time came, like it or not.

Simon hadn't liked it. But he liked being left out of it even less, and his unease grew as he watched Bert and John shifting their bottoms on the bench and their feet on the floor, looking everywhere except at him, while Hamon gave him a short glance and snatched it away. Only Walter met his eyes but with a frowning worry that told Simon nothing except that there looked to be something to worry over, and that much he had begun to guess already.

He looked away to Dickon standing with his half-grown boy's awkwardness between the jurors' bench and the table and found the boy's eyes fixed on him much like Walter's, save that instead of only worry, there was fear.

At what? Simon wondered but just then Gilbey Dunn came in, brought by another of Master Montfort's men and looking none too pleased about it. As the crowner's man made his bow and stood aside, Gilbey gave a quick, assessing look at everyone, then stalked forward to Simon's side, gave Master Montfort an ungracious bow, and demanded, "Yes? So? I'm here."

"And good thing, too," Master Montfort returned as ungraciously. "Otherwise I'd have had you dragged in by your heels."

Cockerel meeting cockerel, Simon thought, and no sense to it, just matching dislikes, left over from when they had last dealt together, once though it had been and years ago, Simon recalled.

He braced himself for whatever was next, ready when Master Montfort spread his glare and bristling displeasure to include him. "You're both here because I have evidence that says you had to do with this Tom Hulcote's death. This is your chance to confess and be done with it. Do you?"

Simon felt his mouth drop open, snapped it shut on a gulp, and said hotly, "What?" as Gilbey after an equally startled pause exclaimed angrily, "Are you crazed? We're not confessing to anything. I'm not, anyway. Are you, Perryn?"

"Of course not!"

"You may as well. The evidence says you were both there when this fellow was killed and so either you killed him yourselves or you know who did."

"Says we were there when he was killed?" Simon said. "No one knows where he was killed!"

"Don't play cunning with me," Master Montfort snapped.

"What's cunning about that?" Simon demanded. "He . . ."

Quietly from where she stood aside, Dame Frevisse said, "If it please you, master crowner."

"I said you weren't to speak, Dame," Master Montfort snarled.

Dame Frevisse bowed her head, acknowledging that with all possible outward humility but said anyway, "Mightn't they be better willing to admit their guilt if they knew the evidence?"

Master Montfort glared at her. "I'm crowner here, not you. This business is mine and you'll keep quiet or you'll not be here. Do you understand?"

Dame Frevisse made a small curtsy and a slight backward step, and Master Montfort faced Simon and Gilbey again, ready to go on, but Gilbey said, "She's right, though. What's this evidence you're claiming?"

Master Montfort sneered at him. "First, you both quarreled with him more than once and the latest time was not long before he died."

"Better to say he quarreled with us," Simon returned.

"There was quarrel and threats were made," Master Montfort declared.

"He made the threats," Gilbey said.

"Threats were made," Master Montfort repeated stubbornly. "Now the fellow is dead, and a belt of yours, Gilbey Dunn, and a hood of yours, Simon Perryn, were found with the body."

"You said they were found where he was killed," Simon cut it. "He wasn't killed where his body was found."

"Ahha!" The crowner pointed a triumphant finger at him. "How do you know that if you didn't kill him?"

"Because there wasn't any blood where the body was found," Simon returned angrily. "If he'd been killed there,

there would have been blood from those stab wounds he had. Any fool can reckon that well enough."

"This belt," Gilbey bulled in. "Who says it's mine?"

The crowner jerked his head toward the jurors. "They do."

"Oh, aye," Gilbey scoffed, with a scorning look at them. "Like that lot would know one strip of leather from another."

"Here!" Bert Fleccher stood up, definite as always in his dislike of Gilbey, despite one of his own sons working for him. Or maybe because of that. "It don't take much to know that gilt buckle like no one else around here has except you, let be your belt is all stamped and patterned and painted and twice as long as a man rightfully needs except he's prideful as sin and that's you right enough, Gilbey Dunn!"

"If it's sin you're talking of, you might have a look at yourself before starting in on others, Bert Fleccher," Gilbey shot back.

With no need to hear what he had heard often enough before, Simon put in, "Belt or not, how do you go about knowing it's my hood? There's no telling one piece of cloth from another that easily."

"It's green," Hamon said. "Yours is green."

"So are a few other men's hereabouts," Simon retorted.

"But not so new, or near to, as yours," Bert said, sitting down.

For the first time, Simon began to be alarmed at more than being stupidly accused. Anne had indeed made him a green hood for his New Year's gift this winter just past, from her last year's weaving. But as discomfiting as that was his sudden feeling that Bert, John, and Hamon at least were going to this like terriers to a hunt, seeming to enjoy he was the quarry.

That they could so much dislike him jarred him out of swift use of his wits, but Gilbey—probably too used to being disliked to be put off—shoved in with, "Let's see this belt and hood, eh? Do you have them? Or are you just making will-o'-the-wisps to see who you can lose in the bog?"

"You want to see them?" Master Montfort slapped the table with an open hand in front of his clerk's nose bent low over paper and scratching pen. "Show him!"

The clerk straightened, laid down his pen, bent over to take a bag from the floor beside his chair, and with great care—as if the things might break unless he went slow about it—took out first a green hood and laid it on the table beyond his inkpot, then brought out and laid beside it a long, embossed, painted leather belt with gilded buckle. Still with great care, he set the bag back onto the floor and took up his pen again, all without raising his head, while Simon stared glumly at both belt and hood. The belt was beyond doubt Gilbey's; most days he wore one like everyone else, enough to keep his tunic cinched in and hang purse and dagger from when need be, but a few years back, for his marriage, he'd bought a "gentleman's" belt such as no one else in the village had—trust Gilbey to that—and wore it holidays and holydays and to Sunday church, and there was no question but that this was it. Nor could Simon deny the hood, either, worse luck. It was his own, dyed a particular dark green from a dye batch Anne had made last fall for the summer's wool-weave; Adam and Colyn had tunics and Lucy a dress all the same green, there would be no trouble matching the hood to any of those even if he denied it was his. And belatedly, too late to make a difference, he realized that what he had seen laid over Tom's face in the ditch and paid no heed, taken up with Dickon's need, and forgotten ever since had been his hood. How had it come to be there? And why had no one said aught to him about it until now? Or about Gilbey's belt, come to that, since it had to have been there, too, from what was being said.

"How likely is it, I wonder," Dame Frevisse murmured, seemingly to no one in particular, "that they'd both be so careless to leave belt and hood there with a man they'd killed?"

The crowner broke off his pleased smiling. "Dame, I said I didn't want to hear from you!"

"But it's a good point," Gilbey said sharply.

"And whatever are Lord Lovell and Abbot Gilberd going to say if all this ends up hindering the harvest?" Dame Frevisse murmured, still seemingly more to herself than anyone.

"I told you, Dame . . ."

"Oh, aye," Simon said quickly. "There's that, isn't there? Lord Lovell and Abbot Gilbert, they'll neither of them like having the harvest messed the way it will be if Gilbey and I be arrested, that's sure."

With a harried edge that had not been there before, Master Montfort snapped, "There's been no talk of arresting anyone!" The surprise on the jurors' faces said that was not what they had thought. "I'm making inquiries, assessing facts. That's what I'm supposed to do, you dolts. I've begun with you, that's all. There are plenty of others I'll question before I'm done."

With a mildness that Simon was more wary of all the time, Dame Frevisse murmured, "Since it's certain Tom Hulcote was killed somewhere else and his body was only a little while where it was found, it must have been moved in the night before?"

The clerk laid down his pen and began sifting among the bits of paper scattered in front of him, apparently looking for the one that recorded what had been said, while Master Montfort blustered, "Yes. Well. Yes. That seems to have been the way of it. Yes."

The clerk left off shuffling the papers and took up his pen again, writing down that, Simon supposed, while Dame Frevisse asked, slightly raising her head toward him and Gilbey, "Where were you that night?"

"The night the body was moved?" Simon thought back rapidly. "In the church. All night. So Anne could sleep some. There'll be witnesses enough to it and to say I never went out at all."

"And I was at home with my wife and servants," Gilbey said, "and they'll all say so."

"For what that's worth," Master Montfort returned. "Their word in the matter is no good at all and you know it."

"But he was gone from the village when Tom Hulcote was killed," Dame Frevisse said.

"How do you know when he was killed, Dame?" Montfort pounced.

Seeming to see no possible threat to herself in that, Dame Frevisse answered gently, "Everyone knows he was last seen alive on Saturday, near to sundown. He wasn't seen again, that anyone admits to, until his body was found Tuesday dawn. From how far gone it was then, he must have died closer to Saturday night than Tuesday morning. But you know that," she added softly to the floor. "You've viewed the body."

"Of course I have," Master Montfort said ungraciously. View of the body was the first thing a crowner was supposed to do at any murder inquest. View it, study it for cause of death, then give the order that it could now be buried. In Tom Hulcote's case, with the days of hot weather since he had died, the order to bury him was come none too soon, and Simon guessed Master Montfort had taken none too close a look before ordering the burial.

"So where were you," Dame Frevisse asked Gilbey Dunn, "between Saturday afternoon and Tuesday morning?"

"Midday Saturday I left for Banbury, to fetch a doctor for my sons." Gilbey's voice had a hard, self-satisfied edge. "I brought him back with me on Sunday, and he was in my house until Monday morning and can say I was there the while."

"Who saw to your livestock then?" Master Montfort demanded.

"My man," Gilbey returned as sharply.

"I thought this Tom Hulcote was your man."

"He wasn't my only one, and God help me if he had been. He was worthless most of this past quarter year, gone as much as he was here half the spring and all this summer and besides I'd let him go as useless more than a week before he was killed. It's Jack Fleccher still works for me, and it doesn't matter anyway because I wasn't here to kill Hulcote."

"And I couldn't have moved the body," Simon said. "That means we're both clear, and belt and hood be damned."

"All it means is that you worked together at his death!" Master Montfort snarled. He pointed at Gilbey. "The reeve killed him while you were gone, kept the body hidden until you came back, and then you moved it while he was safe in the church, all to confuse that you were together in it all along. But you've been caught out at it and may as well confess!"

"That's daft!" Simon burst out as Gilbey exclaimed, "You're mad!"

"You watch your tongues, or there'll be fines on you both!" Master Montfort shot back.

"But if that was the way of it," Dame Frevisse asked softly of no one in particular, "if only one of them could have been there when the body was moved, how did the belt of one of them and the hood of the other come to be left there together?"

"Come to that," Gilbey said, "why would I be so idiot as to be moving a body about while wearing my best belt, eh?"

Master Montfort slammed a fist onto the table, jarring it, making his clerk's pen skitter on the paper. "That's enough from you! From both of you. From all of you! You've my leave to go. All of you. You, too, Dame. Out!"

# Chapter 12

oping her bowed head and hidden hands concealed her fine shuddering of anger, Frevisse followed Perryn and Gilbey out of the house and across the foreyard to the street. Montfort had always brought her to anger and, at his worst, fear, because he was an arrogant and dangerous fool, disliking anyone and anything that came between him and whatever his present purpose was, and what she saw of his present purpose here frightened her.

Ahead of her, at the green's edge, Gilbey turned on Perryn and said angrily, "He wants us guilty."

They were well away from any of Montfort's men but not out of their sight and maybe not out of their hearing, and Perryn said back, "Not here."

"My house then," Gilbey said, and Perryn nodded terse agreement.

They must needs talk somewhere and quickly, Frevisse thought, because she doubted they would have much time. All Montfort need do was bring the jurors around. When once he had their agreement—and she had seen no sign they would make much trouble over it—it would be small matter to put together a full jury to have an indictment and Gilbey and Perryn arrested.

Gilbey's messuage was not far. Most of Prior Byfield stretched out down both sides of the long green, but at its churchward end a short lane pushed out and Gilbey's was there, the farthest and nearly the only house along it, Frevisse saw as she followed the two men that way. Of the other two on the lane, one was no more than a poor toft— a small house set in a small garden and no more—while the other had some time been lived in but was now turned into a cattleyard, its house into a byre.

Beyond it was Gilbey's, and even taken up with the tangle Montfort was making, Frevisse nearly came to a stop at full sight of it across the low withy fence between the street and its wide yard. Most villeins' houses were serviceable but simple: of timbers, wattle, daub, and plaster, long and low, easily put up, easily taken down and shifted around in the yard as desire or need required, with thatch likely to be the greatest expense in keeping it up and nothing much changed from one generation to the next because what was the point in putting much money into something that belonged, when all was said and done, to the lord rather than the man who lived in it? But although Gilbey's house was of timber, wattle, daub, plaster, and thatch well enough, there was nothing long and low about it. Beyond its foreyard garden, it stood square, with gable ends high enough, roof steep enough, it must have an actual upper floor instead of merely a loft tucked among rafters; there was even a small window poked out under a little gable of its own from the thatch along the side of the roof Frevisse could see and a fireplace chimney showing on the other side.

Elena was at the door, looking out over its closed lower half, either watching the chickens at work in the dust between doorstep and garden or for Gilbey, and she waited there while they came across the yard but stepped out as they came along the garden's path and asked, her failure of other greeting betraying her worry, "How went it?"

"Badly," Gilbey answered, and as they reached his doorstep turned on Frevisse with, "You, with those questions of yours. You're so sharp you'll cut yourself one of these days."

"Gilbey!" Elena said.

Gilbey ignored her. "What if what you asked hadn't brought the right answers? He'd have us under his arrest by now!"

"I wasn't asking those questions to keep you from arrest," Frevisse said back at him. "I was asking them to find out what the answers were."

She heard Perryn's soft, hissed intake of breath as he understood she would have asked her questions whether she thought them dangerous to him and Gilbey or not.

Gilbey, realizing the same thing, started to swear, "By God's holy . . ."

"Gilbey!" Elena said.

This time Gilbey cut off, though he looked more irked than penitent, and Elena laid a hand on his arm as she said, "If it went that badly, we'd best go in to say whatever else needs saying." Belatedly she curtsyed to Frevisse. "If you would do us the honor, my lady?"

"With pleasure."

"Here then," Gilbey said and led the way, with Perryn asking Elena as they went, "How goes it with your boys?"

Belatedly in her turn, Frevisse saw that Elena looked very much the way most other of the village mothers presently looked—unkept, plainly dressed in a workaday gown of rough-woven linen, with simple cap and unstarched veil, gray-shadowed around her eyes with too little sleep and too much worry. But her fine-boned beauty was still there and woke, startling, as she smiled and said with open gladness of her sons, "Their fevers broke this morning, St. Roch be praised. Both of them. They've been mostly sleeping since."

"Agnes with them?" Gilbey demanded.

Without apparent offense at Gilbey's rudeness, Elena said, "Of course." Or it might have been she was simply too tired to bother with being angry at him just now. Or else she was dangerously capable of hiding what she felt.

"And your children?" Elena asked of Perryn. "I heard Colyn was past the worst. But Adam and Lucy?"

"Lucy's fever broke last night. Adam's hasn't," Perryn said tersely.

The quick darkening of Elena's face showed she understood what that meant, but "Soon then," she said kindly as Gilbey stood aside to let Frevisse go into the house ahead of him and Perryn after her.

Gilbey, following them in, said, "Hen," at a beady-eyed red one that had taken advantage of the door Elena had left open to come in and peck for crumbs under the table.

With a soft laugh Elena took up a broom from beside the door and shooed it out in a ruffle of feathers and clucking, giving Frevisse a chance to see around the low-ceilinged room. Well-lighted by a window beside the door and another in the southward wall, it took up almost all this floor of the house, with a board wall and doorway at its far end closing off what looked to be storage space. Against one wall narrow stairs went steeply up to another room or rooms, probably where the children and Agnes must be since there was no sign anyone slept down here where most of the living and all the cooking were done. The furnishings were usual—table, benches, joint stools, chairs, chests—but all of better quality and quantity than usual in a villein's house. That and the chimneyed hearth and that the floor was of boards instead of dirt told Frevisse much about how well off Gilbey was and something more about what Elena must have brought to their marriage because all this was more what a well-to-do townsman would have, rather than a country-bred peasant.

What if the rumor was true and there had been something between Tom Hulcote and Elena? What if she had come to choose him openly over her husband? It would have been a choice condemned by law and the Church, impossible ever to be anything but illicit, but women enough made that kind of choice. If Elena had, how much of all this would Gilbey have lost? Because Frevisse judged Elena would not have left behind anything she could take.

As Elena turned to her husband and guests—hen disposed of and the door's bottom half shut and firmly latched against return—Frevisse clamped off that thought. All other consideration aside, Elena frankly lacked the look of a woman who had lately lost a lover for whom she might have done desperate things. That, from what Frevisse had heard, was Mary Woderove's part; the talk among the women in the church was that she had gone wild at word of Tom Hulcote's death, had been kept from harming herself only by quieting draughts from Mistress Margery, and had needed much counselling and consoling from Father Edmund.

And none of that was to the present need, and Frevisse said, abrupt with impatience at herself, "These jurors. Tell me about them."

"Tell you what?" Gilbey asked. "Fools, the lot of them."

"You'd better hope not. Perryn, tell me, how did it happen they were the ones helped you bring Tom Hulcote's body in?"

"They were who came to hand first, that's all. John Rudyng and Bert Fleccher at the alehouse, Walter Hopper and Hamon Otale at Walter's place on the way. That's all there was to it."

"What sort of men are they?"

"That's not the problem here!" Gilbey said.

"It's part of the problem," Frevisse said back at him. "How long there is to find Tom Hulcote's murderer depends on how well they can hold out against Montfort wanting it to be one or both of you." Elena gasped but Frevisse asked Perryn again, "What sort of men are they? Hamon I remember from manor court. He's not likely to be happy with you just now."

"No," Perryn agreed, "but Walter Hopper is solid enough."

"He's the one who didn't say anything while we were there?"

"Aye. He's hard to push where he doesn't want to go."

"And the others?"

"Bert Fleccher . . ."

"A troublemaker," Gilbey said.

"He's that," Perryn agreed slowly, "but not mean-hearted about it."

"Nay, just a fool, and that can be as bad," Gilbey said. "He'd not mind seeing us down if he could do it without hurt to himself. Then there's John Rudyng. He's no use either. Without his mother-in-law there to tell him what to do, he'll go whatever way looks easiest."

"Aye, maybe," Perryn agreed glumly.

Gilbey sat down in the chair beside the table, fingers drumming angrily at the broad wooden tabletop. "And that crowner will likely . . ."

Elena, turning back from a wall-hung aumbry with pitcher and fine blue-glazed goblets, said on a soft but rising note, "Gilbey. Guests."

Gilbey twitched a startled look toward her, then at Frevisse, realized he was sitting and she was not, and stood abruptly up, making an awkward gesture toward the room's only other chair, saying, "Pray, sit, Dame. If you will."

He did not have it smoothly down but he was trying. Frevisse made a slight bow of her head to acknowledge his manners and sat. "You, too," he said at Perryn less graciously but waiting until the reeve had sat on a bench end before sitting again himself. Elena put the pitcher and goblets on the table and began to pour a clear, golden ale while Gilbey, going back to what he had been saying, said, "That shit-witted crowner will bring them around to indicting us by suppertime, so what are we going to do?"

Elena's hands jerked, making the ale she was pouring miss the goblet. "Indict you?" she repeated. "For what? For Tom Hulcote's murder?"

"What else?" Gilbey returned.

She set the pitcher down, looking at Frevisse and Perryn's faces, wanting a different answer. "Truly?"

Perryn nodded.

"On what proof?"

"Fool's proof," Gilbey snapped, "but since he has fools for jurors, it'll be enough."

"It won't be enough when it comes to county court," said Perryn. "Not with men he can't force the way he can here."

"He'll have us ruined long before it comes to that," Gilbey said. Because in the while until then, all their property would be taken into the king's hands for keeping, forfeit to the king if they were found guilty, returned to them if they were found innocent, but either way, some officer of Montfort would likely have the running and profit of it all in the meanwhile—officially on the king's behalf, and surely much would reach the royal coffers, but a great deal would go into the crowner's purse along the way, and Frevisse no more doubted it than Gilbey or Perryn did.

Nor did Elena, who said slowly, wiping up the spilled ale, "So it's not so much who's guilty that he's looking for as that you two are the wealthiest men in Prior Byfield, yes?"

"And justice be damned," Gilbey agreed grimly. "He's reckoning what a pretty profit he'll make out of his share of our property if we're found guilty and how much he'll make off it even if we aren't, and since there's not much profit to be had in finding a poor man guilty, we're his murderers of choice."

"More than that," Perryn said, "if he settles for us being guilty, then the true murderer goes unfound and that's as bad a wrong."

Elena paused in holding out a goblet to Frevisse. "Worse still," she said quietly, "is that it has to be someone of the village and they'll go on being here, with none of us knowing who he is."

In the silence that answered that, Frevisse took the goblet Elena was holding out to her, before a small knock at the door made them all look that way, to see Dickon Naylor looking over it uncertainly.

"You weren't at your house," he said to Perryn, plainly unsure of his welcome, "so I came here . . ."

"Come in," Gilbey snapped. "Don't stand there looking lost. That ass of a crowner let you go, then?"

Shutting the half-door carefully behind him and snicking the latch, Dickon answered, "He's finished for today, he says. He's sent everybody home."

"Finished?" Frevisse repeated, surprised along with Perryn and Gilbey.

"I don't see any guards with you," Gilbey said as Dickon crossed to stand beside Perryn. "We're not for it yet, then?"

Perryn took the boy's hand and pulled him down to sit on the bench beside him while Dickon shook his head and answered, "After you left, Master Montfort tried to lead the men back to where he'd had them before you came in . . ."

"Damn him," Gilbey said.

". . . but they wouldn't go."

Frevisse had never paid the boy much heed but seeing him now, she realized he was not much the "little boy" she had been thinking him when she thought of him at all. He was already well into the lanky growth that came on some children earlier than others, and there was enough of his father in the contained way he had answered just now that she thought it likely it wasn't only in body he was ahead of himself. Attending more to his answer than she would have earlier, she asked, "What happened after we left?"

Dickon regarded her gravely. "Just that. Master Montfort wanted them to say the hood and belt were reason enough to find Simon and Gilbey guilty of Tom's murder, and Hamon might have, just to make trouble, like, but the rest of them dug in their heels and wouldn't. They said it didn't make sense, the hood and belt being there when both men couldn't have been. Even Bert said there was more looking to be done before things should be called settled, but I think that was because he liked the color Master Montfort's face was turning and wanted to see how purple it would go. Then Hamon went along with them."

"What's this about a hood and belt?" Elena asked.

Gilbey told her, briefly, both about them and what had passed with Montfort, ending, "So all he's got is nonsense and no proof of anything."

"But it's your belt?" Elena said.

"Oh, aye, it's my belt, right enough, and Simon's hood, but they'll do Montfort no good."

"Unfortunately," Frevisse said, "Montfort is able to believe whatever he wants to believe, ignore whatever he wanted to ignore, unless he's forced to go another way. We held him off a while with mention of Lord Lovell and Abbot Gilberd and putting questions to him that he didn't like but none of that will keep him back for long, set against the chance for profit your guilt offers him."

"You mean disproving Gilbey and Simon could have been there together isn't going to be enough?" Elena said.

"Not if he wants to believe in it, and that brings us to the need to prove who did kill Tom Hulcote."

Gilbey rapped impatient knuckles on the table top. "How likely are we to be able to do that?" he said scornfully.

"Not likely at all if we don't try," Perryn said curtly. He rubbed a large hand over his face, took a deep breath, and looked to Frevisse. "You have some thought on how to do it?"

For answer, she asked, "What do we know for certain about Hulcote's death?"

She waited but no one said anything, all of them—Dickon, too—waiting with gazes fixed on her.

"Begin this way then," she said. "He was last seen alive late on Saturday, yes? By whom?"

There was a pause, the others looking at each other, before Perryn said, "By me."

Frevisse failed to choke off her surprise. "By you?"

"Near as I've heard anyway." Perryn was faintly defiant about it, understanding it was not to his good to have been the last who saw Hulcote living.

Frevisse rethought how to ask the next question, but there seemed only the one way. "He was by himself?"

A unreadable mix of expressions crossed Perryn's face and he shifted awkwardly where he sat, as if the bench had sudddenly become doubly hard under him, before he answered, "Nay. He was with me."

Hopefully keeping her thoughts hidden, Frevisse asked, "Doing what?"

"Quarreling."

"Over what?"

Perryn did not try to hold in his bitter disgust. "Over Matthew Woderove's holding, surely. Tom wanted I should tell him I'd change my mind over the holding, let him have it after all, or at least tell him you'd not have it either."

"Did you?" Gilbey snapped.

"How likely do you think it?" Perryn snapped back. "Nay, I told him naught. I was going into church to see how it was there and he overtook me at the church gate, demanding, like there was nothing else in the world but him and that damned holding, and I was that angry at him for it that when he wouldn't let it go, I told him I wouldn't even tell him what day of the week it was if he'd asked me, and I certain as hell wasn't going to tell him about the holding."

"And then?" Frevisse asked.

"Then he cursed me and said I'd be sorry for it and flung away along the field path there, and I went into the church."

"Did anyone see or hear the two of you there?"

"Not that I know of. They might have. But if they did, they saw him go off alive and well."

And angry. Angry enough to come back later, when Perryn was home and quarrel with him again?

Frevisse did not ask that, only, "No one has admitted to seeing him after that?"

"Not anybody."

"He was at the alehouse," Gilbey said. "Folk have said so."

"But that was before he met me," Perryn said. "The sun was just to the horizon when he left there, Bess has said. It was half gone below when I was talking with him."

"You didn't tell the crowner that," Gilbey said.

"Right enough, I didn't! That's all he needs."

"If somebody else saw you, they might," Gilbey persisted.

"If somebody else saw us, they saw us quarreling and wouldn't have kept it to themselves this long, given the way tongues run on wheels around here. It would have been all through the village long before Tom was found dead and you know it."

"But you said nothing about it to anyone?" Frevisse asked.

"What was to say? That we'd quarreled? No new tidings in that. I had other things I was worried on more than him. I doubt I even thought on it again until after I knew he was dead, and that didn't seem a good time to say aught about it."

"Judging by his body, then," Frevisse said, "we can guess that he was killed sooner rather than later after you last saw him."

"Aye."

"And it's certain the body wasn't put into the ditch until soon before it was found. That tells us someone kept it somewhere the while between. Why?"

The men and Elena passed puzzled looks among themselves before Elena said, slightly a-frown with uncertainty, "Because they couldn't move it until then?"

"Why not?" Frevisse asked. "It's easy to understand why they couldn't leave it where they'd killed him if it was somewhere that would give their guilt away as soon as it was found, but what was different about Monday's night that made it a safer time than Saturday or Sunday's night to move the body?"

They all thought again a long moment, before Gilbey said impatiently, "There was naught particular about Monday night. Nothing about Saturday or Sunday either."

"It rained once in there," Dickon offered.

"At dawn on Monday," Perryn said. "Just before sunrise and for a little afterwards, not in the night. There was no rain any of those nights. And what would rain have to do with moving the body anyway?"

"The moon?" Elena asked but answered for herself, "No, there wasn't that much difference in it from one night to the next those nights."

"Nor point in waiting in hope of an overcast night

when he couldn't be sure of one," Frevisse added. Not when waiting meant the risk of a decaying body betraying the murderer's secret.

"And if an overcast night was what he wanted, why didn't he use the overcast there was Sunday night before the rain?" Elena asked.

"Aye," Perryn said, impatient, frustrated. "Why wait until the next night?"

"To give him a chance," Frevisse said, "to lay hands on your hood and Gilbey's belt."

# Chapter 13

erryn stared at her as if he understood what she had said but disbelieved she meant it. Then belief caught up to understanding and angrily he said, "Yes."

Gilbey looked from Frevisse to him and back again and demanded, "What d'you mean?"

"Some one took them to make us look guilty," Perryn said.

Gilbey shot to his feet. *"What?"*

Watching him, Frevisse said levelly, "Whoever the murderer was, he kept the body hidden until he could have something of yours and Perryn's to leave with it, to make you both look guilty."

Gilbey dropped back into his chair. "Damn the bastard."

"Gilbey," Elena said.

"Pardon, Dame," Gilbey muttered, not thinking about it. And added, after a moment's thought, "But damn him anyway."

Whoever had done it likely was damned, unless he turned penitent, made confession to a priest, and did penance, Frevisse thought, but aloud asked Perryn, "Why didn't you recognize your hood and the belt when you went for the body?"

"I didn't see them. Nay, I saw the hood but didn't heed it, didn't look close at it, not to know it was mine until I saw the crowner had it and thought back."

"You didn't look closely at it until then?" Frevisse asked doubtfully.

Perryn shifted, gave a sideways look at Dickon. "I was heeding him."

"I was crying," Dickon admitted, a little defiantly, refusing to be ashamed despite he likely was. "Simon took me away while I did and we didn't see anything of Tom's b . . . body being put on the hurdle. Then there was a blanket over it."

"When you found the body," Frevisse said, "did you see the hood and belt then?"

"The hood was lying in the grass on the ditch side, not all the way to the bottom." Dickon frowned, thinking. "Like it had been tossed there, maybe. Tom looked like he'd been rolled down into the ditch and the hood looked like maybe it'd been tossed after him."

"But it was you put it over his face?" Perryn asked gently.

"Aye." Dickon swallowed thickly. "The birds had been . . . at his . . . eyes. I didn't want to leave . . . leave him . . . to them . . ." Hot color rushed up his face with memory and still-fresh anger. "They could at least have rolled him over, whoever put him there! Left him face down so the birds couldn't . . . couldn't . . ."

He shut his eyes and bent his head, to keep in or at least hide tears, and Elena came quickly around the table to him, to lay her hands on his shoulders from behind and say with some of the same anger, "They should have. You're right. It was cruel not to. You did best for him and bravely, too."

Perryn took hold of his nearer arm and gave it a kind shake. "You did well, Dickon. Better than most would have."

Dickon raised his head, wiping tears. "I didn't see any belt there except what he was wearing and that was just his old one."

But the other men had seen Gilbey's and yet had said nothing, not then or afterward. Why? Frevisse wondered but asked aloud, "Perryn, did you or anyone look around for any signs of whoever else had been there?"

"I looked a little after the body was moved, but there was nothing. The ditch is all grass that wouldn't keep tracks, and the lane near to there is hard dirt besides being used enough no tracks on it would mean much."

"It had rained the morning before."

"Not so much everything hadn't dried by Monday noon."

Long before Hulcote's body was brought that way.

She looked to Dickon again. "What did you hear about the hood and belt while you were at the crowner's court? Who said they were found with the body? Who gave them to him?"

"I don't know," Dickon answered toward his bare feet, wriggling his toes uncomfortably. "When I was let go in, the belt and hood were lying there, and the crowner already knew whose they were and all."

"Is this taking us anywhere of any use?" Gilbey bulled in impatiently.

"It's taking us out of knowing nothing into knowing

something," Frevisse said back at him. "And every something we know takes us a little farther toward maybe
knowing enough. Perryn, when did you last have your
hood?"

"When?" He thought, with an absent nod at Elena offering to refill his goblet while he did. "It's been warm.
I've not needed it since it last rained. That was . . ." He
stopped, seeing what he was about to say.

Gilbey said it for him. "Monday morning. Today's the
first it's rained since then." He held out his goblet for his
wife to fill.

"You're sure that's when you had it last?" Frevisse
asked. "That you had it then?"

"Certain of it," Perryn said. "I went before milking to
see how things were at the church. I mind I stood in the
house doorway putting on my hood, watching the rain and
wondering if there'd be enough to help the corn along."

"When and where do you last know you had it?"

"At my house, when I'd come back from the church
that morning. The rain was stopped and the hood was wet,
and I took it off before I sat down to breakfast." He
thought a moment longer. "I've no thought of it after
that."

Frevisse looked to Gilbey. "Your belt. When did you
last have it?"

"Sunday," he said. "After that . . ." He shrugged and
looked to his wife questioningly.

"He wore it Saturday when he went to fetch the doctor
and was wearing it when he came home again," Elena
said.

"For all the good it did to bring that fool," Gilbey
grouched. "I had to pay him above his fee to make him
come at all, and then when he's here all he says is that
the thing has to run its course, keep them in the dark and
their fevers down, and then he offered some medicine we
could have for a gold piece but if that swill was medicine,

I'm a peascod. I wouldn't have taken the filth myself if I was dying, let be give it to the boys."

"Nor did we," Elena said. She had set the pitcher down after Frevisse had refused more to drink and went now to stand behind Gilbey, putting her hands quietingly on his shoulders much as she had with Dickon. "What Mistress Margery gave us . . ."

A thin, unhappy wail from overhead turned all their heads toward the stairs, and, "That's Ned," Gilbey said, rising. "I'll go, before he can have James awake."

Frevisse hoped she covered her surpise that he would go to tend to a sick child and maybe to two if the other awoke, but Elena only said to him as he went, "Send Agnes down if it's possible. She's as like to know about your belt, about who's come and gone from the house since Sunday, as anyone."

"Aye," Gilbey agreed, disappearing up the stairs.

Suddenly not trying to hide how tired she was, Elena sat down in his place, her hands dropping into her lap, her shoulders slumping; but she managed her lovely smile, shadowed though her eyes were, and said, "I'm sorry. It's not been a good week."

Frevisse smiled back at her with full understanding and agreement. "No, it's not been." But that did not change what had to be done now, as quickly as might be before Montfort made things worse. "What else do you remember about Sunday and Monday? Who came and went from here is what matters, I suppose. Or maybe we should begin with what you last remember about the belt."

Elena put a hand to her forehead and shut her eyes, thinking before answering, "I remember it Sunday night, Gilbey taking it off. We'd given the doctor our bed." She gestured toward upstairs with a small twitch of her head. "Gilbey was going to sleep down here and Agnes and I with the boys, but Gilbey and I stayed talking a time before I went up after Agnes. He was angry about the doctor. I was angry he'd gone for him at all. Mistress

Margery . . ." She broke off, said with a smile, "That's neither here nor there. About the belt. I remember him taking it off while we talked because he was starting to ready for bed. He coiled it up and put it down here on the table." She reached out to lay a hand on the nearest corner of the broad tabletop, fell silent with more thought, then shook her head. "I don't remember seeing it after that. The doctor went very early the next morning. He'd brought his own man with him, so Gilbey didn't have to go back with him. Ned and James were worsening by the moment by then, and I hardly heeded anything else all day. Or the next or next. I never thought about the belt at all from then until now."

An older woman came down the stairs, sidewise as if she did not trust her knees on their steepness. Like Elena, she showed both the tiredness and untidiness of too many days spent caring for someone else and not herself, but when she turned from the stairs, the look she gave them all was sharp-eyed enough to show she was ready for more, if need be, and after a deep curtsy to Frevisse and while making a lesser one to Perryn and Elena together and ignoring Dickon, she said, "They'll settle again now their father is there. He said you wanted me for something, mistress?"

By her speech she was from Banbury, rather than country bred, had probably come from there with Elena who nodded her toward one of the joint stools, saying, "Sit while you have the chance. Dame Frevisse has questions she wants to ask us about Monday last."

"Monday last?" Agnes sat frowning over Monday last. "That fool of a doctor was here who couldn't tell you more than I already knew."

That sounded like something Agnes would talk about at length, given the chance, and Frevisse put in quickly, "After he left, did anyone else come here that day?"

"Monday," Agnes repeated, thinking about it. "The boys were sickening by the moment that day, worse and worse, poor little things." She fixed an accusing stare on Dickon. "You're still well enough, it seems."

"I was meseled when I was little," he said uneasily, as if it were a matter of guilt. Or something he had had to explain too often of late.

"And lived. That's good." She looked to Elena who was making the sign of the cross over her breast. "Ours will do fine now, too. You'll see." But she and Perryn and Dame Frevisse and Dickon all crossed themselves nonetheless before she returned to the point. "Monday. No, I wasn't heeding much else than the boys, would I be? Mistress Margery came. After the doctor was gone. Said we should steep balm in water for the boys' drinking, to help against the fevers rising, and chamomile, and said the nuns were going to send a columbine cordial as soon as it was brewed. She brought that Tuesday morning, yes. And Father Edmund, he was here on Monday."

"Ah," Elena said. "I'd forgotten that. Yes, he prayed with us."

"And that old cat Esota Emmet," Agnes said. "She came in hard on his heels, to see what was what."

"She came to see if she could help with anything," Elena said.

"Since two of her granddaughters are meseled," Agnes returned, "she had more business seeing to them than nosing in here."

Leaving that argument behind, Elena said, "Jack was in here a few times of course."

"Jack?" Dame Frevisse asked.

"Jack Fleccher. He sees to the byre and cattleyard and helps out with anything else that's needed," Elena said.

Frevisse remembered mention of him to Montfort and asked something that had occurred to her then. "He's related to Bert Fleccher?"

"Bert's youngest son. We hire his wife, too, sometimes, to help in house or the fields, as need be."

"Was she here Sunday or Monday?"

"Their youngest is sick with the others. I've not seen her since Friday, I think. Agnes?"

Agnes pursed her lips, thinking. "No, she's not been here. There've not been many folk in and out, but I can't be sure who was here which day, things being at sixes and sevens as they are. Was it Monday or Tuesday Joan Whit was here with those baked apples? And Walter Hopper sent that Hamon once, to ask if there was aught help Jack might need. That might have been Monday?"

She asked it of Elena, who shook her head and spread her hands palms upward apologetically to Dame Frevisse. "I don't know. I would have said Father Edmund came on Tuesday, rather than Monday."

"Not Tuesday," Agnes said. "Monday. And Wednesday, too, and again yesterday. It was Mistress Margery came back on Tuesday to see how the boys did, to bring the columbine cordial and be sure we were using the balm and to say we could send to the church for her any time, which thank God we've not needed to do. It's that Esota who hasn't been back. Monday afternoon. That was when Joan Whit came."

Dame Frevisse prodded a little with more questions but that was as much as either woman was sure of, except that Agnes remembered the belt being on the table Monday morning, after the doctor and his fellow had gone. "I meant to fetch it upstairs to put away but I didn't and when next I thought of it, you had," she said to Elena, then added with sudden suspicion, "Hadn't you?"

"No, but it's taken care of. I'll tell you later," Elena said. "Be so good as to go back upstairs for Gilbey to come down."

Agnes' eyes were sharp with speculation but she simply obeyed, increasing Frevisse's respect for Elena's hold over her household. Family servants and husbands were usually the hardest to manage, but she seemed to have both well in hand.

As Agnes left, Elena rose to offer more ale, which

Perryn took and this time so did Frevisse. Gilbey came down as she was finishing pouring and retook his chair, holding out his own goblet to be refilled while answering his wife's questioning look with, "They're sleeping again and cool, no fever at all."

Elena briefly closed her eyes, lips moving in silent prayer.

"What did Agnes know?" Gilbey asked. "Anything of use?"

He sounded as if he thought it unlikely.

"That your belt was here Monday after the doctor left, but neither of us remember it after that," Elena said.

Gilbey grunted. "Anything about who else has been here?"

"Too much," Frevisse said, "and nothing to the point yet."

"So we're nowhere," Perryn said glumly.

"No," Frevisse disagreed. "We've brought it down to the hood and belt having been taken sometime on Monday. We're certain Hulcote was dead by then. That means they were taken of a purpose to make the two of you look guilty of his death."

"Where does that bring us except still no place?" Gilbey demanded.

"It brings us," Frevisse returned, "to ask who dislikes the two of you so much that they want to make you this much trouble. And to ask, along with that, who wanted Hulcote dead."

# Chapter 14

ho's to say?" Gilbey said impatiently. "Nobody cared enough about Tom Hulcote to want him dead. I'd like to have taken a stick to him for laziness, but that's not wanting him dead. As for Simon and me . . ." He made a wide two-handed gesture. "We're disliked and by more than a few, that's sure. Him for being reeve, me for having money."

Frevisse looked to Perryn, who shrugged as if he neither liked nor could deny what Gilbey said. "But it was Tom who was making threats," he said. "Nobody'd made any against him I'd heard of."

"Who had he been threatening besides the two of you?"

Perryn looked at Gilbey who said bluntly, "Just us. Me

the most. What you heard at manor court and other times. Bess in the alehouse finally told him to shut his gob or get out that Saturday."

"Aye, but Tom was all talk and no doing," Perryn said. "That was always his trouble and everybody knew it."

"You weren't worried by his threats then?"

"We'd be right fools to say we were, wouldn't we be?" Gilbey said back. "That'd be reason we'd want him dead, wouldn't it be?"

"But not reason to leave your belt and Perryn's hood with the body. Who is there lately might want to make trouble against you both?"

Perryn answered slowly, thinking on it, "There's usually somebody not happy with how I've done things, but the only one I know who's been full angry with me lately has been Tom and he's out of it, isn't he?"

"And your sister," Elena said.

"Oh, aye. Mary," Perryn agreed. "But she's always in a fret over one thing or another, and I don't see her killing Tom of all people."

"Let be keeping his body hid a few days," Gilbey said, "then hauling it out to Oxfall ditch and . . ."

"Gilbey," Elena said.

Gilbey broke off and Perryn went on, "There's those might have spite against me for things I've forgotten I ever did, but that's no help, since I don't remember them."

"Nor no way I see either," Gilbey said. He stood up. "And no time for it either just now. Jack Fleccher's been left to the work alone too long as it is today. By your leave, my lady, I'm off."

Frevisse could not keep him if he chose to go but along with her dismissing nod she asked, "Did Tom Hulcote and Jack Fleccher do well together?"

"Nay. Jack works and Tom didn't. Even when he was here, Tom left too much to Jack, and half the time of late he wasn't even here."

"It was only that last month before he quit he was so

slack about being here," Elena said. "Before then he was none so bad."

"When did he quit?" Frevisse asked.

"The next day after St. Swithin's," Gilbey said, "but he'd been worthless for more than a month before then. Here and gone and come back and gone again, I lost count how often."

"Gone off to where?"

"Who knows?" Gilbey asked back, leaving. "Who cares?" he added and was gone.

Perryn stood up as if against a weight of tiredness. "I'd best go, too, my lady. Dickon."

The boy rose readily, but Elena said, "A moment, please you," and crossed to the hearth where the smell of beans, onions, and herbs was bubbling up from an iron kettle set on a low tripod over the little fire there. "Take some of this with you."

"Likely Cisily has something ready to our supper," Perryn said. "No need."

"There's no harm in having a bit more," Elena said as she ladled thick brown pottage into a wooden bowl. With a smile, she held it out to Dickon. "You could probably eat all Cisily has fixed and this too, I'd guess."

Dickon nodded eagerly and reluctantly Perryn said, "Well, yes, thank you then. That's kind."

It would have been reasonable for Frevisse to take her leave with them, but she stayed where she was while Dickon collected the bowl from Elena with a wide grin and thanks; and while he and Perryn left, Elena filled another bowl, shifted the pot off the fire, lidded it, and brought the bowl and a wooden spoon across the room to Frevisse, saying, "If you're hungry, my lady?"

The savory smell decided Frevisse against denying her hunger. Years ago, in her early months as a novice, she had tried to subdue her pleasure in food, eager to discipline herself to holiness by every means she could think of. Disappointed at her failure to cease noticing what she ate, she had gone to Domina Edith, the elderly prioress of St. Frideswide's, confessed her failure, and asked help. Domina Edith had told her, gently, that there was no spiritual fault in taking pleasure in food. "There's likely greater fault in scorning God's good gifts, given to our bodies' needs," she had said.

"But gluttony is a sin," Frevisse had protested.

"Gluttony is the indulging in food and drink to excess, past need or common sense. Is that what you've been doing?"

A soft rowling of hunger in Frevisse's stomach had served for answer and brought both her and Domina Edith to laughter, and she had given up guilt over food.

Nor was she over-indulging here, because although her meals and Sister Thomasine's were being brought from the nunnery, what had sufficed her while she was in the cloister was not enough these days spent in nursing ill children, and she took spoon and bowl gladly, asking as she did, "You'll join me?"

"By your leave, no. I'll wait for my husband."

"Sit with me then and talk, if you would."

"If you will." Elena sat again, wiped her hands on her apron, folded them into her lap, and with her gaze on Frevisse, openly waiting to be asked something.

She was too ready, and Frevisse took time to ease her hunger first, finding the pottage savory and saying so with unfeigned pleasure.

"It's been good growing weather for herbs as well as all else," Elena said, "and it's herbs that make the difference between plain beans and something worth the eating. Now, before someone comes or the boys waken again, what is it you want from me?"

Frevisse returned the favor of Elena's forwardness. "Tom Hulcote. You would likely hear talk among the women that the men never would. Did you ever hear he was out of the ordinary disliked by someone? Or did he ever say anything to you about someone he was afraid of?"

"He worked here, took his meals with us. That was all I ever had to do with him. The only times he talked with me much about anything, it was to spin tales about why he hadn't done some piece of work, hoping I'd make it straight with my husband."

"Would you?"

"No. It was my money he was being paid with, too. Why should I help him cheat me? He was a weak man. One of those who go on about how luck never goes their way and how they mean to change it but never seem to do much to make it happen."

"He was bidding to have the Woderove holding."

"He was bidding to have Mary Woderove."

That was put curtly enough that Frevisse let go circumspection and asked plainly, "You didn't like him?"

Just as plainly, Elena answered back, "No. Nor much disliked him either, come to that. He wasn't worth the bother. To me or anyone else, that ever I heard or saw."

Except to Mary Woderove.

It was constantly clearer that Tom Hulcote and Mary had had no one but each other, and now Mary had not even him.

Nor Tom even his life.

"And if you've heard that there was anything between him and me there shouldn't have been," Elena went on, calm about it and maybe a little bitter, "there wasn't. But then I'd say that, no matter what, wouldn't I?"

"No. You'd more likely hope the question didn't arise at all."

Elena gave a small, unwilling laugh. "True enough. But there's no point denying I know what folk say about me, what they think."

"Do you wonder that they do?" Frevisse asked, deciding boldness would serve her as well as it did Elena.

"No, but I can wish they'd find something else to talk on."

"They won't."

Elena laughed openly this time. "No. They won't. There's too much sport for them in believing I must have married Gilbey for no more than his money and therefore surely serve him the way young wives always serve their older husbands in all the stories. I'm too young and he's too old and I'm too lovely and therefore I must be adulterous. That's what they say, isn't it?"

"Not," Frevisse said dryly, "quite so bluntly."

"It's what it comes to, though. I knew it would when I set out to marry him but didn't think I'd care."

"And now you've found you do."

"More for Gilbey's sake than mine." Elena smiled. "But then he minds it more for my sake than for his, so all evens out, I suppose."

"It wasn't for his money you married him, then?" Frevisse asked.

"Of course I did," Elena said, surprised. "And he married me for mine. We're neither of us fools. My brother will have the bakery for his inheritance, but my father has settled other Banbury properties on my sister and me. They give a goodly income from rents and all."

Trying to balance between question and statement, Frevisse said, "You could have married well in Banbury."

"Oh, yes," Elena agreed. "With this face and that property, I was offered for by everyone from the butcher down the street to the squire's younger son from over the county border."

"But you took Gilbey in preference to them all."

"And a hard time I had bringing him to it, I promise you."

Frevisse had no chance to hide her surprise at that, blurting without pretense, "What?"

Elena laughed with open pleasure. "Gilbey has a sister who bought her freedom years ago, married and lives in

Banbury and is a friend of my mother. I heard of Gilbey long before I ever met him and liked what I heard. When the chance came, I tried to catch his interest in me but he wasn't having it."

Frevisse was still trying to accept that Elena had liked what she'd heard of Gilbey Dunn as Elena leaned toward her, surely able to read her face and said, seeming suddenly to want her to understand. "Every man who ever offered for me made it plain they thought I must have less wits than a cabbage because I have this face. They also made it plain that they didn't care, that my pretty face and fat dowry were enough to satisfy them. None of them ever thought to ask what would satisfy me."

"Until Gilbey?"

"Gilbey—he told me so later—never bothered to look at me above once and forgot about me afterwards because he wasn't minded to go after trouble, what with him being villein and me being freeborn, and besides, he reckoned he needed a young wife like he needed plague."

What that lacked in charm it had in truth, from what Frevisse knew of Gilbey.

"I thought, even before he told me, his lack of interest in me was from something like that, and I liked him the better for it. It was more sense than some men had shown. But I also liked what I'd heard of him in his sister's talk, about what he wanted and how he was going about to have it."

"What did he want?"

"The same thing he still wants. More than what he has. Though that's common enough," Elena added before Frevisse could. "The difference is that he enjoys the doing what needs to be done to have the more. He enjoys finding out ways other men don't see and turning them to his profit."

Like taking pasture another man had let go to waste and turning it to milk and cheese and beef that he could sell in Banbury, Frevisse remembered from Anne Perryn's talk.

"And so do you," Frevisse guessed.

"There's hardly better pleasure to be had, than to take little and turn it into much." Elena said simply, "unless it's to be able to share the pleasure with someone else."

The way she and Gilbey must share it with one another, Frevisse thought.

"All I had to do was make Gilbey see past my face. I went deliberately with my mother to visit his sister when I knew he was there and made chance to say aside to him that there was a tenement and messuage the owner was looking to sell in Market Street. He wanted to know why I'd bother to tell him that, and I said, because the innkeeper next door to it had said he didn't want it but was secretly waiting for the price to go down before he offered for it while spreading rumors to keep anyone else from it while he waited. The price was already gone somewhat down, and whoever bought it now could then drag a better price out of the innkeeper than had been asked to start with because he needed the property."

Caught now into open curiosity, Frevisse asked, "How did you come to know all that?"

"Gilbey asked that, too. It was simply that the innkeeper is my father's friend. I'd bring their ale while they sat and talked and drank in our parlor, and they never cared what I heard because they never thought I'd understand it anyway. I told Gilbey that and he asked, sharplike because we didn't have long to talk alone, what I hoped to gain by telling him any of this, and when I answered back, 'Your interest in me,' that was that." She fixed her coolly certain gaze on Frevisse. "I'm telling you so you'll know I wouldn't bother looking half an instant with any interest at someone like Tom Hulcote. Despite whatever other folks might think we ought to be, Gilbey and I are glad of each other, and Gilbey knows me too well ever to think he might have reason to be jealous of me that way, if that's what you're looking at for a reason one or the other of us might have murdered Tom."

Frevisse startled with the realization that Elena had not been talking idly this while, had understood the suspicion behind her questioning, and had set out against it. Giving answers she was willing to give so as to forestall questions more dangerous to her?

Hiding her anger at herself for being so easily led, Frevisse asked something that had only to do with her curiosity, not Tom Hulcote's death. "Why, with all his ambition, hasn't Gilbey bought his freedom?"

"Because he'd lose too much by being free," Elena said bluntly. "First, there'd be the cost of buying himself free, then the cost of buying land if he could but more probably leasing it, land not being that readily come by. So long as he stays Lord Lovell's villein, he holds his land here by right. Though we're thinking that it may be better now to give his right up and shift to copyhold, no more work days or fees owed, just a flat yearly rent, everything to be held in survivorship between us, with the boys to inherit."

"Will Lord Lovell agree to that?"

"It's common enough anymore," Elena said as if she had no doubt about it. "The lords prefer cash in hand to the bother of reckoning workdays owed and trying to collect past-due fees, and Gilbey is a good enough tenant that the steward won't want to risk losing him. It will come to much the same as being free without the cost of buying his freedom."

"What about this house?" Because whatever actual practice was, in legal fact what a villein owned belonged to his lord, and if it came to law the lord's claim would very possibly be upheld.

"The house and everything in it are my father's. He leases it for a penny a year to Gilbey in return for use of the land it stands on, and it's tied to pass to my children when he dies. That way it will never be Gilbey's and at risk to the lord. Though if for some fool's reason, Lord

Lovell decided to make trouble over it, worse come to worse, it can be taken down and moved away if need be."

Worse come to worse, it could be taken down and moved away, too, if—for some reason—Elena's marriage to Gilbey failed.

Some reason such as Tom Hulcote.

How right was Elena in thinking Gilbey would never be jealous of her, when he had so much to lose if he lost her?

And how honest had she been in claiming she had no inclination to Tom Hulcote?

But those were hardly questions Frevisse could ask outright and, ready to be done with Elena for a time, she took her leave gracefully. Elena saw her to the door, making equally graceful farewell but saying in a worried voice as Frevisse started away, "My lady, is anything you've learned so far of any use?"

Frevisse turned back to her, paused, almost said, "I don't know yet," but said instead, matching Elena's worry, "Only that there's someone so hurting in himself with anger or unhappiness that it isn't enough he killed a man. He wants to be sure someone else suffers for it in his place."

# Chapter 15

he last of the day's clouds were gone, save for a few wisps strayed across the west, gold and cream and touched with scarlet, above the setting sun. The day's warmth had thickened through the afternoon, and walking slowly away from Gilbey's messuage, Frevisse found herself wishing for the cool shadows and deep quiet of St. Frideswide's church and cloister walk, wanting to be enclosed and silent with nothing needed from her but prayers, even if only for a little while. Her thoughts were tired and twisted into pieces with all the different ways the day had gone—from the dark, wearing hours with the ill children to facing down Montfort to questioning how Tom Hulcote had come to his death. She was used to days that held together, flowing in a steady pattern from their beginnings to their ends, not sharded into pieces that jarred and grated against one another and against her peace of mind.

She did not want to be part of Prior Byfield and its troubles.

But she was, and *Deus adjuvat me; et Dominus susceptor est animae meae*. God helps me; and the Lord is the protector of my soul.

And if God was her help and protector, she was likewise bound to help and protect where she could, giving to others what God gave to her, and just now her help was needed here, partly because Montfort would do his worst to believe what he wanted to believe—that Perryn and Gilbey Dunn were guilty—and partly because she could not rid herself of the fear that had come to her in the churchyard—that Tom Hulcote's death was not the first there had been in this and might not be the last.

His death and Matthew Woderove's had been so alike.

She paused in the midst of the street, caught between returning to the church and turning toward Simon Perryn's with the questions she wanted to ask there, now being maybe better for them than later. But she had already been gone from the church far longer than she had meant to be and the questions could wait until morning; the children's needs could not. And nonetheless, after a moment more of hesitation, she turned toward Simon Perryn's.

There were others seeing to the children but no one else would ask the questions that needed asking.

Perryn, his two servants, and Dickon were still at their supper when she paused on his threshold, her shadow thrown ahead of her through the open doorway telling she was there before she need knock, and in the moment until her sun-brightened eyes were used to the house's shadows, Perryn said, "Dame Frevisse," in surprise and then in welcome, "Come in, please you, my lady."

By then she could see him rising from his place on a

joint stool at the table's head and Cisily and Dickon and a man who must be Watt on benches down its sides all turning to look at her, and she had a sudden sense of how comfortably crowded it would be at the table when Anne, Adam, Colyn, and Lucy were all there, too, and how empty it must be to Perryn without them, how hard the days of not knowing who would come home again and who would not must have been.

And even now they were not sure that Adam would.

She put the thought away from her. They had finished eating, she saw. The meal's end looked to have been applemose and some sort of wafers that were probably supposed to be thin and crisp and golden but were thick and brown and somewhat blackened around the edges and Dickon had been scraping the burned part of one away with his knife, into the remains of what looked to be overcooked pease pottage in the bowl in front of him. If this was Cisily's usual cooking, no wonder he had been eager for Elena Dunn's, Frevisse thought. But Cisily, Watt, and Dickon were rising to their feet with Perryn, and she said quickly, "I pray you, sit, please," as she entered at Perryn's invitation. Watt and Dickon did but Cisily began to bustle from the table, saying, "Let me fetch you some supper, my lady, if you'd eat with us, if it please you."

"I thank you but no," Frevisse said. Besides that she was satisfied already, the smell from whatever Cisily had cooked suggested there had been scorching at the bottom of the pot.

"Ale then?" Cisily said.

"Thank you, yes," Frevisse said though she did not much want that either.

"Is there aught wrong, my lady?" Perryn asked, still on his feet and worried. "The children?"

Sorry she had not realized that would be his first thought, she said hurriedly, "Not that I know. I've only come with some of the questions I asked at Gilbey's. About Monday."

Cisily, fetching another cup to the table, grumbled, "None of us know aught about naught at Gilbey Dunn's. They keep themselves to themselves there, they do."

Frevisse was a little used to Cisily from her helping Anne in the church: an older woman with a sprout of gray hairs on her upper lip and grumbling ways but part of the Perryns' household for a long while past and a good worker and good with the children, who, like their mother, never seemed to heed her grumbling. Nor did Perryn now, asking, "Will you sit, my lady?" gesturing to the joint stool at the end of the table from where he stood. To put everyone at better ease, Frevisse sat while Cisily poured ale from a pitcher already on the table and Perryn named Watt to her. Watt stood again, made an awkward bow, and sat. Frevisse thanked Cisily for the ale and said, because she could think of no subtle way around to it, "In truth it's you I want to talk to, Cisily."

Pleased, Cisily sat down on a bench and smoothed her apron over her lap. "Yes, my lady."

"But if the rest of you will listen and put in anything that comes to you, that would be to the good, too," Frevisse said. The men and Dickon nodded and she turned to Cisily. "I need to know about this Monday, the day before Tom Hulcote was found dead."

"Aye, I mind Monday," Cisily said.

"Perryn went to the church early that morning. In the rain."

"And came home to breakfast and complained the oatmeal was over-done. I told him I'd been seeing to the hens, that was why, there being only me to see to everything about the house and that's what happens when there's only one and too much to do. Then he said there shouldn't be that much doing, with only him and Watt and the boy to see to, and that made me want to cry, thinking of the poor babies all sick and gone, and . . ."

Cisily remembered Monday well enough, it seemed. More of it than Frevisse wanted to hear about, assuredly, and she slipped in hurriedly, "And we pray they'll be home soon and everything back to the way it was. Who else was here on Monday?"

It took Cisily a moment to change course, then she said, "Watt and Dickon."

"No one else?" Frevisse prompted. "No one else came here all day?"

"Oh, aye. You want that, too?"

"Please," Frevisse said, afraid it might be all or next to nothing from Cisily.

"Esota Emmet," Cisily said promptly. "I remember her. The old cat. Come snooping, that's all she was up to. Bess Underbush, too, to bring that ale you asked her to, Simon, because we were almost out." She thought a bit, her lower lip twitching with the effort. "Was it that day Walter Hopper was here, wanting something?"

"Aye, Monday," Watt said. "You sent him on to me. Like I'd know what work Simon'd want from him this week."

"How was I to know you wouldn't? If naught else, you'd maybe know where Simon was, for Walter to go ask him."

"Were you here in the house all day?" Frevisse asked.

"I mind I took some of the new ale to Anne at midday, and I was in and out and about in yard and garden now and again." She suddenly brightened, remembering more. "Mary was here. I told you, Simon. Came to the door bold as you please, demanding to see you. That was Monday, sure as anything, because Tuesday we found Tom and she's been shut up in her house ever since, carrying on like nobody in the world ever felt a loss but her, so it had to be Monday she was here because it wasn't Sunday. And Ienet Comber, she came by about cheese. Anyone else?" Cisily thought on that a moment, then decided, "Nay. That was all."

Except for whoever might have come while Cisily was

out. "Watt," Frevisse said, "can you mind anyone else here that day?"

Watt shook his large, grizzled head. "I was out at hoeing from morning until almost time for evening work."

"Where did Walter Hopper find you?"

"Here. 'Twas early he came by. I was just done morning milking."

Frevisse turned back to Cisily. "Do you remember anything about Perryn's green hood that day?"

Cisily shifted to indignation. "You mean that hood that crowner fellow has? Do you know how we go about getting that back from him? It's too good a hood to be lost to such as him."

"We'll have to see," Frevisse said. "Perryn, when you came in that morning, what did you do with your hood?"

"Hung it there by the door." He pointed to a pegged rack on the wall.

"Nay, that you didn't," Cisily shot back. "You left it lying like usual on the bench here, wet though it was. I hung it up, or it'd not be dry yet."

"Hung it there?" Frevisse asked, nodding to the pegs.

"Aye. There."

"What do you remember of it after that?"

"Remember of it?" Cisily frowned, thinking about it. "Nothing, I don't think. Nay. Nothing."

"Not whether it was there or not there after that?"

"If t'wasn't there, Simon had it. That's all I'd think about it. It was there or else he had it, no great matter. As long as t'wasn't lying about for me to pick up, I'd give it no thought and wouldn't now, except Esota Emmet came to tell me about it, right enough, while I cooking supper just now. About master's hood and Gilbey's belt. Somebody's been up to no good with those," she added darkly. "That's what Esota says, and so do I and anybody else around here with sense."

But until Montfort said the same, Perryn and Gilbey Dunn weren't safe, Frevisse thought, and took the thought with her as she took her leave, declining with thanks Perryn's offer to see her to the church, wanting the chance to be alone.

The west still glowed yellow above the lately set sun, the long summer twilight had hardly begun to fade, and from other times in other villages, Frevisse knew that on such an evening people should be out and about, work done for the day but with light enough left for visiting among neighbors, and surely there should be a scatter of children at play on the green, their laughter and shouting bright through the darkening hour or so until they were called in to bed. But this evening there was no one in sight except for a pair of the crowner's men on the bench under the oak tree, a stoup of probably ale between them since one of their fellows was coming out the alehouse doorway bearing another. Save for them, Prior Byfield was outwardly empty of all the life there should have been, because somewhere among them was a murderer and they did not know who. While Tom Hulcote's body rotted in its grave, the rot of his death was spreading here, and not helped in the least by Montfort corrupting where he should have cured.

Was it greed that made a person so stupid? Or was it that stupidity led to greed?

Frevisse turned toward St. Chad's, tired with this gathering of pieces. And now, whether she wanted to or not, she would be sifting and shifting them around, trying to make sense from them without knowing if she even had the pieces needed to make sense.

And meanwhile there were her slacked duties waiting to be answered for. For that, she would not only to ask Sister Thomasine's pardon but offer to take both their duties through the night in reparation. Unhappily, no matter how little she minded asking pardon, the rest of her resolve brought her to falter in the nave doorway. These past days' duties had not grown easier with doing. If anything, they had grown harder for her. But that gave her no right to scant them, especially when she knew Mistress Margery purposed to spend tonight at her own cottage, tending a needed herbal brew through its simmering and sieving and more simmering, and with firm hold against what she would have preferred to do, she went on in.

The little family clusters of straw-stuffed mattresses laid on the floor down both sides of the nave were as they had been, the low, shielded lamplight showing here and there the restless shifting of a child, pale faces and glint of eyes as women looked up to see who had come and then, Frevisse being of no great interest to them, turned back to what they had been doing, which looked for a merciful number of them to be settling to sleep beside their sleeping children. Only Anne Perryn stood up and moved away from her children, bedded near the rood screen, to meet Frevisse and ask, low-voiced, "Have you seen Simon? Do you know how is it with him? Is he going to be arrested?"

"He's at home and well. As things are now, he's not to be arrested, no."

"As things . . ." Anne began worriedly but behind her Lucy whimpered, "Mama," and Anne turned back to her, whispering, "I'm here, lamb. Don't wake your brothers, there's a good girl."

This afternoon Lucy had been sitting up on her bed, blinking owlishly into the church's twilight and declaring she wanted to go home. Tonight she was more querelous, whimpering for a drink, but beside her Colyn lay curled into a quiet, sleeping bundle. It was Adam's restlessness on the mattress beside theirs that was troubling. Even in the low light Frevisse could see his fever-flush and that he was awake but not much conscious, she feared, and silently praying for God's mercy on him, she passed through the rood screen into the chancel, where Sister Thomasine was kneeling with bowed head in front of the altar.

With a spasm of distress, Frevisse realized she had let

the hour for Vespers pass and Compline come without a thought. Contrite and dismayed, she went to kneel beside Sister Thomasine, able to catch enough of her low murmur to join in, head bowed low over her clasped hands, "... *peccavi nimis cogitatione, verbo et opere: mea culpa, mea culpa, mea maxima culpa.*" ... I have sinned greatly in thought, in word, in deed: by my fault, by my fault, by my most great fault. And on through Compline's heart-comforting web of prayers and psalms to the familiar end. *"Divinum auxilium maneat semper nobiscum. Amen."* May divine aid remain always with us. Amen.

In the right way of things, after Compline there should have been only a silent going to bed and sleep, and at St. Frideswide's the nuns were probably doing exactly that, but here as she sat back on her heels, waiting penitently, patiently, while Sister Thomasine prayed alone a little longer, Frevisse worked to hold to Compline's peace while she could, knowing that the night was only beginning and sleep would be brief if at all.

Sister Thomasine finished, made the sign of the cross over her breast, and they rose together, bowed to the altar and moved aside to the sacristy doorway, where Frevisse said, her voice kept low, "My apology for being gone so long. By your leave, I'll take the whole night watch in recompense."

Sister Thomasine looked at her, seeming still half-lost in her prayers, but after a moment said softly, "You were about God's work as surely as I was. There's no need of recompense."

One of the graces—and, occasionally, annoyances—of Sister Thomasine was that she never feigned what she did not mean, but Frevisse searched her face anyway. Bodily there was little of her to begin with, and Dame Claire forever worried that, left to herself, she paid insufficient heed to whether she was well or ill, other things mattering to her more. Tonight she looked well enough, but Frevisse asked, "You're not over-tired? You're not going to bring yourself to sickness with this?"

Sister Thomasine's eyes widened with surprise. "Tired? Not beyond anyone else, surely. I'm . . ." She seemed to look inward a moment before saying, simply, "I'm happy."

"Happy?" Frevisse echoed and was discomfited by her voice betraying her own unhappiness.

Seeming not to hear it, Sister Thomasine answered, "How could I not be? All these days and nights I've been living inside of prayer instead of only praying, been nowhere but here, in prayer and at God's work with never need to do anything else."

To live inside of prayer instead of merely praying. It was something Frevisse was sometimes able to do but not often, only sometimes and never for very long but enough that she understood what it meant to Sister Thomasine who had never wanted anything, since she was a half-grown girl except to live in prayer, as near to God as she could come; and she said, admitting her own weariness, "Then thank you, yes. I'd like to take my turn at bed now."

"Your supper is here. Father Henry brought it."

"Gilbey Dunn's wife fed me well enough. You're welcome to my share if you wish it."

Sister Thomasine regarded her gravely. "May I?"

Frevisse covered her surprise. In the priory Sister Thomasine rarely ate even all of her own portion, let be want more, though now Frevisse thought on it, she had been eating well enough here, and quickly she said, "Yes, please, if you like."

"I think I'd better," Sister Thomasine said as it was something she had considered seriously. "With all that needs doing for the children, I seem to need more food than otherwise."

"Then, please, eat it all. I've no need of it tonight."

And would find some way to see Sister Thomasine had more after this.

Sister Thomasine bowed her head in thanks, and Frevisse bowed hers in return, with the doubt that Sister Thomasine would ever cease, in one way or another, to surprise her.

# Chapter 16

he awoke in thick darkness, for a moment confused, the room around her wrong for her cell
in the nunnery's dorter, until the narrow, door-
shaped outline of lamp-yellow light told her she was in
St. Chad's sacristy, not in bed but on a mattress on the
floor; and if she was awake, then the hour was probably
near to midnight and time for Matins and to take Sister
Thomasine's place. Used to her cell's darkness, she rose
and with little trouble found by feel her wimple and veil
where she had laid them carefully aside, with unthinking
familiarity put them on, pinned the veil in place, stood,
and shook out her skirts. With nothing else needed to be
ready, she paused to gather herself with a murmured *Deo*

*gratias* and slipped from the sacristy to find the nave re-assuringly sunk in silence and shadows.

After so many other nights of children whimpering or crying, miserable and in pain, with women moving back and forth in the low-kept lamplight, the stillness was like balm. Even Anne Perryn was sleeping, stretched out narrowly between Colyn and Lucy, though it was likely unbearable weariness had taken her down, rather than desire, because on the mattress next to them Adam lay awake—or something like awake—his eyes closed but his head turning restlessly from side to side. Sister Thomasine was with him, one hand laid lightly on his chest's uneven breathing while with the other she soaked a cloth in a basin of water.

As Frevisse came toward them, she glanced upward but said nothing, and Frevisse waited while she wrung out the cloth and was reaching to lay it over Adam's forehead again when suddenly his eyes were open, staring at her, startling both her and Frevisse to stillness, before his head began to turn again, his fever-bright eyes roaming as if he searched for something to fix them on, then suddenly did, staring upward past Frevisse with such fear that she turned and found herself looking up at the tall figure of St. Chad painted on the narrow wall flanking the rood screen between chancel and nave. Unnaturally lean, it rose through shadows toward the rafters, but the face was caught by some trick of lamplight that gave life to the large eyes staring away into the dark.

Adam whimpered and Sister Thomasine leaned over him, asking, "Adam, what is it?"

Eyes still on the painted saint, Adam tried to speak, choked dryly, managed to whisper, "That man. He never smiles. He just stands there." The boy gave a dry sob. "He just stands there staring and waiting for me to be dead!"

"Adam." Sister Thomasine touched his cheek, bringing

him to look at her, and gently but certain, said, "He never smiles because what he's seeing is too beautiful for smiling at."

Adam lay still. "Too beautiful for smiling?" he whispered, his voice a bare thread of sound.

Sister Thomasine nodded, as unsmiling as the saint as she asked, "Haven't you seen a summer sunrise, just when the light strikes out of the darkness and across the fields and every drop of dew turns to diamonds and the sky to a blue you never see another time and any clouds there are to gold and everything is changed and strange and more beautiful than you knew anything could be?"

Slowly Adam nodded.

Sister Thomasine nodded with him, saying gently, "Heaven is even more beautiful than that and the saint is looking into heaven. That's why he doesn't smile. Because what he's seeing is too beautiful for smiling."

His gaze still clinging to her face but unfeared now, Adam took a deep, slow breath. "That's why you don't smile, either, isn't it?" he whispered.

Sister Thomasine touched his cheek and laid the wet cloth over his forehead and eyes, and in a little while, when he was surely asleep, she rose to her feet, stood for another moment over him, hands folded, head bowed to prayer, then turned to Frevisse and said softly, "He'll do well now."

He looked no better to Frevisse, the fever-flush still on him, his breathing still ragged, but she nodded agreement. Together, they made sure all was well throughout the nave before going to say Matins and Lauds together in the chancel until part way through Laud's third psalm, a child roused, whimpering, and when there was no sound of anyone moving to quiet it, Frevisse broke off with a hasty crossing of herself and went, finding it was a little girl who had bettered yesterday and so her mother was gone to see to things at home for tonight. When Frevisse had given her a drink and settled her to sleep again, Sister

Thomasine had finished Lauds and was gone to bed, and Frevisse stood in the aisle between the clusters of mattresses and dark, low humps of sleeping bodies, listening to soft snufflings and snores without finding anything that needed her and, for lack of something else to do, returned to Adam.

Since yesterday's morning Frevisse had been afraid of exactly this watch, midnight through to dawn, when, even at the best, life ebbed low and death so often subtly came. She did not want to watch a child die. Nor see his parents' grief. Nor have to try to give comfort where there was none to be had. With those uncompanionable thoughts, she sat down on the joint stool between the mattresses, feeling that the only present mercy was that Anne Perryn looked likely, at last, to sleep a night through. If Adam died . . .

Frevisse put the thought from her, took the fever-dried cloth from his forehead, soaked it again, wiped his face and throat and arms, and relaid it on his forehead. He never stirred the while except to go on breathing in that light, labored, frightening way, and when she had finished, Frevisse lay her hands in her lap and began to pray, for him, for all the children, for help in the matter of Tom Hulcote's murder . . .

How long and how deep she went into the praying she could not have said, but when the bright caroling of birdsongs outside in the last darkness before dawn brought her back and she tried to straighten, she found herself stiffened with long sitting and, hand pressed to her spine, eyes still shut, had to draw herself upright bone by bone, feeling every one of them. Then froze to stillness as she heard something besides the birdsong. Heard Adam's breathing. Changing.

Quieting.

With a heart-thud of fear, she leaned over him, starkly far from her prayers' peace of a moment before, until she saw as she stripped the cloth from his forehead and laid her hand there that his face was sheened with sweat. With blessed sweat.

He was drenched with it, all over. The fever was broken.

Quickly she shook Anne by the arm, telling her even while waking her, forestalling her fear, and watched while she felt of her son's face, kissed his damp forehead, laid her hand over his even, easy breathing, and began to cry.

Frevisse had expected prayers and thanks to God but watching Anne's huge, silent tears swell and slip down her face, she knew they served as well for thanks as any prayer ever could.

Behind her, come so quietly Frevisse had not heard her, Mistress Margery said, "He's strong. He'll do well now." She was carrying a cloth-covered pottery jug and to Frevisse's glance at it, she answered, "It brewed well." But she was looking at Frevisse in return and asked, "How do you, my lady?"

"Tired is all," Frevisse said though her head felt as stale as the nave's air.

Mistress Margery's look at her did not lessen. "Best you step outside a time, maybe. I can see to things here the while."

Frevisse accepted the offer gratefully and found, even before she had left the church porch, that the cool dawn air worked on her much as a strong draught of rich wine would have done. For a few deep-breathed moments she simply stood on the churchyard path, breathing, feeling, deliberately not thinking. The day was barely there, the world still mostly only shapes and shadows in the cool and colorless dawnlight, with no more than the barest trace of rose and peach tinting the eastern sky but the birds still in full-throated song, and Frevisse softly joined them with a prayers from Prime. *"Domine Deus omnipotens, qui ad principium huius diei nos pervenire fecisti . . ."* Lord God all powerful, you who to the beginning of this day have made us come . . .

It was a prayer that almost always served to lift her heart but its other words struck too near to what else the day was going to ask of her. *". . . semper ad tuam iustitiam faciendam nostra procedant eloquia, dirigantur cogitationes et opera."* . . . may always our words lead, our thoughts and works be directed, to fulfilling your justice.

Because today she would have to go on with what she had started yesterday.

But not yet, she prayed. For just now let there be simply the dawn and a quietness of heart and mind and soul.

The riot of birdsong was ending as the daylight grew and the world took on colors—summer greens of grass and trees, gold of the grain in the field beyond the churchyard wall, subtle blues rising across the sky. Without haste, Frevisse began to walk, her gown's hem sweeping over the churchyard's long, dew-damp grass, keeping her mind away from what she would all too soon have to deal with, thinking instead that the worst of the plague was past now Adam's fever had broken. Even better and for a wonder and against all likely hope, it seemed no one was going to die. And three and more days were gone by without any new mesels now, and that made it likely there would be no more, and soon she and Sister Thomasine would be free to go back to St. Frideswide's.

There was still the harvest to face but that seemed simpler now . . .

And the matter of Master Naylor's freedom . . .

And Tom Hulcote's murder . . .

Frevisse sighed to find she had come back to that.

And that she was standing looking down at the raw brown, clodded earth of Matthew Woderove's grave mound.

Even as she said a prayer for his soul, she noted there was no sign to show that more had happened here than a hole been dug and the dirt then shoveled back into it for maybe no good reason.

She had talked to Elena Dunn about Tom Hulcote's

murderer being someone who was unhappy, but now that she thought on it, unhappiness was part of both men's deaths. By all she had ever heard of Matthew Woderove, he had been unhappy in his life and now, to judge by his grave, he was not even mourned in death. An unhappy man come to an unhappy end.

Like Tom Hulcote.

Frevisse paused on that thought.

She had only thought of Tom Hulcote as angry, but behind the anger he had to have been unhappy—unhappy in the life he had and unhappy in not being able to better it, his best hope broken that day at the manor court and no likely way it could ever be mended. An unhappy man brought to an unhappy end.

Like Matthew Woderove.

Frevisse shook her head, still not wanting the two deaths together in her mind.

But what if they should be?

What if the matter of Hulcote's death had to be taken back a step? To Matthew Woderove's. What then?

She didn't know.

Her head bowed, she turned and walked away from the grave and only as she was passing the churchyard gateway heard soft-soled footfalls and looked up to find Simon Perryn there.

He bowed and said, "Good morrow, my lady," as she stopped, and she bent her head in return, wondering if she looked as under-slept as he did.

Then she saw the fear rigid in his face and said quickly, "Adam is better. His fever broke just ere dawn."

Perryn sagged against one of the pentice posts, letting go his taut hold on himself. "It did?" he breathed, wanting to hear it again.

"I left him sleeping quietly."

Perryn crossed himself. "Praise be to all the saints. And the others?"

"All doing well."

"None . . . ?"

He hesitated over the question, asking after not only his own but all the children, Frevisse realized, and she answered, "Mistress Margery says we'll lose none of them. They're all going to live. It's over."

The worst of it at any rate, and as easily as that there were suddenly tears in Perryn's eyes, not falling as his wife's had but shining in the morning light as he said, finally smiling, "Thank you."

"God's doing, not mine."

"But your help and your prayers. And Sister Thomasine's."

Now Frevisse met his smile. "And yours. All of us. Your wife was awake when I left, if you're thinking of going in."

"I was, aye."

Smiling, he went and, smiling, Frevisse watched him go, taking pleasure in his pleasure. The more she knew of Simon Perryn, the more she liked him.

But it would take more than her liking to save him from Montfort.

The sun's rim slid clear of the horizon, its low rays striking long across the fields, changing the world to sudden brightness and long-reached sharp shadows, the dew to glinting silver, the rising dawn mist along the stream into a golden veil. With its dazzle in her eyes, Frevisse turned away, toward the village, and found that Perryn had only barely been the first out and about. Folk had been at their first work around their houses and byres before light, surely, and now they were bound, men, women, older children, most with hoes as well as scythes or rakes over their shoulders, for probably Shaldewell Field to weed in the beans until the hayfields dried and they could turn to those.

Frevisse held where she was, caught between returning inside to join Sister Thomasine for Prime and all the first-of-a-morning work there was or setting out to ask more questions before Montfort did worse than he already had. Both were her duty, in their different ways, but she knew which was the one only she could do and, bearing the weight of her choice, she went out the gateway.

Going along the street beside the green, she met folk on their way to the church, bringing food and to see how family or neighbors did. The children were too shy to more than give her a quick bow of the head and sidewise looks as they passed, and Frevisse discouraged their elders from talk by giving them a brisk nod and a bare smile to acknowledge their bows or curtsies without encouraging more, thereby reaching Perryn's messuage unhindered. Neither Watt nor Dickon was in the yard, but she was not seeking them and before ever she knocked at the house door, standing open to the warm day, she could guess where Cisily was by the rasp of sand being scrubbed over wood, and indeed, when at her knock Cisily called, "Come in then. No need to hang about out there," Frevisse found her with sleeves rolled to above her elbows and a rag in her hand, stretched over the table, scouring at a stain. At sight of Frevisse, though, she stopped, pulled up to straight and said, "Pardon, my lady, I didn't know 'twas you. Pray, come in," as she dropped the cloth out of sight below the table and began to roll down her sleeves.

"No need for pardon," Frevisse said easily. The last thing she wanted was Cisily on her manners. "I've come to tell you Adam's fever broke at dawn."

Cisily crossed herself with huge relief. "Praise God and the Virgin. The master was bound for the church, so he knows?"

"He's there now."

Smiling as if unable to stop, Cisily came around the table. "Come in. Sit you down, please. There's oatmeal still from breakfast and the cream is fresh if you'd like. Please."

Despite what she had seen of Cisily's cooking yesterday, Frevisse accepted; she was here to talk with Cisily and the woman might do it more easily across food than otherwise. Or maybe not, because when the bowl of oatmeal and cream was in front of her and she asked Cisily to join her, Cisily did readily, sitting on the other bench, across the table, with mug of ale in hand and talk on her tongue, beginning with how blessed they were that the children were past the worst. "Though trying to keep our three a-bed from now until they're full well, that's something I'm not looking forward to. And what with Anne worn out with all this, I can see already where the burden is going to fall."

"They're fortunate to have you," Frevisse said with shameless flattery.

"I've known them since they were born. Known Simon and Anne all their days, too, come to that."

"You're village-born, then?"

"Oh, aye. Born, bred, and never been out of it except twice to Banbury," Cisily said with pride.

"You knew Matthew Woderove then, too."

"Matthew?" Cisily clucked her tongue. "Aye. All his life, poor man. Never had a chance, he did, with a father like that and then wedding Mary Perryn, though I say it who shouldn't, seeing I work for Simon who's as good as Midsummer Day is long."

"And Mary isn't?"

"Good as the day is long? Not even nearly," Cisily said bluntly. "Never has been. Never will be."

"Not even for Tom Hulcote?"

Cisily tutted fretfully. "Well, there's no surprise you know about that, is there? People talk, that's sure."

"Do you think Matthew ran off because of his wife and Tom Hulcote?"

"Who's to say? Though he'd put up with it two years and more already, so why go hot over it all of a sudden?"

"He maybe didn't know until now."

"Who's to say? He never did. Still, everyone else knew, didn't they?"

"And Father Edmund never sought to put stop to it?"

Cisily put down her mug, frowning a little. "Now there you have me. He didn't know because nobody would tell him, would they? Him being new-come here and all."

"But Matthew Woderove never said anything to anyone? Not about his wife or Tom Hulcote or running off?"

"Not that I've heard, and I would have." Cisily seemed quite sure of that. "My own thought is that, Mary or no, losing his land was too much shame for him, that's all. He just wanted to be away, once and for all, and he went."

"How did he go?"

"At night." Cisily shuddered. "That shows you how desperate he must have been, to be away in the dark like that."

"With no warning either?"

"Oh, he'd had a yelling time that afternoon with Mary, out at the end of their furlong at west end of Shaldewell Field."

"What over?" Frevisse asked.

Cisily shook her head, looking put out. "Now there, no one else was working that end of the field that afternoon. No one was near enough to hear more than that they were angry. But they were that, right enough. The way I've heard it, they were at it a while and while, then Mary threw down her hoe—a wonder she didn't throw it at him, I'd say—and went home on her own and that was the last she saw of him."

"He never went home?"

"Oh, aye, he did, but not until he'd worked the afternoon out, there in the field, and came home when everyone else did. Wouldn't talk to anyone nor didn't want them talking to him neither. And then what do you think he found when he was home?" Cisily leaned a little forward over the table and said with slow relish, "She'd barred the door. Wouldn't let him in. Not into his own house, with half the village passing by on their own ways home and able to see it. That's what she did to him."

.

It briefly crossed Frevisse's mind to wonder why it was not Mary Woderove who was dead instead of her husband, but all she asked was, "What did he do?"

"Matthew?" Cisily was as free with her scorn as with her tale. "Some of the men asked if he wanted they should bring a timber, they'd have the door down for him, and that's what he should have done, if you ask me, and given her a beating she wouldn't forget. But then he should have done that years ago, God's truth. I've heard Simon tried to bring him on home to here, but all Matthew did was shake his head at everybody and skulk away into his byre, to spend the night in the hay, it was reckoned. Like always."

"She'd done this to him before?"

"Oh, aye. More than once. Have a screaming quarrel with him, bar the door, and leave him to sleep in the byre, and the next morning he'd be asking her pardon and thanking her for letting him back into his own house, fool man. Nobody thought but it'd be the same this time, but next morning he and one of Gilbey's horses was gone." Cisily slapped the tabletop with a merry hand. "And you should have heard Gilbey swearing over that horse!" She changed her mind. "No. Pardon, my lady. No, you shouldn't have." But the memory was too ripe for her; she could not help adding, "But it was worth the hearing anyway."

Frevisse did not doubt it had been, if your humor went that way. Trying to make the question sound like idle talk, she asked, "That was about Midsummer, wasn't it?"

"Two days past. They held the court where Matthew lost his land—and wicked that was of Gilbey, he doesn't need more land—the day after Midsummer's, and a day later was their quarrel, and Matthew disappeared that night."

"How did Mary take his leaving her like that?"

"Well, I mind she came to the well that morning with the rest of us, and when some cat asked after Matthew,

she answered that she hadn't seen him and hoped she
didn't. She thought he'd gone out early to the fields somewhere, you see. It was only later, putting together that
Gilbey's horse was stolen and Matthew nowhere to be
found that we started to guess he'd gone and didn't mean
to come back. *Then* there was some caterwauling, let me
tell you."

Frevisse supposed that sooner or later she would have
to talk to Mary Woderove but doubted she would enjoy
it when the time came and asked, "What did she do when
Tom Hulcote disappeared?"

"Now that I don't know," Cisily said with deep regret.
"She was that upset over them not being given the holding
that she'd taken against everyone, and being I'm Simon
and Anne's, she'd have had nothing to do with me, even
if I'd not been taken up then with the childern and all.
What I've heard is she racketed on to anyone who'd listen
and to Tom most of all that everything and everyone was
rotten against him here and he'd never have a chance in
life at all except he left."

"Ran off, you mean?"

"He'd have to. He'd never money enough to buy himself free, that's sure."

"And she was going to go with him?"

"Nothing so good as that, and not that most everybody
here wouldn't mind seeing the last of her, but no, she was
saying, too, she meant to stay and keep the Woderove
holding in the teeth of whatever anyone tried to do to her
and be damned to her brother and everyone. That's what
I've heard. She has hot humors, does Mary."

And not overmuch sense, to be telling the world at
large you wanted your lover to break his bondage and
run, Frevisse thought, but aloud she only said, "When
Tom disappeared then, nobody thought anything about it
but that he'd run?"

"If they thought about it at all, that's what they
thought," Cisily said. "Or just that he'd wandered off like

he was always doing and would come back when it suited his own self. Nobody much cared except Gilbey and only because Tom was supposed to be working for him. This time there wasn't even Gilbey to care. Nobody but Mary, I'd guess, and likely she thought he'd run, sure, like she'd been telling him to do. Else we'd have heard about it. Loud and long." Cisily shook her head, lips pursed. "The way we're hearing about him being dead. You think no one had ever been grieved but her." She suddenly crossed herself. "It's being said, my lady, there'll have to be things done, for fear he'll walk, dying the way he did. Have you heard aught about that?"

Caught by the changed direction, Frevisse hesitated, then said, "Not once he's been laid in consecrated ground and prayers said over him. Not with Father Henry and Father Edmund both to pray for him. And I will and Sister Thomasine."

Cisily gave a little shudder of pleased fear. "That's well enough then. I shouldn't like to meet him of a twilight, that's all, with him all bloodied and angry about it."

Frevisse readily agreed that neither would she, and Cisily, diverted to remembering village stories of ghosts there had been—none she had ever seen herself, mind, and all of folk dead before her time but nonetheless . . .

With much thanks for the breakfast, Frevisse escaped out into the warming day.

# Chapter 17

F revisse crossed the green slowly from Perryn's messuage toward Father Edmund's with head bowed, eyes down, hands folded into her opposite sleeves, thinking on what she had so far learned. None of it looked to be of use in finding out Tom Hulcote's murderer, and nothing in it linked his death to Matthew Woderove's. Nothing even linked one man to the other except her own unease and that they had both known Mary—in the several meanings of "known."

She feared that more questioning, no matter who she asked, was only going to bring out, over and over, what she had already heard. That Matthew Woderove had been pitiable and Tom Hulcote troublesome. That Tom had been given to wandering and Mary was a shrew. Worse, sooner or later, she would have to question Mary and so far had found nothing yet to like about the woman. But then, she was purposing to talk to Montfort and there was nothing she liked about him either.

There was no guard at Father Edmund's gate, only on the bench beside the house door, a young man in the crowner's livery who rose to tell her with good manners instead of the usual surliness Montfort's men seemed to catch from him, that the crowner was still at breakfast.

Frevisse, thinking that Montfort kept comfortable hours if he was only to breakfast now, said, "Best I see him then, not to interrupt him later when he's set to work."

The guard looked doubtful her consideration would make her any more welcome, but he stepped inside to say, "Dame Frevisse begs leave to see you, sir."

She had begged nothing but supposed there was no harm in saying so if it brought Montfort to receive her more graciously.

It did not.

At the crowner's grunted agreement, the youth stepped aside from her way with a slight bow to her, and she entered to find Montfort seated at the head of the priest's table, with Father Edmund on his right and an array of dishes set out cold in front of them that must be from last night's supper—sliced pork in some sort of sauce, the remains of a cheese tart, a loaf end of brown but not coarse bread, and wine. She had not known the priest lived that well, but then the village living was his, not some other priest's who paid him poorly to serve in his place; and very possibly, if he were skilled at ambition, he had income from somewhere else, too. What disconcerted her more was that he seemed at ease in the crowner's company, sitting pleasantly with him over the end of their meal, and momentarily she could not help wondering if that spoke well or ill of Father Edmund, then decided it spoke well, because Christian forbearance toward Montfort could not come easily. For her, assuredly, any forbearance she had ever managed toward him had always come with gritted teeth.

As she curtsyed to them both, Father Edmund said welcomingly, "Dame Frevisse," and Montfort managed, "Dame."

"Sir," Frevisse returned.

"Am I needed at the church?" Father Edmund asked.

"God be thanked, all's well," Frevisse said. "Adam Perryn's fever broke at dawn."

Father Edmund crossed himself. "Blessed be God and the Virgin. We've prayed long and hard for him and the others."

Montfort echoed his gesture with his usual impatience at everything that was not to his purpose and said, "Why are you here, Dame?"

There being no point in coming to it subtly, she said, "About Matthew Woderove's death. Is everything about it sure?"

"Matthew Woderove?" For a moment Montfort looked as if he could not place who that was, then remembered and said disgustedly, "Of course it's sure. We boxed what there was of him. His folk here buried him. There's no more sure than that. He's dead."

Frevisse bypassed wondering if Montfort meant that for a jest and asked, "Is it sure he was killed where he was found? That he wasn't killed elsewhere and moved?"

Montfort's small eyes narrowed with displeasure. "Shouldn't you be at your prayers, Dame?" And aside to Father Edmund, "She does this. Makes trouble where there isn't any." And back to her, "Leave these matters to those whose business they are, Dame. Go back to your prayers and stay there after this."

It was utter dismissal. Frevisse managed a curt curtsy and to say without strangling on it, "Pray, pardon me," and to Father Edmund, "By your leave."

Looking as if he regretted what had passed, Father Edmund made a sign of the cross in silent blessing toward
her, and to him she gave another curtsy, more graciously,
before she retreated.

She was across the yard and to the street again before
she realized there was someone behind her, and because
she meant to go to the church anyway, she swung left-
ward, to be out of the way of whichever of Montfort's
men was going to the alehouse, but behind her someone
said, "Dame Frevisse," and she stopped and turned to find
the guard who had been at Father Edmund's door bowing
to her with hurried awkwardness.

"My lady. If you please. A word."

"Of course, sir," Frevisse answered, puzzled but
matching his courtesy.

"About what just passed. In there."

"Yes?" Wary now as well as puzzled.

"This Matthew Woderove's death. I was the one who
inquired about it. After he'd been identified."

That meant he was one of the crowner's serjeants in
stead of merely a guard, and suddenly he had all Frevisse's attention. "You made investigation? You learned
something?" she asked, trying but knowing she failed to
hide her eagerness.

He failed as badly to hide his pride. "A little, yes."

"What?"

It was abrupt but all the encouragement he needed. "I
found out he went from here to Banbury. He sold the
horse there."

"You found Gilbey Dunn's horse?"

"The dealer had sold it again. It's gone. But he admitted he'd had it. From the description."

"He's a more forthcoming horse dealer than most I've
known," Frevisse observed wryly.

The youth, whether or not he wondered how she had

come to know horse dealers that well, answered, "He sees that if he helps us in a matter where he's not at fault, it'll go better for him if ever he is. At fault. And we find out he is."

Frevisse wondered who had pointed that out to the man but only asked, "He was certain it was the same horse?"

"A dark chestnut with an off hind white stocking and a finger-long scar above the near hock."

That was certain enough, at any rate. "And it's certain it was Matthew Woderove sold it?"

"The man described him and what he was wearing. It was how the widow described him and what he was wearing when he left here."

"When was he in Banbury?"

"The day after he left here."

Frevisse paused, feeling her way along the wrongness of that before she said slowly, "He sold the horse the day after he left here, then set away on foot to somewhere west and was robbed and killed not many miles out of Banbury."

"It seems so. Yes."

She liked the caution in his answer. Moreover, she was starting to like him and asked more openly than she might have otherwise, "Why sell the horse? Why walk when he could have gone on riding?"

"Come to that," the youth said back, "why did he go north from here instead of simply west? Horses sell as well in Worcester as in Banbury."

So he was dissatisfied with it, too; but Frevisse had had time now to notice more about him—his hair's color, for one thing—and she asked at a guess, "Are you kin to Master Montfort?"

The youth flushed a dark red, close to his hair's shade, but answered steadily enough, straightly meeting her gaze, "I'm his son."

And was well-witted enough to know that was not necessarily to his advantage, so that, at a loss for better comment, Frevisse offered, "I didn't know he had a son."

"Three of us, actually. And two daughters. I'm Christopher."

Frevisse slightly inclined her head to him. "Master Christopher."

He slightly bowed in return. "My lady."

And for no good outward reason they smiled at one another, unwarrantably at ease on apparently no more than the basis of good manners. Another thing in which he differed from his father. And he asked, turning the questioning around, "Why your interest in this man?"

Frevisse hesitated, then said, "It's that I keep thinking how he and Tom Hulcote died much the same way. By blows to the head and stabbing. And . . ." She trailed off, not knowing to where the "and" should lead.

"And they're both from here and . . . interested in the same woman," Christopher offered. To her questioning look, he added, "There's always talk in plenty in a village alehouse."

She was coming to approve of him more by the moment but, looking past him, had to say, "You may need to go back. The jurors are coming."

Christopher glanced down the green toward the four village men going toward the priest's house and agreed, "I'll be wanted." He began to back away, saying as he did, "It's just that I thought there was no reason you shouldn't know what's known about this Matthew Woderove's death. If you wanted it."

"Thank you."

He gave her a brief bow, hesitated as if inclined to say more, but did not, only bowed again and left her.

Frevisse went her way, too, but not back to the church. Head down and hands in her opposite sleeves again, crossing the green to Gilbey Dunn's, she considered what

Christopher Montfort had given her about Matthew Woderove. More than she had had but still very little, and the very little made no sense. Why had he sold the horse so soon? He had to know that on the whole Lord Lovell was not one to let his villeins simply leave. Why hadn't he sought to put as much distance as might be between him and possible pursuit before being rid of the horse since he'd gone to the trouble of stealing it?

She needed to know more.

But what?

About Tom Hulcote, she supposed. Matthew Woderove had died elsewhere but Tom Hulcote had died here and here was where she had the only hope of learning anything of use. The trouble was that Montfort's impatience was as much a threat as his stupidity and might leave her too little time to learn enough. If she could learn enough. Because she was guessing at what she needed to know.

But since guesses were all she had, they would have to do.

Elena Dunn was gathering chives from the herb bed beside her door among a scattering of hens. She straightened when she saw Frevisse coming toward her and wished her good morrow, and when Frevisse returned the greeting and asked after her sons, smiled a tired smile, answering, "They're recovering far faster than Agnes and I will. She's told them already today that if they don't stay quiet, she'll take to her bed and leave them to look after her instead. How is it with the others?"

"Adam Perryn's fever broke at dawn. We think that means the worst is altogether past."

Elena gave thanks and crossed herself but was watching Frevisse's face while she did and asked, "What else? More from the crowner?"

"Not yet, but I have more questions, if you'd be willing to answer them."

"About Tom Hulcote?"

"Yes."

Elena sighed. "He's proving as much a trouble dead as he was alive. Yes, of course I'll answer what I can. Best come in and sit down."

She went first, to open the half-door and let Frevisse enter first, while she fended off the red hen with skilled skirts, warning it, "There's nothing in here for you, you ninny. You're going to find yourself as Sunday dinner you keep this up."

Inside, an eastward window let in the morning light and Agnes was busy at the table chopping vegetables. Elena asked, "May she go on, or is this only between us?"

"There's no reason she can't stay," Frevisse said, keeping to herself the thought that Agnes might have answers, too.

Agnes nodded greeting and, deft of knife, wrist, and fingers, went on slicing carrots while at Elena's invitation, Frevisse sat, accepted an offer of cider, and waited while Elena poured three goblets full, handed her one, set one in Agnes's reach and, taking the third, pulled a chair around to sit facing her, asking as she did, "Questions about Tom Hulcote, you said?"

Agnes made a harumphing noise and slammed the knife through an onion with unnecessary force. "Worthless man."

"Not in the eyes of God," Elena said.

"Unfortunately what I want to know," said Frevisse, "is how he was in the eyes of men. You said he quit at St. Swithin's."

"The day after."

"Why had you kept him on so long when he was forever going off for days at a time?"

"Forever going off for days at a time?" Elena repeated as if puzzled. "His going off like that only began this summer. Until then, he'd go for a day now and again, no word to anyone, but show up the next day."

"With no excuse, and it's not as if he did much of his work when he was here," Agnes said. Having reduced the onion to small bits, she reached for another.

"It was only lately that he'd started taking off for three and four and more days at a time. It's what finished it for us. He wasn't worth the bother."

"But I thought . . ." Frevisse stopped. Yesterday Elena had only said he was gone too much. It had been Cisily who said he was forever being gone for days at a time, and Cisily had been enjoying herself and likely as not had gone to excess with it. Frevisse shifted her question to, "When did he begin this?"

"Being gone for days at a time, you mean? About Whitsuntide." Elena looked at Agnes to confirm that. Agnes shrugged. Elena thought a moment, then said, certain, "That would be when. It was early haying the first time he went off and didn't come back for three days, I think it was, that time. It was the worse surprise because he'd never done that until then and we were haying."

"Hiding in Mary Woderove's bed most likely," Agnes said.

"That was before her husband left," Elena pointed out.

"As if Matthew'd notice. Or say anything if he did," Agnes said. "He . . ."

Elena cut her off, going on, "He—Tom—was back for the most of the haying, I remember, so Gilbey held off being over-angry at him that time. But then he was gone again just before the sheep-washing and shearing, and we were feared he wouldn't be back in time at all."

"Just past Midsummer," Frevisse said.

"He was gone Midsummer Day, and we didn't see him again until . . ." Elena looked to Agnes. "How long was it?"

"He was off nigh to a week that time." Agnes was definite. "Was here Midsummer's eve but gone Midsum-

mer's morning. He wasn't here for all the going on when
Matthew Woderove ran off a few days after that, I mind,
and he didn't come dragging home for . . ." Agnes paused,
tapping the knife tip on the table as if counting something.
". . . for four more days. A week and a bit more, I'd say."

"Were those the only times he was gone for long?"
Frevisse asked.

"He did his usual gone-a-day at least twice after that,"
Elena said, "but there was only once more he was gone
three days together."

"When?"

"St. Swithin's day," Agnes said.

"He came back on St. Swithin's," Elena clarified.

"And had a fiend's quarrel with Gilbey the next day,
and that's when he quit. Half a word before Gilbey would
have told him to . . ."

"Dame Frevisse isn't here for talk of private matters,"
Elena said.

Private matters were precisely what Frevisse was there
for, but since she could hardly say so, she settled for
mildly commenting, "What I wonder at is why you hadn't
been done with him long since."

While Agnes savaged into a summer squash, Elena answered easily, "We have need of two men besides Gilbey
here. When Tom worked, he was good enough at what
he did."

"When he worked," Agnes muttered at the squash.

"Mostly it was that there aren't many who can put up
with my husband for very long. Tom Hulcote did. At least
better than most we've had."

Probably by leaving those days when he had had
enough of Gilbey and could bear no more, Frevisse
thought, but only said, "It was the quarrel at St. Swithin's
that finished things?"

"There would have been an end soon anyway," Elena
said. "Besides being gone so much that last month or

more, he'd taken to being churlish in the bargain, angry more often than not or else ill-humored."

"He hadn't always been that way?"

"No." Elena frowned a little, as if thinking on it for the first time. "No, he wasn't. What he was, was lazy when he could be. Slack at his work unless he was watched. But not ill-humored, no. Not until around Whitsuntide?" she asked of Agnes, who left off assaulting the squash, thought about it, too, and agreed, "From around then, aye. From then on and growing worse."

About Whitsuntide, when he had first gone off for longer than a single day.

"You never knew where he went those days he was gone? Those times he was gone longer than usual?"

Agnes mumbled something under her breath that might have been, "Mary Woderove's bed," but Elena considered before saying, "The last time at least, he was in Banbury. Gilbey saw him there."

"In Banbury?" Frevisse echoed, surprised. "What was he about in Banbury?"

"Gilbey didn't know. It was a market day, crowds and all, and Tom was on the other side of a street and didn't see Gilbey nor Gilbey let on he'd seen him either."

"Not until they were quarreling after Tom came back," Agnes said. She paused in scraping the squash off the cutting board into a pot to relish the memory. "In the midst of their yelling, Gilbey twitted him with being in Banbury when he ought to have been here, and Tom went up like a scalded cat."

"Agnes," Elena said quellingly. "That's more than Dame Frevisse needs to know."

It was not, and Frevisse asked, "What did Tom say?"

"Nothing to the point," Elena said. "As Agnes said, he just went angrier."

But anger could be cover for so many things. Frevisse looked for another question, but before she found one, there was a bustle of noise in the yard. Both she and Elena rose to their feet and Agnes put down her knife, all of them turning toward the door, in time to see one of Montfort's guards looking in, and past him Frevisse could see another.

tiffly, as if her throat were suddenly too tight, too dry, Elena said, "No, Agnes. I'll go," but as she started forward herself, Frevisse held out a hand into her way and asked, too low for the guard at the door to hear, "Where's Gilbey?"

With a twist of fear across her loveliness, Elena answered, equally low, "Gone to Banbury. I couldn't talk him from it."

"Mistress," said the man at the door.

With her face suddenly all smiling for him, Elena said, "Coming, sir," and went, graceful with her skirts and prettily hurrying. Agnes, as bid, stayed at the table but Frevisse followed, keeping distance and to the side as Elena said across the door to the man, smiling upon him with no trace of trouble and deliberate charm, "Yes? Is there something I can do for you?"

Staring at her, the man fumbled, "Mistress. Your husband." He managed to gather himself. "Your husband. Is he here?"

"I fear not, sir," Elena said brightly. "Might I be of help to you?"

Her calm seemed to fluster the man the worse, but behind him his fellow said, trying for more authority, "Where is he then? We've come for him."

"My husband?" Elena repeated.

"Gilbey Dunn. We've come for him," the man repeated. "Where is he?"

From somewhere across the yard Montfort yelled, "Get on with it!"

The two men swung around, the first one yelling back, "She says he's not here, sir!"

"Then where is he? Ask her, you fool."

Elena unlatched the door and the two men fell back a few paces as she stepped out onto her doorstep and with the air of a puzzled housewife not understanding all the trouble, answered for herself, lifting her voice, "He's gone to market, sir."

Frevisse, shifting into the doorway behind her, saw Montfort on his bay horse beyond the foreyard garden, already red-faced with impatience. "Gone to market? You mean he's run!" he snarled.

"Sir!" Elena's voice scaled up in what sounded for all the world like innocent protest. "He's never! The green cheeses were ready, and I couldn't take them because of the children. The mesels, you know."

One of the two men at the door took a hasty step backward.

"Stay where you are," Montfort snapped at him without shifting his glare from Elena. "Your husband has run and you're lying for him!"

"I wouldn't!" Elena protested. She sounded far more

peasant than Frevisse had ever heard her, and far less clever, as if she could not understand what Montfort was at. "He's only gone to market, to Banbury with the cheeses, like I said, sir."

"He's run," Montfort declared. "And he's in the wrong even if he hasn't! I gave him order yesterday, him and that reeve, not to leave the manor until I was done with them."

"He never said anything about any order, sir," Elena said with respectful puzzlement. "He wouldn't have gone if you'd told him not to, sir, I'm sure."

"He was told!"

Montfort had brought the rest of his guards with him, including Christopher, Frevisse saw, but they had stayed at the gateway, as if there might be need to keep back the handful of old men and a few women not gone out to the fields today and come to see what the crowner was about gathered beyond the ditch, bird-busy in talk and listening. They were none of them offering to come nearer except— Frevisse saw with mingled relief and worry—Perryn with Dickon behind him and both priests, circling them toward the yard's gateway. But they were not there yet with whatever help they might have given. It was Christopher who stepped forward and said, his voice carrying maybe louder than he meant it to, "I beg your pardon greatly, sir, but I think he wasn't."

Montfort jerked around to look at him. "What? What d'you mean he wasn't?"

"He wasn't told, sir. I mean, I was there, sir. Yesterday. They weren't told, either he or the reeve, that they weren't to leave the manor. Sir."

Montfort purpled. "They were!" He pointed at Perryn, now coming into the yard with Father Edmund and Father Henry. "See. He's still here."

Frevisse stepped forward from behind Elena and said, deliberately loudly, "I most humbly beg your pardon, sir, but I was there, too, and nothing was said to either of them not to leave the manor."

Montfort's glower swung around to her. "You. What're you here for, Dame? Go away."

Perryn had stopped in the street, but the priests were come into the yard now, and from beside Montfort's horse Father Edmund said, calm with the authority of his priesthood, "The Dunn children are ill. Dame Frevisse is here to comfort the mother, by right of God's charity."

"And so are we," Father Henry rumbled behind him.

They made a strange pair, the slender, dark haired, graceful-mannered younger man and Father Henry with his crest of yellow curls and height and muscled bulk, but they served the Church as surely as Montfort served the Crown and were therefore as much to be reckoned with as he was, and despite the crowner looked as if he would have gladly chewed them both down to gristle and spat them out if he could, he said after a short, choking silence, "Yes, well. But Gilbey Dunn is still gone and he shouldn't be. There's guilt in that, whatever *she* says." He made a curt nod at Elena. "There's a man dead and evidence against Dunn and by the law when there's suspicion of guilt and the man has fled, I'm bound to see into everything he owns, how much he has, and what it's worth, and that's what I'm going to do now. In the king's name."

Elena drew a sharp, frightened breath. For all her outward calm, she was rigid, and all Frevisse could offer was a hand on her arm to steady her from showing more, because Montfort was within his rights with what he meant to do. A criminal's goods were seized and sold to pay for the wrong he had done against the king's law. Everything he had, though it be no more than a beggar's bowl, was forfeit for his crime, and because Gilbey was not here when the crowner came seeking him, Montfort was free to assume he had fled until shown otherwise and to begin reckoning of his goods and lands against the time he might be found and tried. Nor would it have been different if Gilbey were there, except he would have been arrested into the bargain; and smoothly, knowing that to argue Montfort's right in the matter would have been to put himself in the wrong, Father Edmund said, "Of course. But since the children are too ill to be moved, we'll stay—Father Henry and I, and Dame Frevisse if she will—to give them and their mother what care and comfort we can while your men do what they must."

For all it was mildly said, the warning was there. Father Edmund would watch that there be no rough-handling of anyone or anything, and to judge by Montfort's glare and tight-jawed answer, "As you choose, priest," the crowner understood him perfectly.

Heavy-handed on the reins, he pulled his horse sharply around, forcing both priests back a few quick steps, and spurred forward out of the yard, making the watching villagers scatter from his way. Low and viciously, Elena said, watching him go, "There's a mean-minded man."

"All mean and no mind, I don't doubt," Agnes said behind her in the doorway.

Simon Perryn said something that served to keep the onlookers in the street and came on into the yard with Dickon still on his heels, while Father Edmund with Father Henry gathered up the guards from gateway and doorstep and set to arranging how things would go. Over her shoulder to Agnes Elena said, "Bring bowls and ale for all the men."

"The crowner's, too?" Agnes protested.

"Would you rather we had friends or foes going through our things?" Elena answered and went forward to join the men.

Frevisse followed but kept aside, only listening while Father Edmund and Christopher Montfort shared between them the sorting out of which guards would see to the barn and byres, which to the house, which the yard and sheds. With Montfort gone and Elena standing silently by, hands clasped beseechingly at her breast, lovely, helpless,

and looking hopeful of their kindness all at once, matters
went quietly. And then, when Agnes had come with the
ale and Elena served each of the guards herself, Frevisse
was left with no least worry that the business would go
far more in Elena's favor than Montfort would have stom-
ached if he had been there.

Simon Perryn had kept his distance, partway between
villagers and priests and guards, ready to go whichever
way looked best. Frevisse wanted a word with him but
waited until it was settled that Father Edmund would
oversee what happened with the yard and outbuildings
and Father Henry keep the boys eased with stories while
Elena and Agnes watched over what was done in the
house. Both priests and Christopher looked then to Frevisse, she supposed in expectation she would offer to stay
with Elena, but instead she said, "By your leave, then,"
and with a quick bow of her head to the priests, walked
away before anyone could say whether they gave her
leave or not. With a small beckon of her head she gathered
Perryn to her as she went, but in the street he paused to
answer the onlookers' flurry of questions with, "She
knows better than I do," leaving it to her to say tersely,
"Master Montfort has accused Gilbey Dunn of Tom Hulcote's murder."

"And arrested him?" a man croaked eagerly.

"Gilbey's gone to Banbury market. For now they're
making do with inquiring into all he has."

"Ho, that'll take them a time," someone else said, and
sharp, eager talk sprang out among them all while Perryn
looked a mixture of dismay and relief because although
it was bad to have Gilbey accused, it had to mean the
crowner was given up on him if Gilbey was the only one
he had gone for this morning.

Frevisse could not fault him for his confused feelings,
but none of the men to whom she wanted to talk was here
and she cut across the general questioning and comments

to ask, "Where are the jurors? They were with Montfort already today. Where are they now?"

"Gone out to the haying," a bent-shouldered old man answered. "Even old Bert. I saw 'em go."

"Aye," one of the women agreed. "The crowner had them in but not for long, and they weren't talking to anyone when he let them out, from what I saw."

"Must have said they weren't to say aught to anyone," the first man put in. "Even Bert wouldn't share a word about what passed, just kept going. We were to have a game of draughts this morning, too." Which seemed to grieve him more than anything else that had happened.

"Didn't look happy, though, none of them," someone else said.

"Have them fetched back, if you would please, master reeve," Frevisse said to Perryn. "I need to talk to them."

"I'll go!" said Dickon, eager-footed at Perryn's elbow.

"You do that, then, youngling," Perryn said. "Where to?" he added to Frevisse.

"The oak on the green, I think." Where they could talk with no chance of anyone unwanted overhearing them.

Dickon left, thrusting away between people while Frevisse said, "I need Mary Woderove fetched to me, too."

"Geva," Perryn said to a well-set, firm-armed, rosy-faced woman. "She likely won't throw anything at you. You tell her she's wanted, will you? And see she comes?"

"You want her at the oak, same as the men?" Geva asked, and at Frevisse's nod she went off toward the green.

"The rest of you," Perryn said, "there can't be that little to be doing you should be standing here doing naught. Off to it, why don't you?"

"Do you think maybe some of us . . ." a woman started with a nod toward Gilbey's.

"I doubt Elena Dunn needs more folk underfoot than she has," Frevisse said, "or I would have stayed."

There being no way to dispute that, what there was of a crowd straggled away, not altogether willingly, but Frevisse and Perryn stayed standing in the street until they were well gone. Then Perryn asked, with a twitch of his head toward yard and house, "You're sure we're neither of us needed there?"

"Even if we were, we're needed elsewhere more. Has Gilbey truly gone to Banbury as his wife says, or do you think he may be fled?"

Perryn shook his head. "There's no saying." But he was thinking about it as they started along the street toward the green and after a moment added, "But why would he run when there's naught against him save the belt? It's not much, no more than what's against me, and I never thought to run."

"Elena said he had to take green cheeses to market."

"That's likely enough, and if he'd planned to do it before yesterday happened, he's that stubborn he'd go ahead with it, whether it made sense or not. And maybe it's a good thing, too, or he and Master Montfort might have had at each other's throats just now."

That had crossed Frevisse's mind, too, but following another thought, she asked, "Have you brought to mind yet anyone at all who most particularly dislikes Gilbey?"

"You asked that yesterday, about us both."

"You've had more time to think on it."

"Not to any use. There were Tom Hulcote and Matthew, but you already know that, and they're both dead." And Gilbey was not. If Perryn thought that, he did not say it, only went on, "And Mary. But I can't see how her hating Gilbey can have aught to do with Tom's death or Matthew's."

Nor could Frevisse and without real hope she asked, "No one else?"

"Gilbey is talked against. Him and his Banbury wife both. But it's only the kind of talk you get when folk keep to themselves as much as they do. They're talked on and disliked, but it goes no farther that I've seen."

"By anyone more than another?"

They had reached the oak, its thick shade welcome, and Frevisse sat on the bench, but Perryn remained standing, staring away at nothing with a thinking frown before he said regretfully, "No one. Just who I've said."

And of them, two were dead, and even if Mary Woderove had for some unlikely reason killed Tom Hulcote, she could not have moved his body the way it had been moved, nor had she been at Gilbey Dunn's, to take his belt.

Frevisse tried going a different way. "When Matthew Woderove left, was search made for him?"

"Aye. Surely."

"Much of a search?"

Perryn paused again, then said quietly, "Not much. Nor for long. There were even some as were glad he'd gone, thinking he'd have better chance elsewhere than he had here."

"Were you glad?"

Again the pause and then, "It made trouble for me, being reeve, him running off. But otherwise I wished him well. There was naught left for him here."

Unmourned and unmissed. That seemed to be the most that could be said about Matthew Woderove.

"Here's Mary coming," Perryn said, both wary and relieved.

Wary at having to deal with her and relieved that now Frevisse would turn her questions away from him to her? Frevisse wondered. Not that it mattered. She was wary herself at having to deal with the woman and relieved she had come without making a fight of it. From the one time she had seen her, she had no good opinion of Mary, nor did it better now, watching her walk across the green. Still in her black widow's veil and wearing a plain brown gown—in further token of mourning Frevisse supposed, since Mary seemed not the sort likely given to plain gowns by usual choice—she even now walked with a sway of her hips and a swing of her skirts that made a— maybe unthought—invitation to any male looking her way. That her eyes were humbly downcast counted for something, Frevisse supposed, but not much.

Frevisse came up short on that uncharitable thought, tried instead to grant that maybe Mary was no more than putting on a brave front against her grief, and nonetheless did not rise to meet her or Geva. Subtlety where Mary was concerned would probably be a waste, and when the two women had curtsyed to her, Frevisse briefly thanked Geva and dismissed her, then fixed Mary with a stare and demanded, "Tell me about your last quarrel with your husband."

Mary raised her eyes from the ground, red-rimmed from apparently much crying, and repeated blankly, "My husband? He's dead." She dropped her gaze groundward again. "Please let him lie in peace," she whispered.

"I would if I could," Frevisse said curtly. "Tell me what your last quarrel with him was about. And look at me while you do."

Mary looked up again, more wariness than grief showing now and a little anger.

Wanting her angry because then she might be careless, Frevisse repeated, still curtly, "Your quarrel with your husband. Tell me."

Mary's face paled with in-held fury, her lips tightened to a narrow line, and her hands, until now neatly folded in front of her, spasmed into fists. But only briefly. With effort, she eased her hands, dragged her face back to a simply puzzled hurt, and said softly, as if resigned to being cruelly used, speaking to some point just past Frevisse's ear, "It was no more than what we always quarreled over. That he wasted every chance we had and didn't care he'd dragged me down with him."

"Only usual things? Nothing about the lease lost to Gilbey Dunn?"

Mary's gaze jerked sideways to Frevisse's face. "Of course about that," she said with an angry edge to the words. " 'Twas where we started. All of our quarreling was just more of the same. Not that any of it ever did any good."

"Why quarrel with him then?"

"Because it made me feel better!"

"Where did you quarrel?"

"Anywhere we happened to be."

"I mean the last quarrel you had."

Mary drew and let go a deep, impatient breath. "In Shaldewell Field. As if you hadn't been told and told again by all the staring big-ears in the village. What's the point of asking about Matthew? It's Tom was murdered here. Why aren't you asking about him?"

"Don't you care who murdered your husband?"

"Of course I care, but it didn't happen here. Why ask me questions? Unless you think I did it!" Mary flung the words and only afterwards, hearing them, went round-eyed with horror. "You do! You think that, don't you?" She turned fiercely on her brother. "And you stand there and let her!"

"What I think," Frevisse said, cutting off whatever Perryn might have answered, "is that I want you to answer my questions and not make trouble over it."

Mary snapped her mouth shut, thought on that, then said sullenly, still angry but willing to try to contain it, "We quarreled. It wasn't anything out of the ordinary." She sent her brother a resentful glance and amended, "Maybe a little worse that last time. I was that mad at him for losing the lease and all."

"You quarreled and locked him out of his house . . ."

"Our house. *My* house," Mary snapped.

"He went to sleep in the barn and in the night ran off,"

Frevisse went on. "Had he ever threatened to run off, this time or another?"

"Matthew? He never threatened anything. Wouldn't say boo to a goose unless he was goaded to it. Was too afraid the goose might say boo back at him," Mary said disgustedly.

"But you weren't surprised to find he was gone?"

Mary shrugged. "I didn't think he was gone far. Not until Gilbey's horse was found missing."

Frevisse looked at Perryn. "Where was Gilbey's horse taken from?"

Careful not to look at his sister, Perryn said, "It was staked out to graze with his other one. In Farnfield." The field that Matthew Woderove had lost to Gilbey. "Well away from the village, close to the wood," Perryn said. "He could be away with no one likely to notice."

"At least he showed that much sense," Mary said.

"Did he take anything with him?" Frevisse asked her, curt again.

"Just what he had with him when he came in from the field. No, he left the hoe, and good thing, too. All he took was what he was wearing and his scrip. A good leather bag, that was. Whoever did for him must have taken it, the bastard."

Frevisse clamped down on her growing unfondness for Mary Woderove. Under all Mary's passions of indignation and angers, there was a coldness to her that made Frevisse doubt she had ever really warmed to anyone except herself. More than that, Frevisse was beginning to suspect that she worked at keeping others hot with anger, the better to work them to her cold will, and not meaning to be worked, Frevisse said coldly, "Now. Tell me about Tom. When did you see him last?"

"Tom," Mary echoed with bitter pain. "Just because he loved me, no one minds that he was murdered!"

Refusing to be drawn into pointing out that if she did not care, she would not be asking questions about it, Frevisse repeated, "When did you see him last?"

"Saturday midday." Brought to it, Mary gave the answer flatly. "I keep telling people that."

"You'd been telling him he ought to leave here, to run. Would you have run with him?"

Mary gave her brother an angry glance. "I'd have gone to him but not with him. I meant to stay here a while."

"Making trouble over the Woderove holding, despite you knew it would do you no good," Frevisse said.

Mary jerked her chin at her brother. "Why should he get off easy? Him and the others that hate me around here. If nothing else, I want my harvest off it."

"Why not have Tom stay until after the harvest then?" Perryn asked, goaded. "Then you could have gone off together with money in hand."

"Because I was that mad I wasn't thinking that far ahead," Mary snapped back at him. "I just saw you wanted Tom ruined, and I wanted him away before you could."

"Did he tell you he was going to run?" Frevisse asked.

"Nay. At the last all I'd had out of him was that he had to think on it a while."

"When you didn't see him again, did you think he'd gone off after all?"

Mary completely refused that thought. "He'd not have gone off without saying to me he was. I thought he was still angry at me for pushing him, that's all, and when I'd had enough of him staying away, I went to his place."

"When?"

"Sunday. Early. When most folk were to Mass, so I wouldn't have to see anyone."

"He wasn't there? Or any sign of him?" Frevisse asked.

"Course he wasn't there. From all they're saying, he was dead by then, wasn't he? But I didn't know that, did I? All I could tell was that he'd not run. Naught was gone that he would have taken with him. So I reckoned he was about, and all I need do was wait till he came back to me.

He always came back to me. But this time . . ." Her mouth
suddenly trembled, making her look like a small child
fighting off tears; and piteously as a small child, she said,
". . . this time he never did. I never saw him again ever."

Unmoved by Mary's sorrow for her own pain, Frevisse
asked, "Has there been anyone angry out of the ordinary
with Tom? Was there anyone he was afraid of?"

"Tom? He wasn't afraid of anyone, was Tom. But, aye,
there was someone angry at him out of the ordinary. Gilbey Dunn. Frighted for his wife with her namby town-
face and hot skirts. As if Tom would have looked at that
flinty bit of bitchdom."

"Mary!" Perryn said.

"You think she doesn't know about those kind?" Mary
jerked her chin at Frevisse. "I'll warrant she knows more
about them than you do. Flinty bitches."

Determined to be untouched by Mary's venom, Frevisse said, "What are you going to do now that Tom is
dead?"

"Do?" Mary's brittle anger was back. "What *can* I do,
now I've been robbed of everything? I'll live somehow.
I'll . . ." She made a sudden, unexpected struggle against
the anger, bowed her head, and said, strangling a little on
the submission, "We have to accept what comes to us.
People die. It happens. Father Edmund's been saying that,
to help me. He's been kind." She gave her brother a sour
look. "Unlike some." She lowered her eyes again and said
stiffly, "I just want to take what's left me and make do.
That's what Father Edmund's been helping me to see.
That I have to thank God for what I have and make do
with it."

And Father Edmund had better take care, Frevisse
thought without trying to curb the unkindness, or Mary
would very likely next be trying to make do with him.

# Chapter 19

In the pause after she had dismissed Mary, as she watched her walk away, Frevisse considered her, so mean-spirited a woman that her grief was only for herself and her lost hopes, her concerns only for the wrongs done to her, not more than a jot for the wrongs done to her husband or her lover.

To put both murders onto her would be no grief at all . . .

Frevisse pulled back from the thought's ugliness. Dislike was proof of nothing in this matter and, besides, she could see no way that Mary profited by Tom Hulcote's death.

From her husband's, in some ways, yes . . .

Glumly Perryn said, now Mary was out of hearing, "You were wondering who didn't wish me well. There's one. Nor Gilbey neither. She'd see us both hung and like it." And before Frevisse could answer that, "Here be Bert and the rest."

The four men were coming out of a narrow way between two messuages, probably the straightest way in from wherever Dickon had found them in the fields, Bert Fleccher first, rake over his shoulder, and Walter Hopper not far behind him with Hamon trailing after, carrying two rakes and a water bag, and finally John Rudyng, talking to Dickon trotting beside him.

Longer-strided, John overtook the others as they reached the oak, all of them red-faced with hurry, pulling off their broad-brimmed hats respectfully and bowing as they came into the shade. With the sun higher, there was less shade than there had been, and to be in it they had to stand nearer to the bench than Frevisse liked, but disappointed in herself to find she had grown nice over sweat nor wanting to put them off answering her easily, she kept her discomfort to herself, thanked Dickon for his service, to which he awkwardly bowed and went to sit aside on the shady grass, eager to listen, while Frevisse turned to the men and said, "Did you indict Gilbey Dunn for the crowner this morning?"

"Pah!" The exclamation was Bert's but all their faces agreed with him as he went on disgustedly, "Not likely. We told him what we told him yesterday, that there wasn't enough to warrant finding anybody guilty of anything."

"Outlander." John Rudyng put fulsome scorn into the word. "Coming in and making it seem we'd no sense over something as fool as that belt and hood."

"He went to arrest Gilbey Dunn anyway," Frevisse said.

Bert's jaw worked as if he was about to spit while Walter Hopper answered, "So the boy said." He nodded at Dickon. "But it wasn't by our doing."

"We knew that's what he was about, though," Bert

said. "It's why we went fieldward, so Gilbey wouldn't see us and grudge against us the worse for it later. He would, the . . ." He thought better of what he had been about to say.

"But the boy says Gilbey's gone off?" Walter asked.

"To Banbury, according to his wife," Frevisse answered.

" 'T'wouldn't stick anyway, the arrest, without there was a jury said so, and we didn't," John said.

"Nay," Bert agreed, regretful. "Not but it'd be sport to see old Simon and Gilbey sweat it a bit." He gave Perryn the side of a grin with teeth missing from it. Perryn gave him a stare back that made Bert's grin widen. "Not worth giving that crowner fellow the pleasure of it, though."

"Hauled us in there like none had aught to do in a day but him," John Rudyng said resentfully. "Then jawed at us because we wouldn't do what he said. Sent us off, saying maybe he'd look to arrest us next."

"Pah!" said Bert.

"When you found Tom Hulcote's body," Frevisse said, "you saw the hood and belt there with it?

"Oh, aye," said Bert, and the other three men nodded agreement.

"Where?" she asked.

They looked at each other to see who would answer and left it to Walter to say, "The belt was beside him."

"How?" Frevisse asked.

"How?" he repeated blankly.

"How was it beside him? As if it had fallen there, or as if it had been put where it was?"

"What would be the difference?" Hamon asked.

For answer, Perryn unbuckled his own leather belt before Frevisse could explain. "Like this," he said and stepped forward, letting go of the belt so it fell away behind him to lie long across the grass. "Or like this." He turned and picked it up, wound it deftly into a coil that would have fitted easily into a belt pouch, then tossed it away from him. It uncoiled as it fell but when it had fallen was still was looped around on itself at one end.

"Do it again," Walter said.

Perryn did, coiling and tossing his belt three more times. The pattern it fell in was different each time, but every time it stayed more looped on itself than less.

"Now, just let it fall again," Walter said.

Perryn did, three times more, and every time it fell stretched out, no looping.

"It was coiled and tossed then," Walter said, "because I mind me it was looped where it lay."

John and Hamon nodded agreement to that, and Bert said, "Besides, how could a belt like Gilbey's have come undone enough to fall off? The way it's run through the buckle, then the end wound around and through on itself and hangs down to his knees, the daft man, how would it come loose enough to fall and him not notice his tunic hanging around him? But we already thought the belt was no evidence anyway."

"Best to be sure," Perryn said. He looked at Frevisse. "My hood was lying by him, too, when Dickon found him."

" 'Twas over his face when we came," Hamon said.

"Dickon put it there," Frevisse said. "Was he wearing a hood of his own? Tom, I mean."

"No. In this weather, who needs a hood most of the time?" Bert asked back.

"Which of you took the belt and hood?"

"None of us. It was Father Edmund did," John Rudyng said, "and told us to say naught about them to anyone."

"Why? Why say nothing about them?"

Uneasy looks passed among the men, with sideways glances at Perryn, and no one seeming willing to answer.

"Well?" Frevisse prodded.

Walter, staring at the oak trunk somewhere above her head and well away from Perryn, said, "I suppose it's because we all knew whose they were, soon as we saw 'em, and so did Father Edmund. Didn't look like a good thing to be putting about the village, with nothing that could be done about it anyway until the crowner was here, Father Edmund said, and 'Be quiet about this,' he said, and we could all see the sense to it, so we did."

"What Father Edmund said," Bert put in less moderately, "was we were all to keep closed about it or there'd be penance on us like we'd not believe."

Frevisse had been close to asking how—no matter that it was good sense to keep quiet about the hood and belt— they had managed to do it, but threat of penance from their priest and their certainty that he meant it was answer enough. It had even sufficed to stopper Bert, and her estimation of Father Edmund rose.

But she still had little more than what she had already guessed about the hood and belt and had been already fairly certain how illegal Montfort's move against Gilbey was. Unhappily, she could think of nothing else to ask and thanked the men and dismissed them back to their work.

"To the alehouse for me," Bert said as they began to move off. "I've had my haymaking for the day."

"No more need to lie low, that's it, now you know there's going to be no dust kicked up over Gilbey," Hamon mocked.

"Aye," Bert mocked back. "And when you've learned to duck as well as I have, you'll look a fool less often than you do, Hamon Otale."

"Hamon," Frevisse called after him, remembering something. "And Walter. A moment more, if it please you."

Quick looks passed between all four men before Bert and John Rudyng kept on their separate ways, though Bert with long backward looks until the alehouse doorway took him while Walter and Hamon, taking off their hats again, turned back into the shade.

"The day before Tom Hulcote's body was found, what

did you go to the reeve's house for, Walter?" Frevisse asked.

Walter regarded her blankly a moment, the question taking him by surprise, before he answered, "To find out when Simon would want my work this week."

"A half-day's weeding of the lord's beans yesterday," Perryn said, "that you still owe, what with being a juror instead."

Walter gave him a narrow stare. "Might change my mind about that hood not being evidence," he said, but it was in jest and he added easily, "This afternoon then, if that'll serve."

Perryn nodded, equally easy about it.

"Why did you let Hamon go to Gilbey's looking for work that morning?" Frevisse asked.

"Hamon's been grumping on about how he's no chance to earn money in hand. I thought Gilbey was likely to be short-handed, with Tom not working for him any more, and told Hamon to see if he could earn a bit of something there, me not needing him that day once I knew Simon didn't want me just then."

"And his wife was wanting to know how things were going at Gilbey Dunn's," Hamon said, "with the sick brats and all, but didn't want to go herself, Gilbey's wife being the way she is. 'Have a look in the door if you can,' she said, so Walter said I could go."

"Hamon," Walter said with no particular heat, just a wish he would be quiet and resignation that he wouldn't.

"Well, that's how it was," Hamon said. "She said I was to tell her everything about it afterwards."

"Did you?" Frevisse asked.

"Wasn't much to tell." Hamon sounded as wronged by that as Walter's wife had probably felt. "I never hardly got past the doorstep. That old thing her servant sent me off to Gilbey in the barn. He didn't want me, and I never laid eyes on Gilbey's wife at all." Which he seemed to feel was an equal wrong.

Unhopeful of learning more, Frevisse let them go with careful thanks, then sat watching them walk away while her mind tracked back through what she had found out, none of it seeming of particular use, but she nodded at Perryn to sit with her on the bench, and when he had, they both sat in silence, Frevisse staring into the distance, Perryn at the ground, with nothing to say between them until Perryn roused with a deep sigh and, "About Mary. I'm sorry for the way she was to you."

Frevisse had let go thinking of Mary. Even the fact that, besides Gilbey Dunn, she was the only strong link between the two dead men seemed to be of no matter in finding why they were dead. But she was Perryn's sister and mattered to him—or at least her ill manners did, and Frevisse said, "No matter. It's forgotten."

But not by Perryn who said, still heavily, "She's a trouble and always has been, ever since she was little. There's never been a halfway about her in things. When she loved Matthew, it was the only thing in the world for her, and when she stopped loving him . . ." He left the sentence hang, no need to finish it. "The trouble is, she'd not stopped loving Tom Hulcote yet. It's made it worse for her than losing Matthew was."

"She didn't look to be much grieving just now," Frevisse said, but that sounded unkind even in her own ears, especially when said to Mary's brother, and she added, "Though she was wild enough with grief at first, by what I've heard."

"Oh, aye," Perryn agreed wearily. "Mary's always enjoyed a good howling when she has the chance."

As when what was left of her husband's body had been brought back to be buried, Frevisse remembered. Back to what mattered, she said, "The question we keep coming short against is who would want Tom Hulcote dead. What happened that someone killed him? By all I've heard, nobody cared enough about him to mind even whether he stayed or went, let be whether he was alive or dead."

"Nobody but Mary," Perryn said.

"And she was telling him to go," Frevisse said, impatient that Perryn would not leave off about what was no use to them.

But he had reason for it, it seemed, frowning at the ground between his feet as he said, "It's not right, her doing that. Telling him to go. She's never been one to let go a thing until she's done with it. Not Mary. And with Tom gone, she'd have been without a man and she's never liked that. Not since she was old enough to want one."

"She still has Father Edmund," Dickon said.

Sitting on the grass aside and a little behind them all this while, he had been out of sight and—Frevisse realized belatedly—out of mind. With a smile as rueful as her thought, Perryn gave her a sidewise look, then looked past her to Dickon and said in what was very much a father's forbearing tone, "She does and that's good. But Father Edmund's not the same to her as Tom was."

Stiffly, showing he knew he was being talked down to, Dickon said, "He kisses her the same way."

Perryn's gaze met Frevisse's, the same, sudden, harsh question in both before Frevisse slowly turned to Dickon and asked, carefully keeping feelings out of her voice, "Does he? How do you know?"

Dickon shifted a little, suddenly uneased, looking from her to Perryn and back again before he said, with equal care, "There's a place up on the wood edge." He pointed vaguely toward where Crossfield made a low rise into woods. "It ridges out some and you can see . . ." He gestured along all the north side of the green.

"I know the place," Perryn said. "Every boy knows it. Its the best place along the woodshore for . . ." He reconsidered what he was going to say. ". . . not snaring rabbits." Because any kind of hunting in the lord's woodland was mostly a forbidden thing. "My grandfather used to not snare rabbits up there, too. And my father and me. None of us ever used to set snares there when we were your age, nor eat the rabbits we never caught neither."

Frevisse saw what he was at and left him to it as Dickon began to grin with a shared understanding that had everything to do with Perryn having been a boy and nothing at all to do with him being the reeve and answerable for keeping village laws.

"That's it," Dickon agreed. "Adam showed me."

"From up there you can see most of the back way that runs behind the messuages that side of the green, and into some of their byre yards, too," Perryn explained to Frevisse. "You saw them from up there, did you?" he asked Dickon.

Dickon nodded. "They didn't think anyone could because there's a shed angled between the byre and the back gate, and the byre in the next yard has its back to there, and even if they'd looked, they'd not have seen me because I was down in the long grass."

"Dawn this would have been?" Perryn asked.

He made no more of it than he had of the snaring so that Dickon went on easily, "Half light, maybe. No more. They came out of the byre together, her and Father Edmund, and they . . . kissed." And something more than kissed, guessing from Dickon's sudden hesitation and then the way he went on quickly as if he did not want to be asked more about it. "Then she went to see out the back gate that everything was clear, nobody about, and there wasn't and he left, back to his own place."

"It'd be not far to go," Perryn said to Frevisse. "There's maybe two messuages between her place and the back way into his."

"When was this you saw them?" Frevisse asked.

Dickon was well into enjoying himself now and answered eagerly, "Two mornings ago. Just after I'd taken the cows to pasture. You have to go out early to snares, before the crows find them, if you've caught anything," he explained to her.

Frevisse forebore to tell him she had known how to

snare rabbits and what to do with them afterwards when she was half his age.

"That was careless of them," Perryn said grimly. "To be out like that when it was light."

But Frevisse had thought of more than that and asked, "Dickon, how is it you know she and Father Edmund kissed the same way she and Tom Hulcote did?"

Dickon squirmed and said with sudden interest in his kneecap, "I saw her and Tom at it a couple of weeks ago." He looked up quickly. "But they were right out in the open, and it was daytime when they did. They didn't care if anybody saw them. I wasn't looking for it, either time. It just happened. Nor I'm not the only one who's seen them. Her and Tom, and her and Father Edmund. Adam even saw . . ."

He stopped, his mouth open, his eyes shifting widely aside in search of something else to say.

Gently but too firmly to let him think she would let him off, Frevisse said, "This matters, Dickon. You've listened to enough of what's passed here to understand how much we're in need of answers. What else has been seen between Mary Wodcrove and Father Edmund and Tom Hulcote, by you or anyone else?"

Dickon looked to Perryn who nodded he should go on, and Dickon took a deep breath and said, "Once Adam happened on her and Father Edmund. They were out beyond that field her husband lost to Gilbey. In among the trees. They were . . ."

There was small likelihood a boy his age did not know what happened between men and women, but he also knew the limits of what was properly not said aloud and, embarrassed, he stopped.

"You mean," Perryn said quietly, "they were doing what only man and wife should do together."

Dickon nodded gratefully.

"They never knew Adam was there, did they?" Frevisse said to set him going again.

Dickon shook his head. "He drew off and went away, and they never knew he'd seen. But he told me about it afterwards. And some of the other boys."

And, being boys, they had probably laughed over it.

Very far from laughter but holding her anger out of her voice, Frevisse asked, "When was it he saw them?"

"Before Midsummer. A little before. He said the next time he saw Father Edmund and Mary was at the court then, and he kept wanting to laugh because he kept remembering . . ."

Dickon broke off, embarrassed again, and Frevisse pushed him for no more. He had said enough, and still keeping her feelings from her voice, she told him, "Thank you, Dickon. You've done well, telling us this. Can you keep it to yourself a while longer? Both what you know and that you've told us?"

"Of course," he said, sounding in his certainty very like his father.

# Chapter 20

ame Frevisse sent Dickon off to the church, to help Anne and keep the children company, she said. He went willingly enough, leaving Simon to wish he could go with him, wish he could go to Anne and hold her and be held by her and for just a little while be done with all of this. Because he was afraid. Afraid of what they had learned and afraid of where it might lead. So afraid that he was cold with it.

And in a voice as cold as he felt, Dame Frevisse said, staring away down the green at nothing, "Tell me about Tom Hulcote's wounds."

"His wounds?" Simon groped to find why she would ask that. "What about his wounds?"

"What way was his skull was broken? You said his

head was broken in on the side. The right side, I think."
She might have been asking which way the street ran for
all the feeling she showed. "Was it from top to bottom?
From front to back?"

"From front to back," Simon said, understanding that
much of what she wanted. As one of the "finders" of the
body, he had had to look it over with Bert, Walter, John
and Hamon, to be able to witness later to the crowner if
asked, but that did not mean he liked thinking about it.
"Or back to front. Could have been either way."

"Was it done with something blunt or edged?"

"It wasn't sliced into, like with an ax. More battered,
like."

"Then it might be crushed in more near the hand-end
of whatever he was hit with, where there'd be more
force," Dame Frevisse said.

A little thick in the throat with trying not to remember
too clearly how Tom's head had looked, wondering how
a nun came to think on something like that, Simon answered, "I didn't look that closely."

"Has he been buried already?"

"Yesterday, soon as Master Montfort had done with
him." And Simon prayed she would not want him dug
up.

"Where was he stabbed?"

"In the back."

"On the right side or left?"

"The right."

"High or low or in the middle?"

"Low. Below the ribs."

"Did the blade go in upward, straight, or down?"

"I never looked! Nor anyone else either, that I know
of. He was stabbed and dead and that was enough."

"With a knife, a dagger, a sword?"

"Not a sword," Simon said. "The wound was too narrow for a sword blade. I don't know there's anyone in the
village even has a sword."

But Dame Frevisse was gone into some thought of her own again, leaving him to his own, and that was no pleasure. Knowing Mary had betrayed Matthew had been bad enough but to know she'd betrayed Tom, too—at the same time she'd been betraying Matthew—and with a priest. Their own priest. With Father Edmund, who in the ten months he'd been here had baptized four babies into the Church's grace, given the Last Rite at their dying to Gil Jardyn's boy and little Jack Gregory, old Peter Whitlock and Joan Cufley to bring them to God's mercy. The man who at every Mass held Christ's Body in his hands. Hands that between whiles held Mary. Another man's wife. Another man's paramour.

These past days, when they'd had neither husband nor other lover to worry over, how "comforting" had Father Edmund been?

Beside him Dame Frevisse said, "It's why she was urging Tom Hulcote to leave here. Not for his sake but to clear the way between her and Father Edmund."

Bitter with certainty, Simon agreed, "Aye. She knew Tom'd not hear it if he found out. He'd have killed her."

"Only it was Tom who was killed," Dame Frevisse said very quietly, leaving Simon to see what lay between his thought and hers.

He did and tried to answer her but could make no word come out before she went on carefully, "If Tom came on them together and went into a rage, Father Edmund could well have had to kill him."

"Aye," Simon forced out. "And then tried to hide he'd done it." By making him and Gilbey look guilty in his stead.

"And then there's the matter of Mary's husband's death," Dame Frevisse said in that same cold, level voice.

"What? Nay, it was some thief off Wroxton way did for Matthew."

"Was it? Matthew's death was as convenient to their

ends as Tom's leaving was supposed to be. She needed to be rid of both of them."

"She drove Matthew off, that's all. Same as she was trying to drive Tom off. It worked with one, not with the other, that's all."

"Miserable though she'd made him, was Matthew all that likely to strike out on his own? And why would he sell the horse he'd stolen before he'd gone even a dozen miles on his way?"

"He was frighted he'd be caught with it. He'd not thought it through when he did it, and when he did, all he wanted was to be rid of it." Simon grabbed at something else. "Anyway, leave be the small chance there'd be of Father Edmund finding Matthew on the road to kill him after he left here, he'd not been out of the village even half a day since Lent. So even if the priest killed him here, there was no time he could have shifted the body all the way to Wroxton." He caught up to another thought and added before Dame Frevisse could ask, his mind beginning to cast the way hers did. "Nor Mary neither. She's not been gone anytime this year and maybe more."

He had a momentary hope when Dame Frevisse held silent as if thinking on that and then seemed to go another way, asking, "Did your sister know how unlikely it was you'd give Matthew Woderove's holding to Tom Hulcote?"

"She knew how little I thought of him and how I thought even less of the two of them. She knew he'd not have it from me, if the choice was mine."

"Master Naylor thought differently on it."

"He saw more in Tom than I could." Simon admitted it unwillingly. "He wasn't so set against him as I was."

"With Master Naylor removed from the decisioning, Tom had almost no chance at all of having the Woderove holding?"

"Aye."

"But Mary, despite she knew better, led him on to think he had a chance. Why?"

Flat under the weight of his anger as he understood where she was going, Simon said, "So that when he was refused and angry over it, she could bring him to leave here and leave her." To Father Edmund. Sickness curdled in the back of Simon's throat, because however Tom had come to his death, Mary had been at the root of it.

"The trouble is," Dame Frevisse said, "we've no proof, only guesses."

"It makes sense where there wasn't any," Simon said heavily.

"What about the rumors of something between him and Elena Dunn?"

"She's been named with nigh every man in the village one time or another, but nobody's ever seen aught that I've heard." But nobody had ever seen aught between Mary and Father Edmund either, save a couple of boys who had not seen fit to say so to anyone.

But Dame Frevisse was away along her own track of thought with, "Gilbey is gone."

It was like an ill echo. Matthew was gone. Tom was gone. Gilbey was gone . . . Sharply Simon said, "He's cleared off to keep out of Master Montfort's hold, is all. His wife says he's gone to Banbury, but I'd wager he's gone to Lord Lovell, to set him against Master Montfort's purposes."

Dame Frevisse said naught for or against that possibility but went back to where she had been. "The trouble still lies in proving anything. All we have is likelihood, not proof." She sat up more straightly and her voice changed, took on an edge. "But it can't be left that way. I need the four jurors brought to me again. And Mary."

"What?" Simon said. "Why?"

"And one of the crowner's men." She stood up. "I know which one. I'll bring him."

Simon stood up because he should be standing if she was but asked, "Not Master Montfort?"

"Never Master Montfort. Send someone to fetch the jurors back. You bring your sister, but say nothing about what we've learned or suspicion. May we use your house for this?"

She had not yet told him what "this" was but he said, "Aye. But best I send someone else for Mary, please you, and go for the jurors myself. She'll not come for my asking."

"So long as she comes."

"And Father Edmund?"

"*Not* Father Edmund," Dame Frevisse said. "Yet."


Walter made the most trouble over it. Stopping where he was, he stared off along what was left of yesterday's cut of hay still needing to be turned for drying and asked, "How's this to be done then? And you said I'm to hoe the beans this afternoon. What's to happen to my own if I'm forever being dragged off for this juror business?"

"I'll count today's time you've spent on jury against your work due Lord Lovell," Simon said recklessly.

"And me?" Hamon said. He was better at whining than any man ought to be. "What's in it for me then?"

"You get to count sitting about as work," Simon said, and since sitting about was the sort of work Hamon did best, that satisfied him.

John left off raking biddably enough when Simon asked him to come, and Bert was no trouble, leaving the alehouse readily enough when Simon thrust his head in at the door and said he was needed, except he started on the same questions the others had already asked and Simon didn't answer him either, just jerked his head toward the others and said, "Ask them. They know as much as you're going to."

His worry that Mary might not obey wasn't reassured

by sight of Geva leaving his house with close-clapped mouth and a glare, but when he asked, "Did she come?" Geva answered tartly, "Oh, aye," stalking past and saying over her shoulder as she went, "She's in there. Her and that nun and they're welcome to each other, they are, and you, too, Simon Perryn."

Today the shutters at the windows on both sides of the house were let down to the day's warm brightness and what little air was moving, sweet with the scent of drying hay, and there was light enough that Simon's pause on the threshold was from habit more than need to usen to the shadows, but it gave him time to take in Dame Frevisse standing at the far side of the table and Mary at its far end with between them a prickling silence and a fox-haired, uneasy young man in the crowner's livery. Cisily at the hearth was bent to stir whatever simmered in the pot there, and Dickon was standing across from her holding a bowl. As the savory smell reminded Simon's belly of how long ago breakfast had been, Cisily looked along the room toward him and said, tipping her head toward Dame Frevisse, "She says you're none of you going to eat now. Is that so?"

Simon cast Dame Frevisse a look of his own but already had answer ready, because despite his hunger, he was afraid his gorge would rise if he sat down to eat with Mary as things were now, and he said, "Aye. We'll wait."

Cisily grumbled, "Well, then," as if he'd taken leave of his senses and turned back to Dickon. "You can take what's going to the church then."

"Dickon will be needed here," Dame Frevisse said with cold command. "Best you take it yourself."

Cisily's mouth, halfway to being open in protest, closed. She settled for giving Dame Frevisse a hard stare, then set to gathering up wooden bowls, spoons, a loaf of bread, and a knife into a basket and took up the pot from the fire with a towel wrapped around its handle for carrying, all in a stiff-backed, offended silence to which Dame

Frevisse gave no heed, going on standing with bowed head, looking at no one in a silence no one cared to break, though Bert, Walter, John and Hamon shared looks with each other and toward Simon that Simon gave no sign of seeing, trying to be as apart as Dame Frevisse. The crowner's man kept likewise warily still. Only Mary gave open, restless show of her impatience, casting displeased looks around at everyone and, as Cisily was leaving, managed to catch Simon's eye and mouth at him, "What?", but Simon looked away and kept on looking away until Cisily was gone and Dame Frevisse raised her head to say cold-voiced into the silence, "Sit down."

It was a general command, not a request, and no one questioned it, not even Mary. The crowner's man moved first, sitting on the bench along the far side of the table with the slight, tense frown of someone trusting her but not sure if he should. Simon went to his own place at the table's head while Bert, Walter and John took the near bench, leaving Hamon to go to the other side, to sit a wary distance from the crowner's man. The stool that was usually Anne's was across the room, near to the hearth, and Dickon claimed it, so that Mary made shift to sit at the crowner's man's other side with a displeased sweep of her skirts and a glare at Simon.

Dame Frevisse waited where she was until they were settled, then went to stand at the table's end opposite to Simon. Her black nun's garb gave her an authority she might otherwise have lacked, but as it was, her silence held them to silence as she gave them each a slow, long look before she said, still cold and clipped, "There are new questions about Tom Hulcote's murder. You're here to hear them and find out what answers there may be."

"What about Master Montfort?" Walter asked, not challenging her so much as worried.

"Master Christopher takes his part." She gave no time for other questions. "Master Christopher, did you take close look at Tom Hulcote's body yesterday?"

Not quite covering his uneasiness, the man answered, "Yes."

"What do you say killed him?"

"His skull was broken and he was stabbed twice. In the back."

Mary made a small choking noise and bowed her head to hide her face, her hands clenched together in her lap.

Master Christopher looked at her uncertainly, but Dame Frevisse said crisply, "The blow to his head. Where did it come from?"

"Where?" he repeated. "You mean was he hit from in front or from in back?"

Dame Frevisse nodded. It was something she had asked Simon, but Master Christopher had a better answer than he had had. "I'd say from behind. The bone was more deeply broken to the back than to the front."

"What?" said Walter. "I don't see."

"Show him," Dame Frevisse ordered.

As if unsure he should be doing this, Master Christopher stood up, stepped clear of the bench, and went to take up a length of firewood from beside the hearth while gesturing to Dickon to stand, asking him, "If you please, turn your back to me."

Dickon, delighted, did.

"Now see." Master Christopher swung the length of firewood slowly at the side of Dickon's head, stopped short of him, and said, "There's enough curve to the skull that where the blow lands the force is greatest, the break will be deepest, while the blow loses force with the skull's curve and the bone isn't broken in so deeply."

"You could see that, looking at Tom's skull?" Walter asked.

"I felt of the bone when I examined the body." Sickened distaste showed on all the men's faces, his own with the rest, Simon feared. Mary had not looked up and still did not as Master Christopher went on, "It was the only way to tell how badly broken the bone was. To tell if the blow had been enough to kill him."

With as little feeling as if considering such things was an everyday part of her life, Dame Frevisse asked, "Was it?"

"Very likely. It might have taken him a little time to die, but he would have."

"And been unconscious while he did?"

"Yes."

"Why was he hit from the side? Wouldn't striking down at the back of his head if you were attacking someone from behind be the more likely way?"

"It would be." Master Christopher lifted the thin log and brought it down in a feigned blow at the back of Dickon's head, again stopping short, but Dickon cringed a little anyway. "The trouble is that the skull is thicker in the back. A blow there would stagger a man but, unless it was heavy beyond the common, not necessarily bring him down. The way a blow from the side more likely would. Particularly if the man giving the blow was shorter than the man attacked."

"Was he?" Dame Frevisse demanded. "Shorter? The man who attacked Tom Hulcote?"

"I don't . . ." Master Christopher stopped, frowning over all their heads toward the far wall, his mouth closed down on his thoughts until, abruptly, his gaze sharpened and shifted back to Dame Frevisse. "He might have been. The blow wasn't level to the side of the head. It went upward from the back. But then, that could have to do with how Tom Hulcote was holding his head at the time."

"It knocked him down, though?"

"I would say so, yes."

"And when he was stabbed, was he still on his feet or down?"

"Down, I would say. The wounds were close together. A man stabbed would probably have moved between the first blow and the second. They would have been more apart."

"How many times was he stabbed? And where?"

"Two times. In his back between his upper and middle ribs. On the left side. One of them reached his heart. If he wasn't already dead, it killed him."

Wishing he could keep from it, Simon asked, "How do you know it reached his heart? He had no hurt on the front. Neither stab went through him."

"I felt into the wounds."

Simon ceased to regret having waited on his dinner, but Dame Frevisse said, unmoved, "You saw what was left of Matthew Woderove's body. What could you tell from it about how he died?"

"There was little flesh left . . ."

Mary made a sickened sound. Master Christopher looked at her, ready to stop, but Dame Frevisse icily prodded him on with, "Yes?"

He seemed no more eager to say it than Simon was to hear it, but he gathered himself and continued, "There was too little flesh left to tell much. Judging by the scrape marks on the rib bones, he had been stabbed at least three times. And his head had been battered in."

"Battered," Dame Frevisse repeated. "Not merely broken by a single blow like Tom Hulcote's?"

"The skull was cracked at least twice in the back and once across the right side. As if he'd been hit three different times."

"A less 'clean' attack than what was made on Tom Hulcote," Dame Frevisse said.

"Far less."

"Or less skilled," Dame Frevisse said. "As if maybe from killing Matthew Wodcrove someone learned how to do better when it came to Tom Hulcote."

Mary stood up with a piteous cry, turned an anguished face toward Simon, and held her hands out pleadingly.

"Simon, please! I can't bear this! I don't want to hear it! Please let me go home!"

As coldly as Dame Frevisse might have, Simon said, "Sit down." He had grown hardened to her trick of turning pitiful when she wanted to. "And be quiet."

Mary must have read in his face how completely he meant it because abruptly her own face closed against him and, taut with anger, she snapped, all piteousness gone, "I don't have to. I'm going home."

"You are not," Dame Frevisse snapped back, her voice as taut as Mary's but with ice instead of anger. "You will sit and you will listen and Master Christopher is here in the king's name to see that you do."

For a tight-drawn moment Mary looked near to defying her, but Dame Frevisse's stare narrowed and harshened, and Mary, against everything likely, sat and again dropped her gaze to stare at her hands gripped together in her lap. Bert, Walter, John, and Hamon looked as startled as Simon felt, while at Dame Frevisse's gesture, Master Christopher and Dickon sat where they had been before, and she faced the table's length again.

In the long quiet then, as the men looked back at her, Simon heard the familiar sparrows scrabbling in the thatch outside the south window and a woman well away across the green calling laughingly to someone else, and then, careful of each word, Dame Frevisse began, "Here's how it came about that Matthew Woderove and Tom Hulcote were murdered."

There was an uneasy, protesting shifting among the men except for Simon who went sitting as rigidly still as Mary, but no one spoke and Dame Frevisse went on, "To begin with Matthew Woderove. As the story runs, he lost a lease to Gilbey Dunn, quarreled with his wife, stole a horse and left here. He sold the horse in Banbury and set out on foot from there, only to be murdered near Wroxton and left to rot."

Mary shuddered. Dame Frevisse ignored her. Or

seemed to, going on, "In the meantime, while her husband rotted graveless, Mary Woderove went on lusting with Tom Hulcote, probably in the comfort of her dead husband's bed."

This time Mary did not move at all and no one, not even Bert, looked at her while Dame Frevisse went brutally on, "Then Matthew Woderove's body was found and Mary Woderove set to urging her lover to claim both her husband's holding and her. When his bid for it failed, she then urged him to flee the manor, but before he could, he was murdered, leaving Mary Woderove bereft of husband, lover, and land."

Mary looked up at that, her breast heaving, her eyes hot with tears. "Oh, aye," she said through shut teeth. "And now I'm being tortured by a wicked nun, and my brother is letting her!"

As if Mary had said nothing, giving her not even a glance, Dame Frevisse went coldly on, "Except that what we've all believed isn't the way any of it was. First, Matthew Woderove was dead before ever he left Prior Byfield."

The men stirred at that, and Bert said, "Now that's wrong. He stole Gilbey's horse and sold it in Banbury. He was seen there."

"A man that Mary Woderove said was Matthew when he was described to her sold the horse in Banbury," Dame Frevisse answered. "That's all we know. The body when it was found had only the tatters of a shirt and small clothes and hosen. Isn't that right, Master Christopher?" The crowner's man nodded it was. "No tunic," Dame Frevisse said, "because that was something the man who bought the horse in Banbury could describe, so it couldn't be left with the body. That way there would be only Mary Woderove's word that the man who sold the horse in Banbury was her husband."

"That's stupid!" Mary hissed. "Your brain's withered

away along with the rest of you, shut up in that nunnery there!"

"Because it wasn't Matthew who sold the horse in Banbury, was it?" Dame Frevisse said, sharp as a whip's crack. "Matthew was dead before he ever left your byre, wasn't he? It was Tom Hulcote who stole Gilbey's horse, used it to carry Matthew's body away to hide near Wroxton, sold the horse in Banbury, then went back to put the body out to be found and came home again while all that while you played the outraged, wronged, deserted wife."

"That's . . . None of that's true," Mary said, furious. "Tom wasn't even here when Matthew left. You remember!" she demanded at Simon. "He was gone before Midsummer court and didn't come back until after Matthew was long gone."

"I mind he was gone then, yes," Simon said, cautious.

"But how far?" Dame Frevisse asked. "Who's to say he wasn't lying up in the woods, waiting for you to quarrel with Matthew and bar him out of his house, both of you knowing Matthew would refuge in the byre as he always did, but this time for Tom Hulcote to come and kill. Or Tom and you. Did you help in your husband's death? Or merely plan it?"

"That's filthy!" Mary cried.

"There would have been blood in the byre if he was killed there," Walter protested.

"Was anyone looking for blood?" Dame Frevisse retorted. "No one even looked for Matthew, let alone his blood, and on a byre's dirt floor, with a little shovelling and some treading down, it'd not likely be found, especially with no one looking for it."

"I mind Tom wasn't back until three days at least after Matthew was gone," Bert said consideringly. "Three days. Four nights. Time enough for shifting Matthew's body around and all the rest you said."

"You old fool!" Mary snapped. "I suppose Tom killed himself, too? Or did I kill him? The only love I had in the world, and I might as well be dead now he is?" Her voice scaled up and broke and she hid her face in her hands.

The lie of that was enough to stop Simon's breath, but Dame Frevisse said in her hatefully cold voice, "Was it easier the second time to smash a man's head in, Mary? From killing Matthew you knew to hit Tom from the side, didn't you? And the stabbing. Once wasn't enough? Were you just that angry with him because he wouldn't leave when you wanted him to so you had to stab him and stab him again?"

Mary's hands dropped from her face as she sprang to her feet. "You lying bitch! You don't know anything about any of it. So shut yourself up!"

"Here now!" Walter said, but to Dame Frevisse, "By your pardon, my lady, but it doesn't make sense, all that you're saying. About killing Matthew to start with. Why would Tom go to all that trouble of moving the body, stealing and selling the horse, moving the body again? If he'd killed him, why not just hide the body and be done with it?"

"Because it wasn't enough to have Matthew dead," Dame Frevisse answered. "They needed it known he was dead. Otherwise Tom Hulcote couldn't bid to have his holding and his widow."

Walter started to say something to that, but she cut him off, saying to Mary, "How hard was it, waiting for word that his body had been found but it never coming? You finally sent Tom Hulcote to . . . what? Make sure it was still there, probably, and then go into Banbury and start a rumor that someone had seen a body out Wroxton way."

"You're mad," Mary scorned.

Dame Frevisse looked to Bert. "Do you remember Tom was gone a few days at St. Swithin's?"

"Aye, I mind Gilbey was swearing that was the last he'd put up with Tom's going off without a word." He elbowed John in the ribs. "You mind that."

John nodded that he did, and so did Walter and Hamon, who said for good measure, "Gilbey was right angry about it, aye."

"That doesn't mean he was in Banbury," Mary said, her voice daggered with fury.

"Gilbey Dunn saw him there," Dame Frevisse answered.

"You're lying!"

"The trouble was that you couldn't wait longer for Matthew's body to be found. There had to be enough of it left to tell who it had been. Did you tell Tom, when you sent him off, to be sure of it? Rotted as it had to be by then, you had to have been worried there wasn't enough of it still there . . ."

"Stop it about Matthew's body!" Mary slammed her fists down on the tabletop. "I don't want to hear about his thrice-damned body, rotted or otherwise!"

"You'll hear about it for as long as I choose to talk about it," Dame Frevisse said, cold with authority.

"I won't! I'm going."

"Master Christopher," Dame Frevisse said, and as Mary started to pull back from the table, he rose and took hold of her nearest arm. For an instant she looked about to strike him, but Dame Frevisse said, "Sit," and Master Christopher pulled her down so that she sat, albeit with the gracelessness of an outraged cat who, baffled though it might be for now, is only waiting to have its own way.

"But even so," said Bert, "even if that's all anything like true . . ."

"Fool!" Mary flung at him. "It's none of it true. It's all lies she's making up because she's ugly and a nun and I'm not!"

". . . what's Tom dead for?" finished Bert.

Dame Frevisse fixed her cold eyes on Mary. "Why don't you tell us how Tom came to be dead, Mary? You struck him in the head first, to bring him down, then stabbed him. He'd not have stood there to be stabbed without fighting back. You'd never have put two knife thrusts into him if he'd been conscious. But you'd learned from killing Matthew what to do. That's what the blow to the head was for, wasn't it? To be sure he didn't fight back while you finished killing him."

Mary was drawing sharp, shuddering breaths through her set teeth, her hot-eyed, hating glare fixed on Dame Frevisse who went on, still coldly meeting her hatred, "And after you'd killed him, in that while until you could haul him out to dump him in that ditch, where did you keep his body, Mary? Under your bed? Or maybe in your bed, for old times' sake?"

"Simon!" Mary shrieked, finally tearing her gaze away to him. "Make her stop!"

But it was Walter who said, "That's not going to work. Even if she did kill him . . ."

Mary's head whipped toward him. "I didn't kill him!"

". . . she'd not be able to move Tom's body far, and we know it was moved. And even if she could have moved it, where's the sense in her killing him anyway? I can see her doing for Matthew . . ."

Mary made a sound like a spitting cat.

". . . and I can see Tom helping her at it," Walter went on despite a startled glance at her, "because he stood to gain by Matthew being dead. He was counting on having Matthew's holding . . ."

"By marrying her," Dame Frevisse agreed. "Because he didn't know she was Father Edmund's paramour as well as his."

Mary sprang up again at that, screaming, "Liar! You liar!" And at Simon, at all of them, "Make her stop! Shut her up! Make her stop it!"

Surprised how far he was from having any feeling for her except disgust, Simon said, "I can't. She's only saying what someone else has said."

Mary swept a look of derision around the table. "Who?

Someone of you who couldn't have me, so you're making up lies about me instead?"

"No." Dame Frevisse made a small hand movement toward Dickon without taking her eyes from Mary and, as he stood up, said, "He saw you with Father Edmund and so did other boys, more than once and in ways they couldn't mistake."

A distant part of Simon willed Mary to answer that—deny it, disprove it, show it wasn't true, say something to change her back into a sister he need neither fear nor be ashamed of.

Instead she stood staring at Dickon, struck to silence, and into her frozen failure to say anything, Dame Frevisse said remorselessly, "It was the one thing needed to make sense of everything else. You used Tom Hulcote to rid you of Matthew, and meant to be rid of Tom after that, to leave you free to your other lover. To Father Edmund."

"You don't believe her, do you?" Mary whispered, turning a hunted look to Simon.

"I believe Dickon." All feeling was dead in his voice. "I believe Adam. I doubt there's anyone who'll believe you."

Mary drew sharp breath through her teeth, flung back her head with an angry cry, and bent to pound her fists on the tabletop, crying out, her voice scaling up to break with cornered fury, "Damn Tom! Damn him! If he'd just left . . ."

"Mary," Father Edmund said from the doorway.

## Chapter 21

ear and dismay twisted tightly together inside of Frevisse. Her carefully used cold anger's purpose and her desperate hope had been to break past Mary's lies before she need deal with Father Edmund. Because whatever Mary was, he was worse.

But Mary was already crying out to him, "They know!" And he was crossing the room, saying back to her, "They only know what you've been telling them," his voice and look warning her to silence.

"I haven't told them aught!"

"Then they know nothing." Circling the table to her, sure of himself, he was set on making sure of her.

"We know you're lovers," Frevisse said with the ice-edge scorn she had been using against Mary, not able to think of better weapon against him.

Father Edmund faltered slightly, lost a margin of his smile as he made a swift look around the table at the other men's faces, but took Mary's out-held hand anyway and said, "Are we?" Matching Frevisse's scorn. Daring her to prove it.

Guessing desperately from that that he had heard nearly nothing before he came in, she jibed back, "You were seen. In the woods and other places. You've been careless with your lovemaking."

She twisted the word to ugliness and his smile left him. He looked longer at the men around the table this time, taking in that they believed her, and with disregard for the shame he should have shown, he laid his hand over Mary's clinging to his arm, scorning them all as he said, "So our sin is known and you're offended. What pity you're such cowards you couldn't face us both with it."

Mary started to say something. His hold on her tightened, silencing her as he readied to say more, showing his displeasure at them, but Frevisse, her anger rising past her cold control, said back at him, returning his disgust, "The worse pity is that your sins of the flesh are the least of what you've done."

"The least?" Father Edmund put a quantity of scorn into that, too sure of himself to think he could lose ground. "There's more?"

"I *told* you . . ." Mary started at him.

"The thing is not to tell *them*," Father Edmund snapped.

"Her husband's death for a beginning," Frevisse said.

Father Edmund dismissed that sharply. "He was killed miles from here by thieves."

"He was killed here by Tom Hulcote. And by his wife. Who'd plotted it with you beforehand."

Mary tore a hand free of Father Edmund's hold to grab the front of his surcoat and demand up at him, "You see?"

Ignoring her, his harsh gaze fixed at Frevisse, he said with contempt, "You're being foolish, Dame."

Ignoring his contempt, she answered, "And then the two of you killed Tom."

"We never . . ." Mary started shrilly.

"Be quiet!" Father Edmund snapped. "She's nothing more than guessing."

"It's gone past guessing," Frevisse thrust back. "It must have been troublesome, Mary having a husband and two lovers all at once. Was that why you decided to be rid of two of them, Mary? Or was it Father Edmund who thought out how to be rid of them? Or the two of you together?"

Goaded, Mary cried out, suddenly fierce, "You're guessing! You're lying!"

With a certainty weighted by her anger, Frevisse said, "The 'clever' part was having Tom kill your husband for you first of all. You told him that if he did, he'd have you and the holding both, didn't you? That's how you brought him to it, isn't it? But how did Matthew come to be both clubbed and stabbed? Tom on his own wouldn't likely have needed to do both. One or the other, but not both. What happened? Did Tom balk at the last or did Matthew put up more fight than you thought he would and you had to club him down for Tom to stab?"

With a snarling ugliness, all beauty stripped from her, Mary let loose of Father Edmund to turn fully toward her, starting to answer that, but Father Edmund caught her by the shoulders, pulled her back against him, said over her head, fierce now in his turn, "Say *nothing*, Mary. Nun, on peril of your soul, be silent."

"I doubt it's *my* soul is in peril," Frevisse answered and thrust on, "Clever, too, to put Tom to all that trouble of making it seem Matthew wasn't killed here at all. Having him 'leave' the day before your deliberate quarrel with Matthew, then steal and sell the horse and dump Matthew's body well away, all so there'd be no suspicion on either of you. He did all that so he'd be able to have you openly, have Matthew's place in every way, and all the time you meant that he'd have nothing."

"No! None of that happened! None of it!" Mary cried.

His arms around her, holding her to him, Father Edmund said contemptuously, "Let her say what she wants. It's the only thing will satisfy them. Hearing her lies. It makes no difference. There's nothing proved, however much she says."

Because that was too true, Frevisse said with contempt to match his own, as if she had proof in plenty, "And while Tom was seeing to Matthew, you went about to be rid of Master Naylor."

Perryn and the other men—save Christopher, who didn't know about it—roused to that, Perryn demanding, "How?"

"He simply sent word to Lord Lovell that he thought he recognized Master Naylor as villein born," Frevisse said, as confidently as if now she were not making an outright, utter guess. "He knew that on your own, Perryn, you'd never give the Woderove holding to Tom Hulcote. Therefore he saw to Master Naylor being out of the way, lest he persuade you otherwise."

Father Edmund's hesitation to deny that told Frevisse, to her relief, that she had guessed rightly. In all of this, his accusation to Lord Lovell against Master Naylor was the one thing of which there would be firm proof. If he denied it and somehow she had the proof in hand, then everything else he had denied would be suspect, too, and while the advantage was still hers, Frevisse said at him, "It's the other reason you couldn't wait over-long for Matthew's body to be found. Tom had to be refused his bid for the holding before Master Naylor was released."

"And that's why Tom was in Banbury at St. Swithin's time!" Bert exclaimed. "To spread rumor of Matthew's body so someone would find it!"

Walter, John and Hamon were at last looking more grim than confused, beginning to see how the pieces, proof or no, all held together damningly. Father Edmund, able to read the shift and trying to regain lost ground, said with new fierceness, "What are you gaining by these lies, Dame? Who set you to them?"

"My brother!" Mary cried. "He hates me!"

Refusing to be turned, Frevisse said bitingly, at Mary again, "That left you only Tom to be rid of. As planned, he was refused the holding and you set to urging him to leave, telling him there was nothing left for him here. But he wouldn't go. He meant to stay. Is that why you killed him? Because he wouldn't leave you? Because he loved you too much? Or did he find you and Father Edmund together in a way he couldn't mistake and was so angry that all you could do was kill him to keep him quiet?"

There was nothing beautiful about Mary now. Eyes hating, she strained forward against Father Edmund's hold, snarling, "You dirt-mouthed bitch!"

Frevisse leaned toward her in return, not caring what her own face showed, demanding, "Was it you he went for in his anger, and Father Edmund struck him down? Or did he go for Father Edmund first, and you did for him? The way you did for your husband. Did Tom have time to know it was you killing him? Did he have time to know just what your 'love' is worth?"

Mary screamed then, wrenching against Father Edmund's hold, too furious even for words, wanting only to come at her. Hamon shifted hurriedly off the bench and away while Father Edmund, struggling to hold her, said, "Mary, no! She's guessing. It doesn't matter what she says! She doesn't *know* anything!"

Frevisse, ignoring him, leaned farther forward, tauntingly near to Mary's reach, and sick though the words made her, said goadingly, "And when you'd clubbed him down, Mary, was it you who stabbed him twice over to be sure he was dead? Or was that something you managed to leave to your other lover to do?"

"Dame!" Father Edmund said with a fury that brought

Mary to sudden stillness in his hold. "Enough! On your obedience, Dame, be silent!"

Frevisse straightened, slowly, her eyes locked to his, letting him see everything she thought of him and what he could do with his priestly "obedience" before she said, cold and deliberate, "And then you hid his body while you remade your plans to cover what you'd done. It took you Sunday to think it out, Monday to accomplish it, and that night, finally, you were able to take him—how? by wheelbarrow, its wheel well greased to go unheard in the night?—out by the back way to dump him in a ditch the way that he'd dumped Matthew."

"Guessing," Father Edmund said.

"The pieces fit," Frevisse returned. "Every one of them. Down to Gilbey Dunn's belt and Simon Perryn's hood."

"What . . ." Father Edmund faltered on that, not shifting swiftly enough to follow where she had gone.

"The belt and hood you told these men to say nothing about," Frevisse said. "The belt and hood stolen from Gilbey's house and here."

Mary gave a vicious, desperate laugh at that. "There! There's your lie! I've never been at Gilbey's house this half year and more, and anyone will say so!"

"No one says you've been at Gilbey's house," Frevisse said sharply back at her. "You came here and took your brother's hood. It was Father Edmund who went to Gilbey's and took the belt."

Mary stared, while Father Edmund's face went tightly shut, with thoughts racing behind it, but Frevisse gave him no time to sort them out, saying quickly at them both, "I've asked. The belt and hood were where they should have been on Monday morning. After that they were gone. Someone took them. The only person both here and at Gilbey's that day is Esota Emmet, and there's nothing against her in any of this. The only others possible are Walter Hopper and Hamon Otale. Walter came here, and Hamon as his man was at Gilbey's."

"There then!" Mary cried. "It could have been them!" And at Perryn, "It could have been! Make her admit it could have been them!"

"Save that there's nothing—*nothing*," Frevisse said in sudden, open, blazing anger, "to tie them to either Matthew's death or Tom's, but *everything* to tie you and Father Edmund. Beginning with your lust."

# Chapter 22

There had been no other way to do it.

Or if there was, she still did not see it.

With head bowed and arms wrapped tightly across herself, Frevisse went on pacing back and forth the length of the path between Anne Perryn's garden beds with the same measured tread she would have paced St. Frideswide's cloister walk if she could have been there. And she deeply wished she was. Or, better yet, on her knees before St. Frideswide's altar, praying herself toward quietness.

But it would be days more before she could be there, and when the men had taken Mary Woderove and Father Edmund off to Master Montfort, with Dickon following along for curiosity's sake, she had stayed here, to be alone until the trembling stopped; until she could undo the sickened ugliness left in her by the deliberate, cold rage she had summoned up to deal with Mary Woderove and then with Father Edmund because she could see no other way. She had come to understand, that little while she had questioned Mary on the green, that Mary's anger was a cunning one—real enough but used like a weapon to have her own way. What no one had ever done before was use anger purposeful as her own back at her, until Frevisse did, and it had worked where maybe nothing else would have, just as proof he had never thought to see set up against him had brought down Father Edmund, had held him silent as Simon Perryn had risen to his feet at the head of the table and, looking at his sister and his priest with a face dark not so much with anger but the soul-deep misery of betrayal, said, "Aye, priest. It wasn't enough to kill Matthew. To kill Tom. To whore my sister and break your vows. You had to try to make innocent men look guilty in your stead."

Stiffly, as if it made a great difference, Father Edmund had answered, "I had no hand in Matthew Woderove's death."

Mary had cried out at that, pulling away from him, turning to face him. "No hand? No! You only urged me on to it, planned it with me. How I'd bring Tom to do it and everything and then how we'd be rid of Tom afterwards!"

"I never meant Tom's death," Father Edmund had answered sharply. "I only meant for him to leave."

"And so did I!"

"But when he wouldn't," Perryn said, "you killed him. Both of you."

"He found us together," Mary had said, sullen against the wrong he had done them. "He would have killed us both, he was that mad. Would have killed you first," she added savagely at Father Edmund. "It was you he was going for!"

"And so you hit him from behind with what?" Christopher had asked.

"A piece of firewood, like you said, you clot! It was what was to hand." She had pointed accusingly at Father Edmund. "And even then I had to tell you to stab him! That he wasn't dead and he had to be!"

Frevisse went on walking, not regretting what she had done, only wishing the anger's sickened residue, still curdled like churned lead in her stomach, would go away. It would, she knew. If not today, then later. Given time and prayers enough, she would finally cleanse its ugliness out of her.

Unlike Mary, who would almost surely take her ugliness to the grave with her, still seeing no reason she should not have killed two men to let her have a third unhindered.

And Father Edmund?

At thought of him the little quiet Frevisse had so far won back shredded away. There were priests in plenty like St. Frideswide's Father Henry, men who held to God's way as closely as they could despite the sins of the flesh that called to them as readily as to anyone else. There were, less often, priests who gave way to those sins. Priests fat with gluttony or corrupt with avarice or damned with pride or lost to lust. But to be a priest and murder a man . . . To take a man's life without giving him chance to save his soul . . .

Frevisse found she was standing at the far end of one of the garden paths, staring down into a cabbage plant, noting with rather desperate care the particular cabbage-shade of its green, the fine patterning of its heavy leaves . . .

"My lady?"

Too deep in contemplation of the cabbage, she had not heard Perryn come and looked around to find him standing a respectful distance away along the path behind her, and said the only greeting she could think of between them. "I'm sorry about your sister."

"I've been sorry about her a long while more than you have," Perryn said steadily. "You did what needed doing. She couldn't be let go. Neither of them could."

Frevisse nodded, grateful he understood, and moved away, out of the path and toward the apple tree at the garden's edge, plucking a tall-grown basil plant's leaf as she passed, crushing it between her fingers, breathing in its spicy richness, something that blessedly would never change, no matter what vileness happened in the world.

Perryn followed her under the burdened branches, out of the sun into the apple shade, and as she sat on the bench there, gesturing him to join her, she asked, "Master Montfort was willing to believe what you told him?"

"Not gladly," Perryn said. "It was Master Christopher he listened to. Master Christopher's his son, as happens."

"I know."

"I reckoned that you did. He listened to him right enough, and believed him. He's furious at losing his grip on Gilbey's goods, though."

"He would be." For Montfort this whole misery of lives put to waste undoubtedly came down at the last to the single hateful fact that he would make no profit from it.

Perryn looked up through the apple branches into a distance of sky, the silence stretching out between them before he said, still gazing away, "They'll hang her, won't they?"

Frevisse nodded.

They neither of them mentioned Father Edmund. Mary would be tried at county court, found guilty, and hanged, but Father Edmund's priesthood put him beyond sentence of death. He would be tried, as Mary would be, and found guilty, but then be given over to his bishop to be kept in the bishop's prison under penance until, inevitably, he was pardoned. There would be no hope of any great preferment in the Church for him afterwards but he would have his life. And Mary, Matthew Woderove, and Tom Hulcote would be long dead.

Bitterly, Frevisse hoped his penance would be hard beyond the ordinary.

Beside her, Perryn said, "One thing. I had the priest write out a confession of his lie against Master Naylor while we were there and Master Montfort witnessed it. Dickon has taken it off to the priory."

"Did you? Has he?" Frevisse said, her heaviness suddenly lightened.

"Will it be enough to have him loosed, do you think?"

"With that in hand, Domina Elisabeth will have him out of guard by this afternoon's end."

Perryn gave a satisfied sigh. "That's all right then. It'll be good to have things back the way they should be. Not," he added as if it was something that surprised him, "that it's been all that bad to work with you."

"Nor with you," Frevisse said and meant it but had to add, "No matter how glad I'll be to give Master Naylor back all his duties."

Perryn made a half-laugh at that. "Aye. Each to his own." He stood up. "That's what I wanted to tell you. Now I'm off to the church, to see how it is with Anne and the children."

"Please, tell Sister Thomasine I'll be there soon."

Perryn slightly bowed, started away, stopped, turned back to her, and said, "I wonder, my lady, if Father Edmund ever thought ahead."

"Ahead?"

Unlikely though it was, what looked to be laughter seemed trying to happen at the corners of Perryn's mouth. "Aye. Ahead."

Frevisse caught his thought. "You mean ahead to . . ." she began but broke off, fighting down laughter of her own.

"Aye," Perryn said. "Ahead to what would likely happen when Mary tired of *him*."

And despite of everything, they both began to laugh, laughter serving, for now, along with prayer, against the ache of mourning.

# Epilogue

ummer was done and autumn come and Frevisse was standing with Master Naylor, with Sister Thomasine to hand for propriety's sake, to watch the cutting of the last grain in the last priory field.

In the weeks since she and Sister Thomasine had returned to the nunnery, she had seen no one from the village and not even Master Naylor until today. He had taken his duties back from her as soon as he was freed, and for the few days between then and when it had been judged safe for her and Sister Thomasine to return into the nunnery, she had simply tended to the children in the church, more than willing to leave all other matters to anyone who wanted them, except for a single harsh exchange with Master Montfort, who had made it plain that her intrusion into business not her own was tolerated only because note of it could be shifted to his son. Master Christopher had sought her out to apologize for that, but she had told him truthfully he was welcome to anything of worth it brought him, so long as he made good use of it.

But today she had had an urge to see something of an end to what she had been part of in the summer, had sought and been given Domina Elisabeth's leave to come out to here, the edge of East Field, to watch, warm in the afternoon sun, the last of the wheat being sickled down by the bent-backed men, to be gathered up in armfuls by women, the larger children, other men, everyone careful to jar loose as little as might be of the grain from the heavy-hanging heads as they piled the stalks on the last waiting cart. This year they had a harvest that made up for the starvation ones, and when this last cart lumbered away to the granary yard and barn, it was harvest-home and feasting for all at the priory's expense on bread, ale, roast meats, savories, and pies at the long trestle tables being set up presently in the priory's outer yard.

And now the cadence of cut-and-gather had ended, Frevisse saw, with all the wheat down, the last armload being laid onto the cart, save for a last golden stand at the field's center. In a slow but unhesitating drift the harvesters were gathering to it, encircling it in a tight cluster of men, women, children so that there was no way for Frevisse to see what was happening in the midst of them, but from all the years of her childhood when she had seen its like in other fields at the end of other harvests, she knew that the oldest man there—the village's oldest man of all if he could be brought out to it—was plaiting the last of the wheat into a simple woman's shape of skirts and arms and head, and when that was done, one of the girls old enough to marry but not wed yet would come forward and with a sickle cut the wheat free from its life. There would be a cheer then and shouting, and harvest would be over and feasting-time come.

But, "Now here's odd," Master Naylor said as the circle of folk parted, and Simon Perryn came from among them and toward Frevisse, Master Naylor and Sister Thomasine.

As Lord Lovell's reeve and holding nothing from the priory, Perryn needed to have naught to do with the priory's harvest, but Master Naylor had hired him to be the priory's harvest lord, in charge of all the priory's harvest work and the workers when Lord Lovell's harvest was done. "Because there's none better," Master Naylor had told Domina Elisabeth. "Whether all goes well or aught goes wrong, Simon Perryn sees to making the best of it."

There was assuredly now no sign of anything wrong in Perryn's stride as he came toward them, nor among the folk left waiting behind him, nor among the boys trailing after him, Dickon and Adam among them, shoving at each other friendliwise as they followed Perryn across the field. Her last particular memory of Adam was of him sitting weakly up for the first time to feed himself but stopping with the broth-filled spoon poised above his bowl to look at Sister Thomasine beside him and say, solemn with certainty, "I'm going to be a priest, you know." Sister Thomasine had said back, simply, "I know," and Adam had nodded as if satisfied and gone on eating. But today the only seeming difference between him and Dickon, scuffling with each other and the other boys as they followed Perryn, was that he was less brown, having lost too many hours of the summer.

At a word from Perryn they stopped, and the reeve came on alone the last dozen yards to make a deep bow equally to the nuns as well as Master Naylor, saying, "My ladies. Master Naylor. A boon, if you would be so good."

"A boon?" Master Naylor did not try to hide his surprise. "For what?"

"The folk want that Sister Thomasine be the one to cut the harvest home."

Master Naylor made a startled movement. To cut the

last of the harvest was an honor vied for among the girls.
For it to be offered away . . . He and Perryn both looked
to Frevisse, Master Naylor slightly shrugging to show he
left the say of it to her, Perryn saying, "By your leave, of
course, my lady."

But it was not her leave they needed, and she turned
to Sister Thomasine to ask, "Would you do this?"

Sister Thomasine gazed away from them toward the
waiting villagers, seemed to consider, and then said softly,
"If they want it and you see no reason I shouldn't, then
yes, in God's great mercy, I'll do it."

Watching her go away across the stubbled field at
Simon Perryn's side, a slender, dark-clad figure beside his
broad one, the children gathering to her as she went, Master Naylor said, "That's never been done before."

Nor would it likely be done again, God granting there
not be another year when so many mercies were needed.
Mercy from plague, mercy from hunger, mercy from the
corruption of secret murders. But given the mercies there
had been, it was a gesture of thankfulness to choose one
of God's virgins for this.

Across the harvest-cut field, hazed golden in the long
slant of setting sunlight, Perryn, Sister Thomasine, the
boys all merged into the waiting villagers. There was a
breathing silence, poised with waiting, and then, at last,
the cheer and the triumphant shouting and the flash of
sickles thrown high and caught as they came down, flash-
ing, in the sun, and the harvest done. There would be no
famine this year and maybe with God's grace the next
year would be as good, too, and the year after that and . . .

# Author's Note

For the curious (or the doubtful), yes, English village government was much as it's shown here, only far more complex. The villagers themselves ran daily matters, governing themselves in much the way of New England town meetings (whose self-governing skills probably developed from these medieval roots) while dealing with the complex bureaucracies of lord, church, and central government. The cases that come before the village court in Chapter One are all taken directly or derived from actual cases in medieval village court records, down to some of the names remaining the same.

Two books I cheerfully recommend if you want a more detailed, nonfiction look at everyday village life are the scholarly but readable *Life on the English Manor*, by H. S. Bennett, and *The Ties That Bound*, by Barbara Hanawalt.

The mesels are of course today's measles, though the word was not applied exclusively that way until well after the 1400s but was used for several different ailments, ranging from measles to leprosy. Mesels as we think of it was considered a children's version of smallpox, less devastating than the adult kind but potentially lethal nonetheless. My own memory of being horribly sick with them in prevaccine days stayed with me darkling enough to be used here—as well as inspiring me to have my own children innoculated against them as early as I could.

Since rashes were—and still are—difficult to tell apart, it was useful that the rash that went with some of the worst forms of plague did indeed form rosy rings, as Mistress Margery observes, and the next time you hear "Ring around the rosy, A pocket full of posy, Atchoo, atchoo, All fall down," know the sweet little game in a circle with everyone collapsing at the end is hypothesized to be a reenacting of the Black Death. Apparently the familiar "Ashes, ashes. . . . " is a variant that came in when the meaning of the whole thing was being generally forgotten, but sneezing was one of the possible symptoms of the plague, and the posies were herbs and flowers hoped to give protection against it. Children, being devastatingly realistic, showed how effective they thought *that* to be.

And by the way, to be pedantic, no one ever died of the Black Death in the Middle Ages. They died of the Great Pestilence, the Great Death, the Great Plague, but the term "Black Death" seems not to have been used until several centuries later.